Will-o'-Wisp

D. S. Blake

Dedicated to Rob Kroese, whose writings and other ventures have been uniquely inspiring.

While lovers speak in such terms as together forever,
many scientists are intimidated by the discourse...
— Paul Pearsall, Ph.D., *The Heart's Code*

"What have the Romans ever done for us?"
"The aqueducts?"
— Graham Chapman, John Cleese, Terry Gilliam,
Eric Idle, Terry Jones, Michael Palin, *The Life of Brian*

Glossary and Pronunciation Guide

*N*ote to the Reader: This is book four of the Exopreneurs series, and while I endeavor to make each book a standalone adventure, the characters have inevitably evolved their own language and point of reference, some of which you may not have read or have forgotten.

Therefore, I provide this glossary and pronunciation guide for your reference, which is spoiler-free to enhance your enjoyment of this book.

Legend (where the entry was introduced):

[S] Silk Unspun

[F] Foul Brood

[W] Wingless

[O] Will o' Wisp

These entries are included for pronunciation purposes and to assure you they weren't introduced earlier.

— *D. S. Blake*

Alvum: (AL-vum) A planet occupied by the Trigonans (hyper-intelligent beehives) and the Myrmidons (hyper-individualistic giant ants). Currently under quarantine. [*F*]

Ambler, Jake: Bailiff for the ICF, grandson and antagonist of Royal Enfield Ambler. The "odd man out" in an organization of odd men out.

The Baron: A young military-minded man who has distinguished himself in Bug Space. (His real first name is Byron, but he never uses that.) [S]

Blood, John "Doc": Chief of medicine on Teila, then on XEE. Rival of Hogar for Ada Lazar's affections. [S]

Brighthart: Inventor of the Stretch Drive, among other things. Born over two-hundred years before Jake. [F]

Bug/Blood Space: "Bug Space" is how humanoids refer to the area of space where insectoids dominate. "Blood Space" is how insectoids refer to the area of space they don't dominate. [F, W]

Chrygenum: (*kry-JEN-em*) An extremely rare substance first theorized by Brighthart and discovered in the meteor known as the Divine Retribution. It makes Stretch Ships, among other things, possible. [F]

Cilydian: (*sy-LID-ee-ehn*) A male of the Lydian species. "Lydian" can refer collectively to the whole species or exclusively to the females. "Cilydian" only refers to males. [S]

The City: New Helena, informally, either the capital or the whole country. [S]

Coleons: (COH-lee-uns) The extremely diverse and specialized creatures of the planet Debrides. They are the only insectoids known to have their own Stretch Ship. [*W*]

The Country: The informal name for the city-states and nations occupying the North American continent and not under the control of The City. [*S*]

The Corporate: The name of the largest and most powerful Exo-preneurial group. The operating arm of New Helena intelligence. [*S*]

Daikhans: (DY-konz) A colloquial term for members of the Eastern Alliance. [*F*]

Dali K: (DAH-lee kay) Jake Ambler's fiancee, one-time princess of Karnata, Captain of the Shiva, leader of the Lost Girls. [*S*]

Debrides: (duh-BRY-deez) Birthplace of the Coleons and home of the dominant financial markets in Bug Space. [*W*]

Derek (Walton): Jake's technical expert friend from the Earth country known as Goryeo. He is known for his impatience and lack of tact. Involved with Mini-Kim. [*S*]

Device: A general-purpose computer/communication device/jack-of-all-trades carried by most humans. Comes in a wide variety of sizes and capabilities. [*S*]

Diana: One of the Lost Girls who is not a fan of Jake. Married to The Baron. [*F*, *W*]

Diptera: (*dip-TEHR-uh*) pl. Diptera [*O*]

Divine Retribution, The: A meteor strike in the late 21st century that was blamed for global societal collapse. (see *Chrygenum*) [*F*]

Eastern Alliance: The remnants of the Daikhanian empire occupying parts of Northern and Central Asia and Eastern Europe. Also, the name of the Exopreneur group representing this confederacy's interests.[*S*]

Elletroid: (EL-uh-troyd) The scientific name for the "will-o'-wisp" of Nidus. [*O*]

Exopreneurs: (Eggs-oh-pruh-noorz) From "exo-," meaning "outside," and "-preneur," meaning "to take," organizations dedicated to developing and exploiting alien worlds through non-violent means. Many work closely with other government, military, religious, or secular organizations. [*S*]

Exos: (Eggs-ohz) Abbreviation of Exopreneurs, used to describe all agencies collectively and the individuals who work for them. [*S*]

Formosa: Self-styled Pope and leader of a faction of Myrmidons on Alvum who captured and tortured Jake. [*F*]

Foulbrood: A deadly disease among the Trigonans of Alvum, which mutated viciously and spread to humans. [*F*]

Glashar Pass: (GLA-shur) A geological formation on the planet Teila, used by the Minosians to invade Lydian cities. The site of Jake Ambler's first battle in Bug Space. [*S*]

Halerd: An Ip who runs the Debrides Exchange. [*W*]

Hekki: Jake's usual partner in the ICF. [*S, F, W*]

Hilda: A slave girl who led a revolt and escaped with her life, joining the Lost Girls. Dali K's first officer. She's wanted in various jurisdictions for her succinct handling of human traffickers. [*F*]

(Heinrich) Hogar: Known generally as just Hogar, chief xenobiologist in Bug Space. [*S*]

Independent Crusader Force: ICF for short, this is the exopreneurial organization Jake works for. [S]

Ip: A type of Coleon with a taste for woods, especially earth woods. (see *Halerd*) [*W*]

Jihadis: The extraterrestrial military arm of certain Islamic interests. Often lumped in with Exopreneurs, their motives are fundamentally different. (cf. The Templars) [*S*]

Kalybus: The not-so-ceremonial weapon of the Lydians. [S]

Karnata: An alien world close enough in environment to Earth to be home to one of the most successful human colonies. Dali K's homeworld. [*F*]

Knuckles: A favored weapon of Jake since Debrides, these are high-tech brass knuckles. [*W*]

Korma: (*KOR-ma*) The alligator-headed chief architects of Nidus. [*O*]

Kurt Hogar: Heinrich Hogar's teenage son. [*F*]

Lauder: The man who runs the public news feed on Space Station XEE. [*W*]

Ada Lazar: ICF's physics and robotics expert. An extremely attractive woman dubbed "Doc Hottie" by Dali K. [*F*]

Leidecker: ICF's regional manager in Bug Space. Jake's immediate boss. [*S*]

Lot, The: On Station XEE, the public areas are named after the ports they're closest to. The lowest-rent port on XEE is known as The Lot. It is the primary public hangout of Jake, Derek, and The Lost Girls. [*S*]

Lost Girls, The: A group of pirates/privateers/mercenaries/errand girls led by Dali K. [*F*]

Lydians: Matriarchal giant spiders with human-looking appendages. The males of the species are much smaller and are known as Cylidians. [*S*]

Melontikopolis: (*me-LON-tih-kop-e-lis*) City of the Diptera. [*O*]

Mini-Kim: (aka Kim Min-hee) One of the Lost Girls. Originally from Joeson on Earth. [*F*]

Minosians: Giant bull-headed cockroaches with a serrated blade for one forelimb and a pincer on the opposite forelimb. [*S*]

Missionaries: Christian explorers who believe the Gospel should be spread into space, even among non-humans. [*F, S*]

Mullis: The signature dish of Mulli, a chef on XEE, consisting of butterflied meat seasoned and grilled, then skewered. A popular dish among young exos. [*S*]

Myrmidons: The giant ants that live underground on Alvum. Recent adopters of Christianity due to missionaries' work, especially Paul. [*F*]

New Helena: A progressive, technologically advanced country on the east coast of North America known for its luxury, its rigid social system, and its exploitation of others through The Corporate. Also known as "The City". [*S*]

Nidus: (NY-dus) Homeworld of the Seyles. [*O*]

Nock: (*nok*) The primary grunt worker of Nidus: builders, diggers, typically answering to the Korma. [*O*]

Notos: (*NOH-tohz*), singular and plural. Tall, thin shock troops and guards for the Seyles [*O*]

Ooga Booga: A practice frequently employed by Exopreneurs to present themselves as supernatural forces to aliens. Against the ICF code. [*S*]

Paul: A missionary and friend of Jake's. [*S, F*]

Peschke: A recruiter and bailiff for the ICF who signed up Jake and later partnered with him on Debrides. [*S, W*]

Rapticores: The insectoids Jake fought on Euphrates. He hasn't talked about the incident, but apparently, they are more ferocious than Minosians. [*S*]

Rosicrucians, The: An ancient group of cyborgs who seek eternal life and domination over humans, though their earlier attempts at domination resulted in them going into hiding. [*F, W*]

Royal Enfield Ambler: De facto ruler of New Helena and head of The Corporation. [*F*]

Seyles: ("SAY-leez") singular and plural. Enormous dragonfly creatures acting as the feudal lords of Nidus. [*O*]

Space Station XEE: ("Eks-Eeh-Eeh" or "Zee"): The hub of human exploration in Bug Space. [*S*]

Spider queens: Lydians [*S*]

Stretch: A manipulation of space that allows for (the appearance from certain positions in space) faster-than-light travel. [*S*]

Stretch Ship: A ship outfitted with an engine that allows for travel by stretch. [*S*]

Tarkanian, Gregor: Founder of the ICF. Jake's boss.

The Templars: The extraterrestrial military arm of certain Christian interests. Their main purpose is to protect missionaries who have traveled to alien worlds, but they occasionally partner with Exos. [*S*, *F*]

Teila: (TEE-la) Home of the Lydians and the Minosians. [*S*]

Telemakhos: (tuh-LEM-uh-kus) A Rosicrucian who really hates Jake. [*W*]

Thrall: a human who rents out their brain and body to act as an avatar to their master. [*F*, *W*]

Trigonans: (try-GOH-nunz) Hyper-intelligent beehives living on Alvum. [*F*]

Vizgirda, Georgia: (vih-ZHEER-da)A scientist working on Nidus. [*O*]

Walton, Derek: *see Derek*

Weir: Angus Weir, chief of security on XEE. [*S, W*]

XEE: see *Space Station XEE*

CONTENTS

CHAPTER 1

INCOMING!

T HWUMP! THWUMP! THWUMP! THWUMP! THWUMP!

Jake pressed both thumbs down on the triggers, swiveling the gun high as the four-winged beast swooped upward.

Dozens of these creatures, called *Seyles,* circled the area, mesmerized by the throbbing, glowing pit in the center but still cognizant enough to know that to get too close meant certain death.

The planet Nidus had witnessed this ritual countless times in its history. Floating in the pit, a creature called the Apothikon gestated, submerged in a nutritive plasm.

Around the pit, a ring of vibrant white-gold flowers grew. Through some physics Jake didn't understand, the Apothikon and the flowers generated an electrical shield—a large dome around the pit that killed the Seyles, their charred corpses becoming food for the creature in the pit.

If a whole, healthy Seyles got through, the Apothikon could be devastated. The electrical shield prevented any of them from reaching the pit without being chewed up—dead or near death.

In this case, however, the shield had somehow developed a gap.

It was this gap that Jake Ambler, acting on behalf of the Independent Crusader Force, had been sent to guard.

The Seyles were a modestly intelligent species, but the Apothikon pulse seemed to strip them of all their higher thinking. Even so, some still managed to discern the gap and that it presented an opportunity. Only Jake, standing on the low knoll where he had mounted the gun, could stop them.

THWUMP! THWUMP! THWUMP!

Hitting the incoming squadron squarely with one shot and winging it once more, his weapon had a similar effect as the Apothikon's shield: the Seyles coming at him lost all its propulsion and sailed on momentum onto the sward surrounding the Apothikon.

He leaned away from the flaming wreckage of one of the besiegers as it flew by.

Sometimes, in the perennial purple twilight with the moons high in the sky, if he squinted, he could see the shimmers of energy that constituted the shield. Other times, as when a Seyles tried to fly through it, Jake didn't have to squint. The whole bubble lit up and turned the once magnificent creature into a desiccated husk, the remains falling into or near the pool of fluid.

Working for the Independent Crusader Force, Jake Ambler had done many things in his relatively short service. Ostensibly, he acted as a negotiator and arbitrator for alien species—a bailiff, in the ICF's terminology.

In practice, he did anything he could to support the organization's primary mission: resolving local issues in a way that would allow inhabitants of one world to trade with other worlds.

Besides being profitable, this was the best proof against a human force invading and exploiting the planet and possibly destroying the native culture and the natives themselves.

The fact that he found himself manning the electroflak against the Seyles, some of whom he had been speaking with only a few hours earlier, might have suggested a certain weakness in his negotiating techniques.

But nothing was ever that simple.

He had not really believed that when the Apothikon sent out its pulse, Seyles across the land would become obsessed with trying to reach the Apothikon until it did.

Early on in his mission, the pulse went out, and one of the very Seyles he had been talking to rose into the sky, entranced, unresponsive to Jake trying to call him back.

It might have made it to the pit first, too, but for the fact that before heading to the pit, all the ensorcelled Seyles stopped by a bed of flowers to cover themselves with a sparkling muck.

They called it *bedizening*, which was as inexorable and mysterious as the call itself.

He could see their bodies reflecting the glimmers even now as the remaining Seyles formed a circle around the pit. He knew what was coming, having seen it several times previously.

They were going to all charge at once.

Sure enough, they did. Most caught fire as they crashed into the Apothikon's shield, which flashed more intensely with every hit. Jake, dazzled, nearly missed the one that flew through the gap high over his head before trying to dive-bomb the Apothikon.

A ring-shaped burst from his cannon exploded, the hot jolt blasting through the creature's wings. It landed, otherwise whole, about two yards in front of the pit.

Jake double-checked the skies, now empty but for puffs of smoke, then looked back at the Seyles, which had enough life left to scrabble through the smoldering corpses of its peers toward the pool.

Leaping from the knoll, Jake dove toward the Seyles and grabbed it by its abdomen, dragging it slowly away from the pit. It was huge, but like all insectoids, it was also very light.

He flipped it over and shuddered.

The colored, translucent wings were now charred and curled in, the enormous, multi-faceted eyes shimmered different colors, and the body normally dressed in rather medieval-looking finery but now covered with sparkling muck presented a pathetic picture to Jake.

For all their insectoid nature, Seyles could look uncannily humanoid. Underneath their eyes, a point resembling a nose and a small, expressive line resembling a mouth added to the effect. The fact that the "mouth" was a thin seam that extended halfway down their body—a gigantic maw—was easily forgotten if they weren't actually eating at the moment.

It spoke in a musical hiss that his translator turned to English.

"Almost made it, Jake W…" The giant eyes and friendly-looking face curved into the equivalent of a smile. The creature shuddered and died with a rattle of its wings.

Jake picked up the corpse and carried it to the pit, dropping it in. Bright lights swarmed the remains briefly; then it was gone, the cloudy darkness of the pit returning.

The Apothikon wiggled almost imperceptibly below.

Chapter 2

Georgia

The planet Nidus revolved around its sun so that one side always faced its star in perpetual day and the other faced away in an unending night. A ring around the middle stayed in constant twilight, a curiously moderate, moist band teeming with life.

It was home to many different types of insectoids, referred to collectively as *Nijins*, most of which had rather short lifespans. Among these, in stark contrast, the Apothikon gestated for decades, drawing in the surrounding life as food.

The attraction began as a sweet-smelling lure, similar to a Venus flytrap. Over time, the lure got stronger and stronger to attract bigger and bigger creatures. Slowly, the flowers Jake called woollyheads appeared and, once in full bloom, activated and shaped the Apothikon's shield.

Then the pulses began.

It wasn't the strangest alien biology he had encountered, and it apparently worked well in most cases. In this particular case, a small wedge of the woollyheads had gone missing.

To cover the consequent gap in the shield, the ICF had decided to deploy a modified electroflak, an anti-aircraft weapon from a war that ended long before Jake had been born. It fired rings of energy that burst like fireworks in the vicinity of an aircraft, or, in this case, Seyles.

The cannon had been scaled back in power so that its effects would mimic the Apothikon's natural shield. It also had an auto-aiming device programmed to target Seyles. This had failed right before the last attack, forcing Jake to man the weapon personally.

He would have to figure that out—after a five-minute coughing jag and a few minutes to recover.

Jake had been sick for a long, long time, with a blend of deadly microbes, inorganic poisons, and destructive nanotech. He had special pills he took—pills he sometimes suspected did nothing but popped one now anyway.

Turning his attention to the electroflak, he disassembled what he could of it and lost himself in trying to figure out the malfunction when he heard a voice.

"You're Gregor's man?"

If there had been something to hit his head on, he would have, jerking upright at the sound of another human being on a planet he had been the lone one for quite some time. Instead, he nearly fell backward, catching himself at the last moment.

He managed to get to his feet, triggering a new coughing jag. When he had recovered from that, finally, he extended his hand, which she acknowledged without actually moving close enough to shake it.

"Gregor—er, Mr. Tarkanian's my boss, yeah," he stammered. The woman was on the short side, square-shouldered but not unfeminine, and had a stern demeanor that, along with her functional clothing, suggested someone who did not suffer fools gladly. She had light, short-cropped hair complimenting her narrow face and a glint in her eye that dared you to challenge it.

"Georgia Vizgirda, I presume, or should I refer to you as Doctor?" Jake asked, realizing that in his oversized grease-splattered coveralls, he must have looked like a child who had stolen his father's clothes and wandered into drydock.

"That depends on how you feel about titles, degrees, and accredited institutions versus actual expertise."

Jake smiled at that. "I guess I can't be surprised that Mr. Tarkanian's friends have a complex relationship with the existing power structures. Tell me, Dr. Vizgirda, what can I do for you?"

The scientist narrowed her eyes, and Jake thought he detected suppressed amusement.

"You can keep this Apothikon alive," she responded simply.

He wiped some of the grease off his fingers and said, "That's why I'm here. But I've been here for weeks and still don't understand it. Clearly, the Apothikon uses the flowers to grind up the Seyles for food, which works out great for the Apothikon. But what's in it for the woollyheads?"

"Woollyheads?" Looking around, she smiled thinly. "Oh, I suppose they do look like woollyheads."

"I know they have a technical name, but they remind me of flowers my grandfather tried to cultivate," Jake said apologetically.

She carried on. "My best guess is that when the Apothikon digests the Seyles, it returns nutrients to the soil, which in turn feed the, as you say, woollyheads."

"OK. But what do the Seyles get out of it? And why do *we* care?"

"You know that the Seyles live in kingdoms that cover most of the inhabitable surface of Nidun."

"Sure," Jake said, swiveling the gun around to see if he could detect any untoward resistance. The movement felt gummy to him. Something must have gotten in the swivel.

Georgia indicated the area to the west of the pit. A river delineated the end of the kingdom Jake was protecting, beyond which lay a narrow, dry plain that quickly turned to marsh, a "bamboo" forest, and a low mountain range that grew taller as it swept southward in a crescent.

"I believe *that* wilderness used to be a kingdom like the one we're standing in. What you see now is what happens when an Apothikon dies."

She held up her hand. "Before you ask how we know, let me say I've just come back from Station KOR consulting with the greatest xenobiologists in the known galaxy. I would've visited you sooner but for that."

"And what did the experts say?" Jake prompted, scraping the inside of the pivot with a small sample-collecting brush.

"Fossils taken from this and several similar sites across Nidus show Nijins die shortly after the Apothikon dies."

Jake frowned a little. "I can accept that without understanding all the details, and I get that if a healthy Seyles gets past me, it could somehow endanger or kill the Apothikon. So why would the Apothikon actually *call* these creatures that can kill it?"

"You eat food—presumably," she looked at him caustically, and he tried not to be self-conscious as he became aware of how rough and thin a figure he presented.

He focused on his sample brush which was thick with mold. Way thicker than he would've expected, even with the humid air. He searched his toolbag for a good scrubbing tool.

"But if you tried to eat a whole potato, for example, you might choke on it. You might get poisoned by it. It might carry harmful bacteria."

She emphasized the point again. "You still need to eat. But that doesn't mean that everything you might consider food is safe under all circumstances."

"The woollyheads are like teeth, then. So as long as it can chew its food, it's fine."

She shrugged a little, apparently finding the analogy not too misguided.

Nidus had been one of the first planets in "Bug Space" that humans had contacted. But since it lacked anything of immediate value for trade and presented numerous engineering and social difficulties, it had remained the domain of pure scientists—and even they mostly looked around and left after a short visit. Therefore, Jake was not overly surprised when she knit her brow and said, "I used to be the only expert on Nidus and the Nijins."

"Used to be?"

"Yes, and now *you* are an expert, which should give you an idea of how low that bar is. My discipline is a subset of astronomy and meteorology, with a bit of xenobiology mixed in. I'm here to gather data on the surface effects of planetary movement."

He grunted an acknowledgment while cleaning the mold out of the swivel mount.

"As for why we care, the eclosion is near—"

"Eclosion?" Jake interrupted.

"I believe that the Apothikon is about to eclose—to break out of its chrysalis and leave its lair—something no human has ever witnessed.

"Furthermore, the planet is in a rare state, astronomically speaking. Approximately every one-hundred years, a combination of factors results in—well, let's call it a wobble, for simplicity's sake."

Jake remembered that from the ICF's documentation. "I read about this anomaly. There are no seasons on the planet, except for very brief, very intense hyper-winters, that alternate every earth century with hyper-summers."

"Quite, and this is also something else no human has witnessed. To see how life adjusts to these dramatic changes will add tremendously to the scientific literature."

Jake filed this mentally with all the other astrophysics he didn't understand about how Nidus had a number of unusual characteristics for a planet of its type. Besides the wobble, it had two moons that "shouldn't have been there" according to astronomers, leading to considerable speculation about their composition.

He slipped the pieces he had been cleaning into the mount. It all fit back together with a pleasing snap, and he wiped his hands before lifting the cannon to reset it.

Jake said, "OK, but if I'm here keeping the Apothikon alive, doesn't that alter the natural order of things? Aren't we tainting the data?"

Georgia looked at him sharply. "I don't think so. Bailiff, I smell a rat."

He smiled at the ancient phrase. He had seen it in his old books and videos but had never heard anyone use it.

"The Nijin taboo regarding the Apothikon is severe enough that I only belatedly realized the creatures were significant at all—that they even *existed*! It was when I saw the Seyles being...*chewed up*, to use your teeth analogy."

Jake chuckled a little. "Yes, it is hard to miss the lights. It's like a giant bug zapper."

"Before I called Gregor, I investigated dozens of other sites. This is the only Apothikon I found with missing woollyheads. These flowers are completely toxic to the native life, quite apart from their remarkable electrical field." She procured a small, clear bag of stems and held them out for him to examine. "Yet, what are these?"

He squinted in the dim light, then finally just shone his work light on the bag. Georgia looked away from the brightness.

"Teeth marks? Incisors, even?" He paused to consider that. "Insectoids don't really have teeth, do they? Even spider fangs are just chitin."

"These look like marks made by human teeth."

"Which raises the specter of a human wandering around Nidus and—very occasionally—eating the vegetation," he concluded.

"Are you one of Gregor's *best* men?" she asked pointedly.

Jake laughed. "I hope not." He activated the computer and ran it through diagnostics as the gun swiveled and aimed at imaginary targets. "I think he sent me here to keep me out of trouble."

"Oh?"

With a smirk, Jake said, "I'm known as 'The Destroyer of Worlds,' and even if that's ninety percent sarcastic, the ten percent still kind of hurts."

"How many worlds *have* you destroyed?"

"This'll be my fifth," he said flatly. "In fairness, I think my effect is exaggerated. The other four planets seem to be doing quite well."

"Well, this may help you somewhat," she said, guiding him to the low embankment that encircled a cluster of farms by his base. She walked along the embankment, which was covered with awa-vines, the most common plant he had seen, reminding him of grapevines, but with golf ball-sized pods hanging off them in thick clusters.

"Ah!" she said, pointing to the reservoir wall.

Jake leaned in and saw a yellowish-white growth that had found space to form under the awa-vines.

"This looks like the mold I found in the flak," he said.

"Quite." With no ceremony, she smacked a group of pods over the mold with her open palm. A wisp of white mist emerged, and as it settled over the mold, the mold began to flake off the wall and fall into the muck below.

Jake reached out to get a sense of the mist and withdrew at the sudden, sharp cold. He smiled at her. "So the mold needs heat. I can fab some small refrigeration units and put them on the cannon, and maybe prevent an incident like earlier. Thank you!"

The doctor seemed to be constantly appraising him, but at least she didn't seem to be disapproving of him at the moment.

"Bailiff, I wonder if—"

At that moment, a Seyles dropped down next to her, and she started but regained her composure quickly.

"Ah, Doctor Vizgirda, meet my friend, Dezzig Seyles."

She moved back casually but quickly to put some space between herself and the nine-foot-long creature hovering there, flapping its wings, eyes glittering, spear casually cradled in two forelimbs.

"Jake Wizard," Dezzig said. "You must come quickly. He's in a *mood.*"

CHAPTER 3

THE WORLD ACCORDING TO GRIGG

B y now, Jake had done enough jobs for the ICF to realize when someone had figured out an angle. Typically, the someone was a humanoid, but some insectoids seemed genetically unable to operate straightforwardly. (Lydians, for example.)

Lord Grigg had taken to summoning him after the Apothikon pulse went out, usually not long after Jake had finished defending it. There was, sometimes, a brief moment of praise. But whatever greeting Grigg started with, it would be inevitably followed by "and while you are there," would he not take care of this issue or some other issue that, after all, was part and parcel of defending the kingdom, given a very liberal interpretation of what might threaten the kingdom, of course.

Jake, who had encountered many alien species reticent about the use of human technology on their worlds, hadn't minded what essentially amounted to a bunch of minor chores. Still, he had taken note of Grigg's willingness to exploit him.

In fact, the mercurial lord had come to take Jake as something like a literal "angel," a messenger from—well, sent by some previously unimagined higher source and at his beck and call—his personal genie or wizard.

Because contact with humans had never become commonplace, and the Seyles only glimpsed wondrous (to them) miracles when humans were around, the creatures regarded the aliens not as an advanced alien species but as actual wizards.

Jake preferred a more low-key approach to things, so he left his battlesuit at his tent and generally walked to the castle when summoned, stopping to talk to the creatures who lived under Grigg's rule.

He enjoyed the walk down from his base, around the high crags that walled it to the south and east, and then up past the farms, tracing the aqueduct to the reservoir.

This slow-paced attitude frustrated Dezzig. Seyles operated at a higher speed than humans—and most of their fellow Nijins as well.

Personality-wise, they reminded Jake of obsessively neat people forced to be around more slovenly types. They existed in a constant state of exasperation with barely repressed rage when it came to dealing with their planetary cohabitants.

The Seyles tapped his lance impatiently. "We really must hurry, Jake Wizard."

"Dezzig Seyles, you are a mother hen."

"A what what?"

"A hen is a creature on my planet mostly used for food. They have wings but can't fly."

"I see. And what's a mother?"

Of course. Insectoid reproductive strategies led to different reproductive roles. "The mother is the one who lays the eggs."

"I see. But I cannot lay eggs, Jake Wizard, and I endeavor not to be food any time soon. So, how am I a 'mother hen?'"

"On my world, a hen lays her eggs, and when they hatch, she watches over all her babies until they can care for themselves."

Dezzig rattled his wings in an expression of confusion. "An entire...creature...a *mother*...who devotes herself—"

"Yes. A mother. Mama. A mom. It's normal among other species, really. Among intelligent species, it's a highly honored position." *Most of the time*, he didn't add.

"Jake Wizard, these hen creatures: do their females not die after laying their eggs?"

Jake suddenly realized why he hadn't seen many "damsels," or female Seyles. "I don't know how it is for hens exactly, but in many species, the males and females live approximately the same length of time. For humans, females live substantially longer."

Dezzig ruminated on that for a while, then asked, "But why are the young so helpless?"

Jake struggled to explain the differences between insectoids and others, and Dezzig seemed to grasp it the way a human might grasp the concept of a giant, garrulous dragonfly.

"I feel *our* way is superior," he pronounced at the end.

Of course you do, Jake didn't say. As they rounded the reservoir, two Korma came into view. They were deeply involved in a discussion and didn't notice the pair approaching them.

Korma generally stood upright, their teardrop-shaped bodies giving them a stable base from which their strong lower legs protruded.

At the point of the teardrop rested an enormous, rather fierce-looking head as if they wore comically oversized alligator masks. Their actual eyes and, Jake was fairly confident, mouths were over and under the fake head, respectively, on the smaller *real* head behind the scary Halloween mask.

"Fugi!" Jake exclaimed. He recognized the Korma from the distinctive orange pattern on his—mostly black—head, which looked a lot like the face of a Seyles.

The two Korma did not respond, and Jake wondered if he had made a mistake, but then he caught a bitter scent. They were afraid. Their natural orange shifted to a bright red, throwing their fierce but fake faces into sharp contrast.

Dezzig said menacingly, "Jake Wizard has spoken, Korma."

Fugi responded meekly. "Greetings, Jake Wizard." He looked about to say something more, then stopped.

The other Korma, known to Jake as Toler and identifiable by the fearsome, many-eyed face pattern on *his* alligator head, couldn't hold back, however. "Jake Wizard, we are debating the maintenance of the reservoir. Bala Korma The Moist argued that the grass in the mortar weakens it—"

"Usually!" Fugi interrupted. "The grass *usually* weakens it, but you can see now," the agitated Korma replied, pointing to areas along the wall, "just as observed by Tyfo Korma The Persistent that the cracks created by the grass are allowing the awa-vine tendrils to—"

Dezzig rattled his wings, and the two instantly grew silent.

"You two," he said, "must settle this dispute soon, or I shall settle it for you. Come, Jake Wizard, we *must* go."

With that, he floated away, Jake following in his wake. They began the ascent to the castle.

Behind him, he could hear Fugi and Toler pick up their argument.

"You were telling me about the inferior young of your world, Jake Wizard," Dezzig said, reviving their conversation. Despite, or perhaps because of, their rigid society, Jake had found a great many Seyles to be intensely curious and distractable when presented with something novel.

"It's not just—I mean—" Jake sputtered a little. "Okay, consider the Trigonans and the Myrmidons: their young require little help to survive, but their parents use their youth to indoctrinate them in the ways of their people."

This led to a discussion of whom the Trigonans and Myrmidons were and how different and complex their cultures were. Jake elided for his sanity the whole discussion of Christianity, which the missionaries had brought to the Myrmidons and dramatically altered their society.

"It is better just to be born knowing your people's ways," Dezzig proclaimed.

"It's a time-saver, I guess," conceded Jake, only somewhat ironically. He wondered if such a thing were possible. Instincts could be complex, but could they ever be so complex as to be a substitute for education?

While primitive in construction, and in essence not much more than some cleverly woven, heavily layered sticks and mud, Lord Grigg's castle still managed to impress, especially when framed by Nidus' large yellow moon—the Dragon moon.

Reminiscent of a hive in shape and as formidable in its own way as the Lydian pyramids, Jake felt a distinct pressure every time Grigg summoned him.

Once in the waiting area of the structure, Dezzig left him quickly, and he was escorted into an antechamber by a Notos, the tall, thin insectoids who might be mistaken for extremely thick bamboo—at least until one jabbed a spear at you with their strong forelimbs.

According to Vizgirda's research, while the Seyles dominated the planet through their physical strength, they employed the Notos as bodyguards, shock troops, and enforcers.

The ones that didn't act in this guardian capacity typically became miners. With that as the main career alternative, royal guard and military Notos expressed sincerely intense devotion to their Seyles masters.

They tended not to speak much, and this one just shoved him into the courtyard at the appropriate moment.

Jake wondered if he should make a show of some "miracles" just to get a little more respect.

"Jake Wizard!" came the voice of Lord Grigg. "Jake Wizard, we have need of your services!"

The translators used by the ICF were among the best in the known universe because, as Gregor Tarkanian put it, "Our mission is to talk to the aliens, not kill them if we can help it."

So while Jake was prone to noticing the translation device's flaws, he couldn't help but admire how it conveyed alien emotion and intention in a way that a primate such as himself could understand.

Insectoids, for example, couldn't "boom" when they spoke. Instead of two big lungs bellowing out, they had dozens of spiracles all over their bodies. When they wanted to emphasize their speech, they had their spiracles operating at different frequencies, including some that Jake could not consciously perceive but which set the hairs on his forearms standing upright.

To its credit, the translator considered those tones and managed to set him just as on edge as if the nine-foot-tall, four-winged monster with myriad reflectors for eyes had said the English words with the same menacing intent.

Jake knew better than to react to the monarch's provocations. Given the accelerated perception of the Seyles, the trick was to pause long enough to convey a lack of concern but not so long as to enrage everyone.

Grigg viewed himself as a preternaturally gifted monarch. As soon as the autocrat had realized Jake was not a threat to him but there to help him, he had enough intelligence to know he could act fairly imperiously toward the human—and that doing so raised him in the esteem of his subjects.

Of all the Seyles Jake had dealt with, Grigg was the only one to wear a crown. He'd had it crafted to fit specifically to his skull shape and size and decorated with assorted metals and gems rather gaudily.

Jake thought it suited Grigg perfectly.

"Lord Grigg," said Jake deferentially, but not overly so. He wanted to let Grigg maintain his sense of importance without seeming weak.

"Far be it from me," the Seyles began hypocritically, "to impugn the wisdom of the great Jake Wizard."

This, Jake knew, would have to be followed by a criticism. He shrugged mentally. These things didn't get his dander up anymore. Or maybe he was just too tired to care about insults.

"And I'm *sure* the Wizard is aware that Matzhin amasses troops beyond Valley Ridge to our south."

Jake nodded. Then he said, "I'm aware," remembering a nod didn't effectively communicate affirmation among the Seyles.

"And I'm sure he *also* knows," continued Grigg, drawing out the sibilants in a language that seemed to Jake to be mostly sibilance, "that Torsk amasses troops to our north, beyond the Great Marsh."

"Mm-hmm," Jake mumbled, tired of the staginess.

"Then this raises the question of why the Wizard who claims to want to help us has done nothing!" Grigg yelled triumphantly to the rhythm of beating wings in the gallery.

"I'm here to protect Lord Grigg's kingdom." Jake avoided mentioning the Apothikon, as it was implicit, and to speak of it directly was a faux pas. "And in this *mild* posture, I have destroyed hundreds of Grigg's people."

Jake looked directly into the faceted eyes. "Should I take an *aggressive* posture? All Nijins will shudder to see it."

The humming from the audience was suitably awed. Sometimes, Jake realized, the most diplomatic posture was a bellicose one. It was too close to "ooga booga" for his liking, but superstition ruled Nidus to an extent he had not seen in any other bug culture yet.

"When the time is right, Jake Wizard will unleash his full strength on the kingdom's enemies!" Jake said, adding a third-person flourish. With luck, he wouldn't have to release even part of his strength, and no one would notice because the Apothikon had survived and eclosed.

So he hoped.

CHAPTER 4

MATING RITUALS

D ezzig had rejoined him after the "council," which mostly consisted of Grigg doing more posturing.

"Jake Wizard, how many Seyles do you think you could kill?" Dezzig asked while tapping his lance on the ground.

Without missing a beat, Jake said, "All of them." Normally, and certainly in the past, he would give more mealy-mouthed answers. He didn't *want* to kill anyone, and he rather hated being put in the position where he had to. He'd always struggled to make that clear.

He thought, *not anymore, not with Grigg*. His body was racked with another hard cough. He slipped a pill out of one of the bottles he carried and swallowed it dry. Then he paused until he felt stable again.

Dezzig watched him through all this. Jake couldn't read the Seyles' expressions well yet. Dezzig had a sense of humor, a kind of dry wit, and a very forthright approach to communication, but Jake wondered if the expression on his face at that moment might be called "dubious."

"What could a *healthy* member of your species do, then?" Dezzig said, and again, Jake didn't know if that was sarcasm, snark, or what.

He didn't answer, and Dezzig brought up something else he'd apparently been brooding on. "Jake Wizard, this concept of mother—"

"It's powerful enough among my species that the word 'mother' is used for our entire planet, 'Mother Earth,' and for factors governing all life, 'Mother Nature,' and for all things that nurture and protect."

"Does Jake Wizard have a mother?"

"He does."

"Where is she now?"

Jake sighed a little, but mostly from fatigue, as they circled the reservoir again. "Mine is on my home world. The mother's job is over when the child has grown up. Sort of. Mothers continue to worry even when children become self-sufficient. The daughters go on to be mothers themselves, and the grandmothers help them, ideally, until the grandmothers are so old they can no longer care for themselves."

Dezzig bobbed his whole body in affirmation and said sagely, "Ah, and this is when you eat them."

Jake stopped. "No! We don't eat each other! That's considered taboo!"

"You let the mother go to waste?" Dezzig cried in disbelief. "I thought they were import—" He stopped mid-sentence and rattled his wings.

Following his gaze, Jake saw the two Kormas arguing about the reservoir at the same place they had left them. They had gotten a Nock involved, though the squat creature sat there with a spade-like tool in hand, looking back and forth between Fugi and Toler as if he were watching a tennis match.

Since Nocks didn't have necks, this meant rotating his whole body as he followed the conversation.

"Dezzig, what are—" Jake was interrupted by a Seyles dropping from the sky.

A damsel.

The female Seyles were thinner and smaller, and they had shorter wings. Their eyes were also much smaller, and, as a result, their faces were more human-looking. She landed next to Dezzig and beat her wings against his, then folded them demurely in front of her narrow frame.

This completely disarmed Dezzig, Jake noted. Whatever he planned to do to the arguing Kormas, he had forgotten.

"Danais," he said. "How fare you?"

Her voice was much softer in the translator and had a light, melodic sound. "Dezzig," she replied. "It is time." And with that, she took off into the sky, Dezzig close behind her.

"What?" Jake had enough time to get out.

As Jake watched, the two jousted in the air for a while, as he'd seen so many Seyles fight before. Then Dezzig clamped onto her, and the two bodies entwined, forming a Valentine-style heart shape.

"Oh." Jake looked away and resumed walking to his base. He passed the spot where the Kormas had been and paused. They and the Nock must have ducked into the service tunnels running under the reservoir because he could still hear them arguing:

"Bajat Korma The Fool insisted that—"

"Bajat Korma was a fool! It's in his very name!"

He chuckled a little and kept walking till his headquarters was in sight.

HQ was, technically, just a tent, but it was a *grand* tent that covered a large area and had a high ceiling, good ventilation, and some very high-tech equipment. Any of the surfaces of the tent could be used as a display, which freed up more space for a workbench, bed, shower, and strategically placed sun lamps. He even had heavy armor, a battlesuit that was just shy of being a full mech suit! He wasn't sure why

Tarkanian had outfitted him so well, but he could live his whole life on Nidus.

Which, he hoped, wasn't the idea.

He coughed again and took some more pills. He wondered if perhaps Doc Blood had just given him a bunch of placebos.

His sickness and the fact that he was alone with only military rations for food were all that kept this from being an easy, if occasionally irritating, vacation.

Dezzig landed next to him as if nothing had transpired in the previous fifteen minutes.

"Congratulations," Jake quipped.

"On what, Jake Wizard?"

"Becoming a father."

Dezzig rattled his wings. "Perhaps. There will be other Seyles who mate with Danais."

"And you just let that happen?"

The Seyles wheezed out something that sounded like a laugh. "Some guard their damsels until the eggs are laid and the damsel dies, but in the time that would take, I could have fertilized a dozen more damsels."

"Where I come from, it's considered an insult not to know paternity or to suggest a mother is promiscuous."

Dezzig, unperturbed, replied, "What greater insult to a damsel than to suggest that she only could have one male?"

Flustered, Jake said, "No, that's not—females can almost always have many males! It's just considered bad if they do!"

Dezzig wheezed a laugh again. "That doesn't make any sense!"

"Well, I guess some humans would agree with you. But because our young are so helpless, a human born with a dedicated mother and father—a male who devotes himself to caring for mother and child—has a huge advantage over one who doesn't. And the male and female being exclusive to each other strengthens their bond and their devotion to their offspring."

"But it's impossible!" protested Dezzig. "I have hundreds of children, probably. I can't even keep track of them, much less take care of them!"

"A human woman, normally, can't have more than a dozen or—"

"Challenge!" Jake heard a voice cry from the sky.

He looked up and saw another Seyles circling overhead.

"Accepted!" Dezzig called back, rocketing into the sky, brandishing his lance. Dezzig's challenger was a dual-wielder with a lance on each side.

Dezzig had once delivered a lengthy lecture to him about how Fosdik Seyles The Ferocious had argued on the value of two lances over one, but like everything else on the planet, it was in dispute.

He sighed and continued to his tent.

Jake found these impromptu jousting tournaments interesting when he first arrived on Nidus. The Seyles moved quickly and gracefully in the sky, each trying to spear their opponent or disarm him. Either would be sufficient for victory.

Death was not unusual, especially when fighting an interloper from a different kingdom.

These days, however, the exercise struck Jake as stupid and wasteful. It's as if the creatures did nothing but fight, feed, and reproduce.

He was somewhat surprised when, not much later, Dezzig entered his tent—once again as if nothing had interrupted their conversation—hunching over a bit and marveling at the technology. Most Nijins gave his tent a wide berth, not the least because of the lamps.

The tent had lamps that mimicked Earth's solar days so that the persistent twilight didn't completely destroy Jake's circadian rhythms.

During the tent's "day," they were brighter than anything the Seyles had seen, but it was early twilight in the tent now.

Jake was setting up the fabber unit to create small refrigeration packs he could attach to the flak.

Besides the fabber, he had an extruder that could create the filaments the fabber used to build just about anything. When he told the fabber what he needed, it told the extruder what *it* needed, and the extruder created a kind of "shopping list" that showed up on his personal device.

Local clay and the Nidus plants that resembled bamboo covered most of his needs, though sometimes he had to go on a kind of scavenger hunt.

Dezzig rattled his wings a little.

"Magic!"

"Of a sort," Jake agreed. "Hey, do you know there's a hyper-summer coming?"

"I didn't understand the words, Jake Wizard. What's coming?"

Jake explained the centennial seasons, and Dezzig listened carefully, seemed to get the concept, and claimed he had never heard of anything like it.

While he explained, he took detailed pictures of Dezzig, making sure his computers "knew" the Seyles. He wondered if he could lure some other Nijins to the area. Perhaps they'd talk if they felt safe.

"That would've been four generations ago since the...hyper-winter...as you call it. No one is alive from that long ago."

"But you know all about your history. How can *that* not be known?"

Dezzig scrunched up his wings in a kind of shrug.

"OK, another question. This you have to know. When you guys respond to...the pulse...the call..."

Dezzig said, "It is called *bedizening*, Jake Wizard. And it is not discussed publicly beyond noting that someone has bedizened."

"It seems like a kind of insanity. And every Seyles that attacks the pit is covered with this sparkly goop. Why? What is that?"

"Why is it? It just is!"

The refrigeration unit popped out of the fabber, and Dezzig grabbed it and held it up to his face.

"Give it a squeeze," Jake said.

Dezzig did and then said, "Cold!" Then he looked at Jake and said, "You've created a giant awa-vine seed pod?"

Jake nodded, "Sort of. It'll stay cold a lot longer, though." He noticed Dezzig eyeing his cup of coffee. "Go ahead and try it," he said. "It should be fine for Seyles."

"This is delicious, Jake Wizard. How is it made?"

"Usually you take beans of a specific plant from my world and boil it. I made those beans with this." He slapped the fabber.

Fabbed food, while digestible, was always unpalatable—to the point that he ate exclusively from the boxes of rations he brought. However, he had set himself the task of making a palatable fabbed coffee bean—a task made doubly hard by the fact that he didn't like coffee anyway.

There had been a fair amount of down time on Nidus so far.

Dezzig noisily enjoyed the pot he made and, wiping his face, said, "Now, Jake Wizard, let me ask you a question."

Jake waited expectantly.

"Why are you so stupid?"

CHAPTER 5

GAME NIGHT

"Jake, get him! Jake! Get him! JAKE!"

The giant forty-limbed monster towered over Derek, who had run out of ammo but had also lured the creature out so Jake and Lefty could kill it.

Fumbling with his controls, Jake finally launched a rocket, which missed. Before the ravening beast could bite Derek, however, it lit up with fire from another attacker and turned its back to Jake.

"Thanks, Lefty!" yelled Derek.

Jake finally got himself under control and fired rocket after rocket into the creature, bringing it down. The boys whooped and hollered, standing over its corpse and looking out over the ruined city the beast had ravaged.

"Crud," whispered Lefty, "Leidecker's coming, gotta go!"

The city faded, and Jake was left with just a picture of Derek's face.

"Kind of an exorbitant use of company resources, don't you think?" Jake said with a chuckle.

Derek shook his head. "Not only do I *not* think that, I think we need to schedule a game night every week at this time."

Jake laughed out loud. "But I'm awful at these games!" He didn't mention that he strongly disliked virtual reality because he knew the games were Derek's passion.

Derek agreed. "I know! You need the practice. You know, there are only a handful of Q-comms in all of the ICF, and Tarkanian insisted we have one for you. For *some* reason."

Although he didn't really understand the technology, Jake knew that Q-comms cost a pretty penny to create and had to be set up in pairs. One side of the pair could instantly communicate with the other, and the connection was completely secure.

Most interstellar communications used Q-comms as a backbone and then branched off into more conventional forms, ameliorating both the cost *and* the security. Derek had apparently given Lefty a terminal so they could all play games together.

Jake said, "Yeah, he's got some kind of investment in Nidus I don't understand."

"Games are a great way to test connections: they'll show lag, any attempted tampering, and so on."

"Uh huh," said Jake.

"And besides," said Derek, "you might go stir crazy down there."

Jake agreed with that. His last mission, where he was often the only human around, had been tough. Even if an insane cyborg *hadn't* tried to drive him crazy, the sense of isolation would still have been profound.

At this point, he'd been sent down alone and in secret. No one would come to relieve him, and no one wanted to work with him.

His usual partner, a taciturn Finn named Hekki, had just emerged from a coma after their *last* outing and didn't even want to talk about partnering up with Jake after the third near-death experience he'd had; however coincidental Jake was to those experiences.

His most recent partner, Peschke, who had joined him after recovering from a long illness, had had a relapse and needed intense treatment to handle a high-tech poisoning.

Jake needed a similar intense treatment for the same reasons, but he'd been sent to Nidus with a bunch of injections to self-administer and pills to handle outbreaks.

He shivered as a chill racked his body but suppressed the cough.

"Tell me the news, Derek," he said, reaching for an injection. The Q-comm actually supplied him with all kinds of reports. He needed something more human.

"It's super weird here, dude. Everyone's on edge. It's, like, war is coming, and we're just waiting for someone to fire the first shot. There's a kind of eerie calm. Even Lauder has been keeping the station news low key."

Jake wondered if his confrontation with Lauder had anything to do with that.

"Byron's on edge like you wouldn't believe," Derek chuckled.

"I would imagine. A war on Earth would keep him pretty busy."

"No, dude, it's Diana. She's got cravings, and she's moody as hell." Derek laughed harder.

"Oh!" Jake smiled. "Wait, are you guys...hanging out?" Byron and Derek historically had a somewhat antagonistic relationship.

Derek shrugged. "Min-hee and Diana—all the Lost Girls—are pretty tight. And I hear Kurt is negotiating with his dad for a peaceful return. He and Hilda eloped!"

Jake shook his head. "How's Hogar taking it?"

"I don't know, really. To hear the girls talk about it, not well. But Hogar's got romantic problems of his own."

"Ah, Lazar, or Doc Hottie, as Dali calls her."

They continued like this for a while, Jake enjoying Derek's voice and the sense of normalcy it brought. Even the unpleasant topics, at least, were human.

He shuddered again and grabbed a pill from a tin he kept next to a small shelf of souvenirs.

Derek stopped mid-sentence to watch him. "How's your treatment going? You...honestly, you look awful."

Jake grimaced as he swallowed. "I feel awful."

"I know Blood's working on a cure. Peschke's out of his coma, and Doc's trying all kinds of things on him."

Jake could only nod. The silence hung awkwardly in the thick Nidus air.

"Hey!" exclaimed Derek. "Did you manage to fix the flak cannon auto-aimer?"

Jake checked his device. "I'll know pretty soon. We're due for another round shortly." Movement caught his eye, and he said, "Gotta go!"

"Are they attacking again?" Derek asked, alarmed.

Smiling, Jake said, "No, if it's an attack, it's a welcome one."

He signed off with Derek and staggered out of his tent. It took him a while to get his balance these days after sitting, but by the time the *Shiva* had rolled out its ladder, he was standing underneath it and smiling up.

Dali K, his future bride, stuck her head out.

"Hey, tough guy! Gangway!"

He stood back so she could slide down the ladder, feet barely on the ground before she bounced and leapt into his arms.

With considerable effort, he stayed upright during this attack and the subsequent passionate greeting.

Then she stood back a few feet to look at him and scowled.

He smirked. "What? Have I forgotten how to kiss since you left?"

She closed in and stroked his face tenderly. "As if. But I thought Doc Blood was gonna cure you of the Rosicrucian's poison."

Jake chuckled. "Eventually. He's worried if he doesn't make a big, dramatic deal out of it, people will take his brilliance for granted."

She got more serious. "Jake, you should be in a good hospital, not alone on some twilight world."

Grabbing her, he said, "But I'm not alone."

His device chimed.

ALERT: APOTHIKON PULSE

His device sounded a klaxon, and he sighed. "I've got marauding Seyles to keep me company, for example."

CHAPTER 6

THE PULSE

They trotted down to the Apothikon pit, Jake cautioning Dali to enter the sward in the gap where the woollyheads were missing.

She was marveling at the ring of gold surrounding the pit. Pollen-like particles floated and sparked, and gossamer electric filaments faintly revealed connections between them.

"Where is it cleared?" she asked.

"Look at where the barrel is aiming, the ground there," he advised.

She looked at the cleared path somewhat dubiously, then ventured in. "And what happens if someone—some bug gets in here?"

"Bad things," he smiled. "And before you ask, I don't really know. The Seyles—" He interrupted himself to point skyward where a squadron of Seyles had caught the moonlight in their wings, reflecting a dark rainbow of colors to observers below.

"They look almost like angels," she observed.

"Or beautiful demons."

She sidled toward him playfully, and he felt the stab of his love and longing. He swallowed nervously, as if he hadn't kissed her a thousand times before.

"The tribes are rather medieval, though with some oddly advanced technology. They constantly war with each other."

She got closer. The shield's pollen hovered around her, giving her a golden aura. Behind her, the Damsel moon framed her head with a pink halo.

"That's not usually our business, is it? Internecine bug conflicts?"

"Not usually. It is in this case because of this path that's been cleared. These woollyheads are deadly to all Nidus lifeforms that we know of. But something cleared them—and then apparently had no interest in the Apothikon at all."

She draped her arms over his shoulders and brought her lips close to his.

"A mystery, eh?"

He resisted the urge, heroically, to kiss her, instead replying, "Yeah. I suspect Tarkanian owes this Dr. Vizgirda a favor, and I'm the means he's using to pay it."

She leaned her head in, kissing him on his face but avoiding his lips. "He assigned his top man. Must be important."

"I think I'm becoming his first choice when something weird happens, actually." Jake interrupted himself again, this time to give up the struggle and kiss her for real.

The whirring of the electroflak coming to life interrupted them next.

"What do we do?"

He smiled and said, "For now, we step back."

The cannon raised its muzzle. On a readout between the manual triggers, a visual representation of the Seyles appeared, with various annotations that Jake had learned referred to the target desirability.

The attached computational brain figured out threat level, likelihood of landing a significant hit, ammunition level—pretty much infinite as long as the power pack it was sitting on held out—and other factors—and used this to calculate and recalculate optimal targets.

The pack itself had so much energy that he stored his blaster batteries in the dozens of charging slots around it.

As far as Jake could tell, it was a near flawless setup. Perfect for siege conditions. He had fixed the targeting mechanism, too, and he felt confident.

Dali held her breath as a squad of frenzied Seyles tried to attack through the shield. It lit the whole bubble up, especially in the spots where they hit, and slowed their momentum considerably.

Then the bodies passed through like comets, and Dali went for her gun.

"No, it's fine," Jake assured her. "They're dead or very nearly so."

Sure enough, some went into the pit with a light splash. Others fell on the surrounding sward.

She said, "What happens now? Do you sweep them in or something?"

Jake smiled a little grimly and pointed. As they watched, the "grass" began to move like giant cilia, and the lifeless bodies slowly followed their companions to become food for the restlessly gestating Apothikon.

"Initially, I tried covering the pit with a grate," Jake explained. "If I cover it completely, the food can't get in. There's no way to secure a net without breaking the barrier. Even if I could risk that, there's no place to sink a pole. So it's down to me and the electroflak."

"I guess you couldn't pass a rope through the barrier, but what if you drove spikes into the ground?"

He smiled, "Tried it. The grass just spit it out."

She glanced at the grass, grimaced a little, and then turned her attention back outward. The Seyles were swooping around menacingly.

A few plunged toward the gap, and the cannon fired rather judiciously, thought Jake, hitting the incoming attackers so that they weren't vaporized but passed through the open area, some landing, once again, in the pit.

She gave him a sideways look and smirked. "Kind of an easy post, eh, tough guy?"

"Not so easy when the flak's not working."

"Seems like it would be a lot easier if you weren't playing pat-ty-cake," she pointed out.

"If we crank up the power, they vaporize, which deprives the Apothikon of its food. It's not a big deal as long as enough are relatively intact. Hit them too little, though..."

Sparks flew as Seyles attacked from all angles. They reflexively drew their weapons while ducking.

"What happens then?"

He shrugged. "We only have lore to go on. We only have lore for most things involving Nidus."

The Seyles, while frenzied, had begun to react to the different stimuli at the missing section of the shield, and a large section broke off from the rest and began aiming directly for the flak cannon. Dali and Jake bobbed and weaved, fingers at the ready, as the creatures' lifeless bodies hurtled through the opening and into the pit.

"No idea at all?" she said rather loudly, as the cannon was firing continuously now.

He stepped to one side as a smoking Seyles split them. "There is a legend. Are you familiar with the Tree of Knowledge?"

She shot a body as it passed overhead, vaporizing it, and looked at him apologetically. "Should I turn the intensity down?"

"No. Better safe than sorry, I think."

She almost blasted another Seyles as it came through but held back and watched it fall at her feet. "You mean The Tree of Knowledge in the Garden of Eden?"

"Yes. God said if Adam or Eve ate of the fruit, they would die. And the serpent said they would become as God themselves."

The cannon had begun a rhythmic firing pattern, and Jake saw why: the remaining Seyles had intuited that the flak could only fire in one direction and had split into two groups.

Each group was feeding into a line on either side of the gun before charging in, and the pivoting mechanism had to keep swiveling left to right to get them. Smoke drifted up from the swivel mount.

"Dali!" he exclaimed, pointing, but saw she had already noticed the same thing he had, and the two began firing into the crowd, trying to relieve the burden on the cannon.

"Concentrate left!" Jake yelled.

Lining up their shots on the left allowed the cannon to re-calibrate and focus on the right.

"It's working!" she called back.

The focused fire had thinned out the attackers considerably. The remainder had clustered far away from the cannon and looked to be circling, almost like they were thinking.

"Something's up," said Jake. Dali just nodded.

Then the creatures broke their circular pattern and dropped out of sight, invisible behind where the cannon rested on the knoll. The cannon aimed itself down, grinding against its mounting block.

Jake and Dali ventured closer, creeping around the knoll.

"They're coming in too low for the cannon to aim!" Jake exclaimed, but Dali had already started firing, and he followed suit.

They picked them off quickly, from two dozen down to a dozen, then to seven or eight.

Finally, only a clump of four remained, barreling at them in an erratic corkscrew pattern. The cannon managed to get off one shot before the clump smashed into it.

The impact stopped most of the mass, but something blurred by, and Jake leapt toward the pit reflexively.

One of the Seyles had gotten through!

It slid to a halt on the sward, and Jake unsheathed his knife, jumping at it. The knife landed deep in the bedizened abdomen, almost to the thorax, and the Seyles gave a sharp cry.

Got you! Jake thought, the words barely forming before he realized his mistake.

The Seyles, determined to get the Apothikon, clawed forward with all its limbs, letting the knife bisect its lower third.

Scrambling, it plunged itself into the viscous fluid of the pit!

CHAPTER 7

FAILURE

Scrambling forward on his belly, Jake looked into the pit.

Dali still stood at the cannon, poking the Seyles' corpses with her pistol. "I think these are dead. I don't see any more."

Jake looked down into the pit. The Seyles had sunk into the fluid, twitching. This left him with the uncomfortable decision of whether to fish it out or—

"Did one get by us?" he heard her say.

"Yeah. I'm worried I'll make things worse if I try to grab it out."

"Maybe it will just get digested like everything else," she offered helpfully, walking toward him. "You did injure it pretty severely."

"Stay back," he said, getting to his knees.

"You're not going to dive in!" she exclaimed, alarmed.

"No! But it's down there still twitching, and I don't know what's going to happen." He paused for a moment. "There's no reason for me to try to go after it. If it stays in there, it'll—"

As the words left his mouth, the Seyles came rocketing out of the pit, only to flop on the sward. Most of the sparkly goop had washed off, but the creature seemed otherwise whole.

After a heartbeat of shock, Jake lurched forward with his knife, this time planting it in the thorax of the supine creature.

Its wings flashed futilely, and Jake had its legs and one set of arms pinned with his legs and its upper arms held down with his hands.

He looked straight into the creature's multifaceted eyes. Though it could be hard to tell, Jake had the distinct feeling the Seyles didn't even see him. Its body thrashed as it struggled to get free.

Dali had approached behind him, pistol still drawn. "Jake, what's going on with it?"

"I don't know." He turned to the creature, which had collapsed after its initial struggles. After a moment, Jake extracted his knife. He turned to Dali and said, "Strangest thi—"

"Jake!" Dali shouted.

The Seyles pushed itself from the ground and launched into his back. He wobbled but kept his balance, looking around, but it had bounced away and now circled the inside of the shield erratically.

Dali had her pistol out, ready to fire. Before she could get a bead on it, it smashed through the bubble—which was just as deadly for creatures trying to exit as those trying to enter—and plummeted to the ground just beyond.

"So...did we lose here?" Dali started to sit on the knoll under the flak cannon, then stood back up as she observed the grassy sward slowly dragging corpses into the pit. "Hey, these can't push us in, can they?"

Jake chuckled as he dropped in the remains of the Seyles that had been cooked in its escape attempt. In its charred state, it offered no clue in figuring out how or whether it had been affected by its brief swim.

"We're too heavy. Especially once they've been cooked, Seyles don't weigh much."

He felt wobbly and slightly self-conscious about his appearance. Except for Georgia, he hadn't seen a human soul in person since coming to Nidus, and he knew his hair was shaggy, and he'd grown lax about shaving.

Standing near the edge and looking into the pit, he answered, "I don't think so. I hope not. At least the Apothikon doesn't look any worse for the wear."

He looked around and assessed the ring, about thirty-five feet in diameter, with the knoll-mounted electrokflak along the center-line with the pit itself which was twelve feet feet behind the knoll.

She joined him, slipping an arm around his waist. He felt her forearm against his hip bone.

"Hard to know what a healthy...one of those...looks like," she smiled.

Distractedly, he said, "I think there are two things at work here. The Apothikon has to be fed, which it can't be if this...broth...is eaten by something else."

Looking at her and managing a smile, he added, "The other is the taboo and less about the Apothikon than what exposure to this fluid might do. But nobody here talks about it, so we're just guessing about that part."

"The Tree of Knowledge?" she prompted.

"Oh, right," he said, remembering their interrupted conversation from earlier. "Yes, there is some belief that the Seyles used to be small, not much larger than Earth dragonflies, and one entered the pit whole and sound and emerged closer to their current size."

She smiled crookedly. "That seems...improbable. Like a fairy tale."

"They don't talk about it," Jake grumbled, "and for their constant references to historical figures, they refuse to talk about the Apothikon."

"That seems odd."

"Or they just don't know, which—how can *that* be?"

With her help, he cleaned and oiled the flak cannon swivel mount again, checking for corrosion and verifying the refrigeration units he had added were working. He felt some relief when he saw that the smoke had come from chunks of Seyles that had fallen into the pivot mount. The gun would've continued to function just fine, if somewhat over-dramatically.

With a few tweaks to the pivot, the cannon could fire at the ground if they came in low again.

As they reassembled everything, Dali said, "I was reading these papers by a Dr. Vizgirda on my way here—"

"We've met," Jake noted drily.

"Oh?" Dali arched an eyebrow at him. "She says these pulses occur in pairs?"

Jake nodded. "They do. She likens them to a very slow heartbeat. Lub dub. There's a day or more between the 'lub' and the 'dub.' Then some weeks later: lub dub."

"She even calls them the systole and the diastole. The systole pushes out, and the diastole draws in."

"It's not a great analogy because the first pulse definitely draws in some Seyles," he grumbled.

"But her theory is that the systole primes the Seyles—weakens their defenses, maybe—so that the diastole draws many more in. The second pulse is always more intense. So which one was this?"

"This was the diastole," he said, collecting his tools.

"Well, we mostly survived it okay, at least."

He smirked. "Yeah, except the pulse pairs are getting stronger over-all—and closer together."

"Like it's getting excited or something?"

Jake said, "Excited. Yeah, maybe. Anyway, these Seyles used a fair amount of cunning. We may have no choice but to crank the power up."

CHAPTER 8

PSYCHICS AND CON MEN

They walked from the pit to Jake's tent, a spacious dome, re-markably well-appointed, with a wide assortment of equip-ment, a workbench, a shower, and a nice bed raised fairly high off the ground. (Hogar, the ICF's head xenobiologist, was concerned about what Nidus' ground life might do to him while he slept, and Jake had seen some enormous tick-like creatures that convinced him to trust Hogar's instincts.)

Dali went to a set of drawers and picked up the bowl the Trigonans had given him. Had it been two years already?

He still felt a pang about Alvum, a pang less and less about what he had done and more a longing to be back there. He had felt an amazing belonging with the hive minds, and he had grown fond of the ant-like Myrmidons as well.

On the other hand, he'd met a dozen Nijins and struggled with almost all of them.

"They moved you out, eh?" she said, handling the gems he had gotten from the Myrmidon mines. Jake Ambler had few personal possessions. She sniffed briefly at the coffee pot, which Jake had refilled in case Dezzig came by, and turned away sharply.

"I've been vanished, yeah. You and Tarkanian are the only ones who know where I am in all of Bug Space. I got dropped off by the pilot and co-pilot of *Stretch One* when they were headed back to...what did the Coleons call it? Blood space?"

"Gross," she said, "but I suppose fair." Looking around, she noted, "There's only one chair."

"Is that a problem?"

She smiled and sat herself on his lap. She looked at him critically, stroking his shaggy hair away from his face. Then she took his hand, reached into her pocket, and dropped in some small colorful metal sticks.

He smiled and looked at it.

"Penny for your thoughts," she said, brushing her nose against his.

"I was wondering when you'd be ready to talk about Karnata," he said softly.

She nuzzled him. "I'm not sure I'll ever be ready." Then she pressed her forehead to his. "My sister and new brother-in-law staged a huge procession, bearers walking for miles while professional mourners wept loudly."

"Sounds...nice?"

She laughed a little bitterly. "Papa would have hated it. The whole affair stretched out for a week."

"Sounds like they meant well."

She sighed. "The only part he would've liked was the laughing saints."

Jake smiled. "I know nothing of Karnata."

She kissed him. "Yet. The laughing saints don't believe in death, so they view funerals like cons or swindles. A joke."

"And your father would've liked that?"

"He loved the saints. He was respectful to those who grieved, but he wouldn't have wanted to cause any sadness himself. He mistrusted...what was the word he used? Lugubriousness?" She softly laughed when she said it.

She imitated his lilting accent: "Dalaja, lugubriousness is not the Karnata way."

Jake stroked her hair. He struggled a bit to find something to say to reassure her and settled for just being there. He dropped the change back into her jacket pocket.

"In case you need to catch a bus," he said, smiling.

Later, she napped while he worked at his table, looking through a large magnifying glass at a circuit he had designed.

He was woozy, his vision blurred, and he felt a coughing jag coming on. Checking to make sure Dali was out, he grabbed a hypo and injected it quickly, returning to his work in the space of a few seconds.

Don't let it slow you down, he told himself.

He had a bare grasp of electricity fundamentals, just enough to experiment with ideas that had been bugging him for quite some time. The sun-lamps shifted around them to a late afternoon setting.

His task absorbed him enough to where he didn't notice when she woke until she started examining some of the equipment he had.

She smirked a little when she saw his electric knuckles. She slipped them on and did a little shadowboxing, leaving light trails behind her fists.

Peschke had introduced Jake to them as useful weapons in bug space, and he had become enamored of them. She slipped them back off and put them back where she found them.

"That's a pretty nice fabber," she commented on the machine that took up the most space at his bench.

"It is. I have to be able to replace all the parts in the cannon. And I've got enough native resources here that I can filter and use to recreate

Doc Blood's pills, in case I need to." He popped a pill when he said that.

"You must have a ton, though, right?"

He nodded. "Yeah, but if something happened to my stash...I don't even want to think about it. You should hear the Doc hollering about this poison in me. 'What kind of savage dreams up ways to torment their fellow man like this!' I haven't seen him this angry since he met Roy's thrall."

Examining the fabber more closely, she said, "How is Grandpa Roy anyway? Still sending those zombies around to talk for him?"

Jake chuckled. "Like I said, you're pretty much the only one who knows where I am."

"So what are you working on?" she asked, finally focusing fully on him.

He paused and looked at her, hesitating.

"What?" she said, amused.

"I have reason to believe that some aliens can read minds."

She laughed. "And?"

"What?"

"On Karnata, we have readers, blockers—oh, and suggesters, which are the absolute worst. They put thoughts *into* your head."

He looked at her nonplussed. "I guess I'm trying to make a 'blocker.' Which is hard because where I'm from, that's all considered legendary. Mythological. *Debunked.*"

She shrugged. "Well, where *I'm* from, it's not commonplace but it is well-known and accepted. Every time someone wanted my dad to set up an intelligence agency, they would talk about using telepaths."

She pecked at him with light kisses.

"But telepaths tend to be like the Laughing Saints. The discipline of acquiring their skills also makes working for political actors an anathema. Well, except maybe the suggesters."

"That's kind of interesting," he said. "Wait...can you read my thoughts?"

She smiled and got even closer. "You're thinking how adorable and irresistible I am."

He frowned. "Too easy. Here..." He flipped a switch on the circuit. "How about now?"

She leaned in close, looked into his eyes, and kissed him again.

"Jake, I'm not psychic," she giggled.

He turned off his gadget. "I've had a lot of time on my hands here between pulses, and I've been researching thought, memory, and the mechanisms that might allow psychic activity. And coffee."

She kissed his cheek, then his temple.

"The coffee's been a disaster. Psychically, I think I'm getting somewhere. Mental effort must have an energy signature, and that's what's being read..."

She kissed his neck.

"And so I thought I could build a noise machine that would blot out a person's normal energy..."

She kissed him behind his ear.

"I just don't know how to test it."

Pulling back, she looked him in the eyes again. "Maybe we can figure something out. Now, I have a question for you."

"What's that?" He was a little dazed from her kisses.

"OK, so you said the Apothikon's lifecycle goes from an egg laid in the pit somehow. That hatches and becomes a larva. Then it pupates into some other state. Then it forms a chrysalis."

Jake nodded. "That's Hogar's theory, based on Dr. Vizgirda's research and some parallels with other insectoids, yeah."

"So the Apothikon in the pit. That's about to hatch, metamorphose, emerge, or whatever, right?"

He nodded again.

"So where are all the grown Apothikons?"

CHAPTER 9

THE AQUARII

"That," Jake agreed, "is a fine question but not easy to answer!"

"Why not?"

He picked her up, realized he wasn't strong enough to do so, and set her down again.

"Let's introduce you to some of the citizens of Nidus." He walked her out of the tent and gave her a chance to survey the landscape.

He had found a nice-sized plateau that overlooked the pit, gave him a clear view of Grigg's castle to his east, a tall hill to the northeast he called Mount Olive, and to the west, beyond the pit, a river beyond which lay a rough wilderness.

To the immediate south, a high crag rose above his base, which the bolder Seyles would mount, silently watching him.

He said, "The first thing you must remember is to watch where you step."

She stopped and looked down.

"Looks like bioluminescent grass."

He pointed to a similar patch in the distance. "And that?"

"Same. Maybe a different shade of green. It's hard to see colors in this light."

They walked over to the patch, and as they got closer, the disordered mass of color resolved itself into a neat series of lines.

He stopped at the edge and said, "If you look closely, you can see movement."

She bent over, then straightened back up. "Worms? Large worms, but still..."

"These are the Nephros, the farmers of Nidus. Let's head up to Mount Olive." He motioned her to follow him as he walked a path up the hill.

She gasped a little when she came to stand beside him at the top. The regular field they had just been at abutted another field, a slightly different color but with rows oriented perpendicular to the one they had been looking at.

And this abutted several more plots, which were in turn surrounded, until the ground looked like a patchwork quilt: each square with its own ordered lines that contrasted with its neighbor.

"Underneath all these fields is a world unto itself. The Nephros are farmers, but they work from underneath as much as from above."

He pointed to some narrow channels networking the fields, which extended to much larger hills in the distance.

She looked for a while, her head tracing the artificial rivers that flowed down from a large structure embedded in the hills.

"An aqueduct?" she marveled.

"As much used to drain water as to supply it. The Kormas architect and the Nocks build those structures. A Korma is inspecting the reservoir right now."

She looked to where he was pointing, but he could tell she couldn't make much out of the odd-shaped blob in the distance.

"That's a Korma," Jake explained. He pulled out his device and showed her a picture.

She looked at it and said, "How...how does it not fall over with a head that big?" Jake chuckled, and she amended herself, "I know, I know. The heads—*everything* about bugs is lighter than it looks to us as humans."

"Here's the wrinkle that I've discovered. I haven't found this documented in any training materials or research: the many different lifeforms on Nidus all live at different rates."

She asked, "Different rates? I know they don't live as long, for the most part, as..."

"Lifespans are all over the place and mostly shorter, true, but I'm speaking of their concept of...I don't know what you'd call it...*now*. So, as we're standing here talking, time is passing for us at a rate we're both comfortable with."

She slid in close and hugged him. "Pretty comfortable."

He smiled and said, "The Kormas would regard our interactions as rather fast. The Seyles, by contrast would think it slow."

"In fact, Dezzig Seyles, the closest of the bugs here I might consider a friend, asked me not long ago why I was so stupid."

She laughed. "You have odd taste in friends."

He said, "No, just imagine it. Suppose. I. Paused. In. Between—"

She laughed. "Okay! Okay, you made your point. It's annoying!"

"Now, there's also a species here called the Diptera who are so much faster, it's hard to interact with them directly. That's one of their cities."

She looked where he pointed and said, "I can see light and movement, but I can't make it out."

He moved his finger up and down to trace the city skyline, saying, "It's only about five or six feet tall at its highest, but it stretches over several miles. It's also surrounded by a wall, probably to protect it from larger creatures stumbling through it."

"Can we go look at it up close?"

He said, "Eventually, but I haven't been able to talk to them yet. Let's start with the Kormas. They're about our speed." He walked her down the side of the hill, which abutted a plateau, through the "olive trees."

"Hey, these aren't olives," she said accusingly, looking at one of the small black fruits that had dropped to the ground.

"They're not even trees! If you look closely, you'll see they're more like stalks of bamboo that have intertwined around each other. Nidus is so dimly lit, it plays tricks on you—you fill in the blanks with familiar things instead of seeing what's there."

"Maybe we should wear goggles," she suggested.

"I have several pairs back at the base. The problem with *that*," Jake began, only to pause as lights flashed and flickered around them. "The problem is the Luca. You'll be enjoying a nicely adjusted view of the landscape, and then these things start flashing, and you're blind."

"What *is* all that flashing?" she asked. "It reminds me a bit of the harbor back home, except more chaotic."

"Honestly, I don't even notice them anymore. The flashes are a communication system, much like signal lamps used to be used on boats. It's far richer than the binary system that ancient sailors used. The Luca can generate at least a dozen distinct color shades and have ten or so distinct durations as well."

He said, "On top of that, they can work in tandem and make chords of a sort. I've only seen a few Lucas up close but they seem to exist solely to act as communication systems. Or that's how the Seyles treat them."

"What do they talk about?" she wondered.

"I've mounted a remote-activated light and receptor on the crag above my tent to decode it all, and—well, it's pretty boring."

"It is?"

"It's small-town news. Crop yields. Water levels. When there are birth and death notices, it's just raw numbers. There's noise mixed in, too."

"Oh. That doesn't sound very interesting."

"No, although they're probably talking about us now," he grinned. "We're news."

She grinned back and then pointed at a passing glowing light. "So, what's that? Is that one off duty?"

He smiled. "No. That's...I don't know what it is. It's not one of the intelligent species. I've been calling them will-o'-wisps because they remind me of lightning bugs from Earth."

"I know the superstition of will-o'-wisps! They would lead travelers to treasure!"

He added, "Or death. These would be the deadly kind. Their lifecycle is..." He struggled for a moment. "Just do me a favor, and don't go wandering around without me. There's a lot of quicksand."

She looked puzzled by that, so he said, "I'll explain later. For now, let's go talk to the aquarii."

They carefully crossed the fields to the reservoir wall. Two of the Kormas were there, animatedly discussing something. The more agitated they got, the more their heads bobbed and swayed, and occasionally, their snouts would collide—which didn't seem to slow either down in the least.

Jake couldn't swear he had learned to differentiate one Korma from another unless he could clearly see the pattern on their fake heads, but the fact that they were arguing tipped him off. "Toler Korma?"

Both Kormas turned to look at them. One said, "Jake Wizard." Fugi, with the scary Seyles face pattern, echoed his greeting.

Every world, and every culture on that world, had its own form of address. For Nijins, species was used as a last name. It seemed impractical until he realized the Nijins had a strict caste system based on species. Your last name was who you were and a good indicator of what you did, a reminder to yourself and everyone else of your station.

The Seyles may have had a word for "human" early on, but they more commonly used "Wizard" now to refer to Jake and other humans.

"This is my friend, Dali K—er, Wizard. How goes the argument?"

The inhabitants of Nidus, as a whole, loved to argue about their work. Jake had seen more arguments than actual work and knew the two Kormas would eagerly take up their points.

"We're discussing the deterioration of the reservoir wall," Fugi replied. He pointed to the wall, which Jake had observed casually on many occasions. Unusual bricks—triangular and laid in complementary patterns with fairly small amounts of mortar between, stretching from the ground to a couple of yards over the Kormas' heads.

In places the mortar had deteriorated, and a thick, grassy plant called a *mud reed* poked through. (Jake had learned that the other side of the wall had a waterproof layer made from a common clay, which reduced some of the pressure against the wall.)

"Still?" Jake asked, unsurprised.

"Toler Korma believes we should scrape out the mortar and replace it, while I say that this deterioration is normal and expected and is meant to encourage the mud-reed to grow here and support the awa-vine."

Jake flicked the grasses on the wall a little. "This is the mud-reed?"

Fugi circled his alligator head in agreement.

Toler knocked his own big head against Fugi's in disagreement. "Larn Korma The Meticulous, one of the greatest in all of history, *demonstrated* how the Mud Reed weakens the reservoir!"

"And Grat Korma The Indomitable *proved* that the weakening scenario only applied after an extended drought *and* plague we—"

"I'm sorry to interrupt you, Fugi, but we wanted to ask you a question."

Toler and Fugi looked at each other. "Jake Wizard wants to ask *us* a question?" Fugi said, awed.

"Yes. We know the Apothikon will come out of its pit soon, and we were wondering where all the already grown Apothikons were?"

The two Kormas looked away from each other now in silence.

Jake said to Dali, "Every time. It's like they're too embarrassed..."

Dali gave a little yelp, and Jake turned his attention to her and the spear-wielding Notos, who had walked up to them unnoticed.

Seven feet tall with six powerful limbs, they seemed to be able to use them interchangeably. Something about their narrow, almost tube-like bodies made them easy to overlook until they were upon you.

"Jake Wizard," the Notos said without ceremony, "Lord Grigg demands your presence."

With a similar lack of ceremony, the two humans followed the Notos, who were leading them to the Castle. Jake found these the most discomfiting of Nidus' inhabitants. As he and Dali followed, he noticed the Notos made plenty of noise now, smashing the butts of their spears rhythmically against the ground as they walked.

Two spears. When Notos walked, they carried one on each side, but they had an incredible facility for wielding both from one side or the other, in either or both hands, driving down with an upper arm and up with a lower.

He'd even seen one hold a spear with his foot while using the other spear from the same side.

Granted, this was from a gladiator competition, which the Seyles loved, but it looked very convincing. Given that he'd seen Seyles joust with two spears, he didn't doubt the Notos also had an ambidextrous facility.

The larger moon—the Dragon moon—had once again settled nicely behind Grigg's castle and presented an ominous picture to Dali, who looked up with a gasp.

Jake quietly slipped himself another pill.

CHAPTER 10

AN EXTRAORDINARY GREED

Despite the Notos, Jake (who was a Wizard, after all) made a point of stopping on the bridge before entering the castle so that Dali could take a moment to see the Seyles' city.

The basic unit of Seyles dwellings was a roundish hodgepodge of sticks from the bamboo forests just beyond the city limits. They weren't actually bamboo, of course, any more than the woollyheads were woollyheads, but from a distance, the long, tall sticks (eerily reminiscent of the Notos body, Jake reflected) recalled the earth plants.

The Nocks, who built the houses, wove separate, bendable fasces over each other with a mud plaster to create an interior area that could be subdivided.

The bulk of the houses were single-story affairs, but the architecture allowed these basic units to be stacked, and Seyles would often do so.

The highest ranking Seyles would stack towers very high, and in spots, the city had the densest clustering of high towers Jake had ever seen anywhere, including Earth and the moon, reaching hundreds of feet into the air. The Seyles compensated for the casualness of the architecture with yet more bamboo, this time used to shore up the towers—which, even supported, often leaned one way or the other, sometimes resting against their equally overly tall neighbors.

Dali smiled, amused. She said, "I guess there's no sun to block out." Looking down she added, "Or any need for streets."

"Gaps between the houses create some narrow ones below, but you're right. If you're patient and watch the horizon, you *can* sometimes see one of the moons peeking through."

Looking around, she pointed off beyond the city. "What is that sea of colorful spheres outside the city before the bamboo forest? The one with the enormous flowers around it."

"Those are the, uh, Seyles eggs," Jake said. "The flickering is the movement of the unborn Seyles. We can go look at them after this."

Grigg's castle stood above this rustic yet oddly forboding vista, glowering at the city below. The Seyles had fire but used glass bowls filled with a bioluminescent algae-like plant for light. The algae throbbed its own unknown rhythm, dimming and brightening at different rates.

As a result, the castle windows looked like actual eyes, especially windows installed with stained glass. Standing before it, Jake had the sense of being watched by a titanic Seyles.

The tall towers of Grigg's castle ringed a courtyard in which the entertainment of the court and the justice of the court (often the same thing) took place. Seyles flew everywhere, so their architecture had little in the way of hallways and passages. Like the Lydians, they did not distinguish between "doors" and "windows."

Ground floor access was for lesser creatures.

The castle roof was nominal, with a pergola over the top towers, mostly to limit the rain.

And from the court-facing balconies, all looked down upon those who entered. Jake realized he felt much happier behind a flak cannon when dealing with this many of the beasts.

He glanced at Dali, who displayed not a hint of discomfiture.

A musical performance by a trio of Seyles who had fitted their spiracles with horns wound down as the two humans watched. The bagpipe-like cacophony died in echoes, and the performers quickly floated off.

The Notos who had escorted them had already withdrawn, and Jake strode into the courtyard with Dali close behind. He put his hands to his sides and bent his knees slightly—the closest he could come to a recognizable Seyles bow, which involved scrunching up into an S-shape.

"Jake Wizard," hum-rumbled Grigg, "who have you brought with you?"

Before he could answer, she said, "I am Princess Dalaja of Karnata. Greetings from my people to yours." The balconies hummed with excitement. "I apologize," she continued, "for my humble appearance. We are far from Karnata and I rushed here when I heard of the challenges facing your kingdom."

Jake smiled inwardly. She had told the literal truth: upon returning to Space Station XEE, she had learned that Jake had been stationed—alone—on Nidus and immediately signed on to help him.

He tried not to lose his self-presence in marveling over how she delivered her words at high speed without sounding rushed. Jake Wizard should not be smitten...well, Jake Wizard *was* smitten, but it was best if he did not show it.

From the very highest balcony, Grigg plummeted down to get a closer look at Dali, who didn't flinch at the monster's approach. "I confess, Jake Wizard, that I brought you here to chastise you for your lack of support, but I believe I have misjudged you. This is your damsel?"

Jake barely suppressed a smile. "Yes, Lord Grigg."

"And this...Karnata?"

Dali smiled perfectly. It wasn't a smile she'd give Jake or one of her Lost Girls. It was a queenly smile, and it found a welcome reception in the imperious Grigg. "A kingdom much like Nidus, founded by my family, and which eagerly awaits the arrival of our new friends, the Seyles."

He drew in his four wings and let himself relax into the natural curl the Seyles' had when at ease, only *slightly* looming over them now. "Perhaps, then, you can answer a question for me."

Grigg's enormous, multifaceted eyes flickered and then shifted colors to appear completely focused on Dali.

"Jake Wizard tells us that there are humans who, should they desire our planet, will invade and conquer us."

Dali nodded. "Some humans definitely would."

"I understand this." Grigg bobbed slightly. "He tells us we must not fight each other, but instead must forestall conflict with humans by engaging in peaceful trade agreements."

"Yes."

Grigg leaned in a little, and the effect was quite intimidating—still, Dali didn't cringe at all. "So why would Jake Wizard want to make it harder for humans to conquer us?"

The gallery batted its wings in approval and anticipation.

Dali removed the change from her jacket and held it out, letting the colorful sticks drop to the floor with musical tinkles.

It was a delightfully dramatic gesture, and an effective one, as the coins glittered on the floor, and—not knowing their denomination or, indeed, much about money at all beyond the disks they exchanged with each other as a token of status—the Seyles doubtlessly imbued them with a greater value than they actually had while inferring tremendous wealth on Dali's part.

"He may have told you that we humans no longer care for these things, which is true and not at the same time."

The court had grown quiet, and she smiled. "We do not value gold or silver, it is true, but we also know that just as other planets value things we do not, they have treasures we comprehend not."

Grigg drew back. "Aha! So you're not interested in our mines but greedy for our..." He looked a little puzzled. "Our what?"

Dali held her arms out disarmingly. "We do not yet know. Perhaps your nectar. Or your music." (It probably wasn't going to be the music, Jake thought.)

She continued. "Very possibly something that means so little to you, you wouldn't even think it important—but which could become priceless to us."

Jake winced a little. He hoped it wasn't *that* valuable. All too well, he knew how that could backfire.

Grigg, however, seemed pleased and reassured. He forcefully expelled air from his spiracles in a Seyles laugh—something Jake had never seen him do before. "Finally, I understand! An extraordinary greed!"

###

"You're good at this," he said later as they walked past the sea of Seyles eggs, piled haphazardly on each other from the back of the giant flower bed all the way to the edge of the bamboo forest. The eggs were more impressive up close, larger than beach balls, and internally lit somehow so that the unborn Seyles visibly wriggled around inside.

The luxury of being at the top of the food chain, thought Jake. *Even the embryonic form creates a shadow close enough to an adult Seyles to scare off predators.*

This was only true of the youngest eggs, he noticed. The older ones grew opaque and sinister-looking.

In front of the clutches, as the groups of eggs were modestly des-ignated, enormous cup-shaped flowers grew, their stamens jutting provocatively upward.

"I'm good at looking around like a rube?" she laughed.

"You're good at negotiating," he clarified. "Perhaps you should be a bailiff instead of a pirateer." He mangled the word "privateer" deliberately.

She stopped and looked upward, leaning into him. "I couldn't do what I do as a bailiff. I address them as equals—or even as slight inferiors."

She said it so naturally, and he had seen her in action, that it seemed a perfectly straightforward sentiment without pretense or arrogance. "It's all about altitude," she smiled.

"I wish you were going to be around for my conference with Lord Matzhin."

"Is he difficult? Types like Grigg can be easy—unless threatened when they become very difficult."

"Matzhin is much easier to talk with. Perhaps because he's the one threatening Grigg. In some ways, it's worse because he's friendly. He seems to like me but doesn't listen to a word I say."

She reluctantly pulled away so she could face him. "And when you tell him that you're going to murder his army?"

Jake shrugged. "I think he presumes I'm exaggerating. I think he wants to test me."

"He'd sacrifice his army for that?"

Jake pointed up and along the piles and piles of Seyles eggs. "You see these clutches of eggs? There are several thousand here, and there are many of these scattered all over the kingdom. Matzhin has just as many himself."

"But...they'll be children! They won't be born ready to fight!"

Jake shook his head. "They are born not just strong enough to fight, but with an instinctual know-how."

She turned this over in her head. "So, if you win, he's just rebuffed. He loses some troops, which are easily replaced. And if he gets through to the Apothikon..."

Jake agreed. "If he gets through to the Apothikon, everyone in Grigg's kingdom dies. That's our best guess, anyway."

She frowned. "The uncertainty..."

He nodded silently.

"And the bank of flowers? They look like giant Calla lilies and make me feel tiny."

"I call them 'Callas,'" he laughed. "I forget their technical name, but their pollen mixes with the air and creates this glittery goop. When the Seyles go crazy over the Apothikon pulse, they first fly here, rub it all over themselves, and then attack."

She looked at him, confused.

"No, I have no idea why. Nobody does."

"Jake," she blurted out suddenly, "let's get married."

He smiled and coughed out a laugh. They had always considered their marriage inevitable, but her abruptness surprised him. Half shocked and half-amused, he said, "Are you going to bring a minister back from XEE? A priest, a minister, or a rabbi?"

With a serious expression, she replied, "Do you need...any of those...to get married?"

He shook his head thoughtfully. "No, I suppose not. All we have to say is, 'I do.' As the captain of the *Shiva*, can you marry us?" He smiled at the thought.

Still serious, she shook her head. "That's not a real thing. Captains can't marry anyone at sea or in space unless they could have married them on land anyway."

"Well, how is it done on Karnata, then?" He began to guide them back toward his base, suddenly feeling oddly exposed.

She said, "Common law is the norm. The two individuals involved simply have to agree they are married. There are some rituals they can do, and they usually exchange a token of some kind. But none of that is necessary."

"What? No clergy? No paperwork? No party?"

"Some rituals involve the clergy, and it's customary to go to the hall of records when children come along."

"Party?"

She giggled a little. "Young couples are often too busy. Parties come later, usually with pregnancies."

"Interesting. So you're saying, if we just say 'we're married' then..."

She nodded gravely. "Before we do that, though, I want us to get everything out in the open."

Jake felt beads of sweat form instantaneously on his skin.

Funny. It's not like I'm hiding anything from her.

He told himself that, but he knew it wasn't true.

"We don't have much time before I have to go, so I'm going to start by telling you something you can think about while I'm gone."

"Uh oh," he gulped comically.

She said, in complete earnest, "Jake, I've loved you from the moment I first saw you."

This provoked a number of responses. First, a sentimental warmth suffused him. Then, when his brain caught up to his heart, confusion. "Wait...you mean when you kicked me in the back in the V-Ring?"

"No, Jake. I saw you months before you ever saw me."

CHAPTER 11

CONFESSIONS

"Wait. What? How? When?"

He could see her trying to smile, wanting to use humor or sarcasm to avoid the truth, but instead, she just blushed fiercely.

"Mars is a great way-point. We had a lot of missions that took us through there."

"I think I would've noticed the Lost Girls parading around Mars," Jake argued.

"Of course you would. In fact, one of the reasons we make such splashy entrances in places is to condition people for when we need alibis. Most of the time, though, we travel singly or in pairs when we're on missions. And quietly."

Jake led them around the outside of the city in silence. He was stunned. He hadn't expected this. Seyles circled above them, their wings glittering with the reflected light of the feeble sun.

"And once on Mars, while passing through the dining hall, I saw the most beautiful creature I had ever seen. At least, human creature."

Jake stammered. "Now...come on...I know you like me, but—"

"Not you, you dope," she poked him. "Though you are more handsome than you seem to realize. No, this was a girl. Gorgeous strawberry-blond hair. A face so clean and pure, you would have thought she escaped from a Renaissance painting. Her every movement was graceful, full of a strong, poetic confidence. Piercing light-colored eyes, yet warm and radiant."

"Jezz," Jake mumbled.

"And she was looking with complete adoration at this total mope who wouldn't give her the time of day."

Jake snickered, though mostly from embarrassment. "I can see how you might find that compelling."

She punched him in the shoulder. "No, I managed to look beyond it. You didn't have *all* the girls hanging on you. Just one who might have been a goddess. And I think she saw in you what I saw—and see—in you."

"Don't punch me again," he pleaded, "but I can't imagine what that is."

"I can't explain how I recognized it since I only saw you eating—or beating up Derek in the ring. The things you've done—on Teila or even Alvum—didn't surprise me. There's something in you that says, 'I'm going to do this, and no one's going to stop me.'"

"Pigheadedness."

"No doubt," she agreed, leaning in almost close enough to kiss him. "But a girl feels like if some of that pigheadedness were directed in her favor, well, that'd be something she could count on."

"You *can* count on me," he murmured into her lips.

She pulled away suddenly, climbing the side of a hill that was part of the chain that led to Mount Olive. "I should have told you all this sooner. You might never have come with me to see the snow on Alvum and..."

He chuckled. "Am I supposed to reject you because you were attracted to me?"

She stood and looked at him seriously. "No, you're supposed to consider what kind of person *I* am. I don't even really understand what I did or why."

"I'm glad you did, you know. You've been in my thoughts since you took your helmet off in the V-Ring."

They walked in silence until they came to the *Shiva*, which she had parked about halfway between Jake's base and Mount Olive.

She gave him a quick kiss. "Think it over for a while. I'll see you in a few days."

"Your move, Jake Wizard."

Lord Matzhin's court had a wilder configuration than Grigg's. While as tall, it had more alcoves and a generally freer layout than Grigg's look-at-me style.

The downside of this arrangement for Jake was that he never knew where to find Matzhin when he arrived at court.

Fortunately the ruler had found *him* and had coaxed him over to a large table where a chess board was set up. Jake had had a hunch that these feudalistic creatures might enjoy the game, and he'd mostly been wrong.

Lord Matzhin had been the exception, wrangling Jake into playing whenever he visited. Matzhin's kingdom functioned more independently than Grigg's: where Grigg wanted to be the center of attention, the primary mover and director of activity, Matzhin had others taking care of as much as possible, only to be disturbed as a last resort.

While far from an expert chess player, Jake easily outmatched the Seyles and had to throw a few games so as not to humiliate Matzhin.

Twice, he had been not subtle enough, and the Seyles had insisted he take the move back.

All-in-all, he was a much more pleasant creature to deal with than Grigg, but also somewhat maddening, in that Matzhin's apparent desire to please was primarily reflected in social grace—and not an actual change in direction.

Jake moved his knight to threaten Matzhin's queen. He could see the scowl appear over the giant compound eyes, giving the face the impression of having a nose.

Matzhin withdrew his queen with something akin to a smile. "You do not know, Jake Wizard, how refreshing it is to play this game. Is there much *material* about it on your world?"

"Material? Oh, yes, games are recorded and studied, volumes of strategy, even drama devoted to it!"

Jake moved his knight again, threatening Matzhin's queen and a forgotten bishop the Seyles had ventured out earlier.

"How delightful it is to know none of that!"

Jake had noticed this about Nijins. Awash in their own history—with certain notable and curious blind spots—they craved novelty, almost to the extent it seemed to Jake that they coveted ignorance.

Around them, the court swarmed with activity, unlike Lord Grigg's, where Seyles sat watching supplicants enter and present themselves under the watchful eye of the Notos.

Matzhin had all manner of species flying and crawling around. The oddly large-headed Kormas consulted with Seyles on plans, and each such group had a fat, squat Nock in attendance. The Kormas acted as an intermediary between Nocks and Seyles. Not, Jake observed, because they spoke different languages, but because they lived at different speeds.

The Seyles spoke at a rate the Kormas could process, but just barely. The Kormas themselves could slow down enough for Nocks to understand. For any big project, the Seyles would tell the Kormas what they wanted, and the Kormas would architect a solution that the Nocks would implement.

Unsurprisingly, a constant irritation attended these conferences. *They're planning a war*, Jake realized.

Matzhin had moved poorly, and Jake set his knight to threaten the king. "Check."

The Seyles emitted a chuckling hum. "Jake Wizard, you are so distracted you are forgetting to let me win."

Jake smiled nervously. "Lord Matzhin, I am concerned that you will attack Lord Grigg."

"Why should that concern you, Jake Wizard? He's merely exuvia."

Jake racked his brain for a moment to recall the meaning of the insult: the Seyles molted throughout their lives, and the material they shed was called *exuvia*. The politest interpretation he had for it was "an empty suit."

Matzhin carried on. "I am playing, Jake Wizard. You do not need to explain the threat of humans again and how we must band together to fight you all off."

Key to the Seyles' dominance on Nidus was their ability to *eat* the other species. Jake didn't think they could manage that with humans, and if they tried, the act might be fatal, given differences in chemistry.

But even with that and his status as a wizard, the size differential made it difficult for Seyles to take him seriously.

This left him trying to convince these flying monsters of the danger that not only humans generally posed but the destruction that he was personally capable of—in fact, *required* by his employer to do.

"It's not just that. Your Highness, if you invade Grigg's land, I will have to fight against you, and I would hate to—" He gestured around helplessly.

Matzhin clearly found it amusing. "You worry too much, Jake Wizard. Or should I call you 'Jake Human'?"

Jake started. The Seyles had labeled him "Wizard," apparently due to some legends of being visited in the long-ago past by humans—or at least something that a giant four-winged monster would perceive as similar to a human. Matzhin's use of "Human" suggested he wasn't impressed by the "magic" he had seen or heard about.

He took a deep breath and fixed a level gaze on the creature.

"Lord Matzhin, with complete forthrightness, I must tell you that I have been called *The Destroyer of Worlds*."

Hell.

He hadn't gotten through to Matzhin. He knew he hadn't. The Seyles had been condescending and spoken diplomatically, all while the court didn't even register a hiccup in its war preparations.

He had even gotten a lift from a lower-ranking Seyles back to his tent, so unintimidated they were by him.

Seyles didn't think much about roads, so the ground-based Nijins traveled on muddy paths or occasional cobblestones, with one exception. Each piece of Apothikon territory was connected to each other by a road called the Node Path.

Longitudinally, it went from Matzhin in the south, through Grigg's kingdom and the Great Marsh to the north, and beyond both to wrap all the way back to Matzhin.

Latitudinally, one end started at the planet's sunny side in the west, ran through the wilderness next to Grigg's kingdom, then through Grigg's kingdom. From there it crossed The Endless Marsh—a vast stretch so big, the kingdom on the other side didn't even bother threatening Grigg. It ended where the twilight band gave way to the wintry side of the planet.

The north/south and east/west paths crossed not far from where Jake had set up his camp, and he often walked the Node Path to the east to get to Grigg's castle.

It was an ancient road, and many arguments were had as to who built it and why.

He watched it wind below him, through the fields tended by the Nephros (who *really* looked like worms from fifty yards up), churning through the dirt to weed and till with their fields demarcated, Jake noticed, by the tendrils of the seed pod vines, the awa-vines that enmeshed all the lands. He saw clutches of eggs on Matzhin's side of the Valley Ridge and the giant Callas blooming against them, identical to the ones by Grigg's castle.

Nidus felt like an eternal autumn, forever in twilight, either just a little cool or a little warm for comfort, damp air smelling of rich decay. The sun, totally eclipsed and visible only by its corona, hung low on the horizon like a flaming wheel.

His ride, a chatty youngster named Zh'mer, asked many questions about space, wizards, and other bug species in the area but never waited for an answer, distracted by some bit of terrain or an unusual structure.

His chief fascination, however, was *stores* and *shopping*. Seyles, he explained, took what they wanted from the lesser species, exchanging gold and silver disks with holes in the center only with each other. They used such coins to gamble or to express fondness.

They also used them to buy things from each other, typically things they had stolen or gotten their slaves to make. There were few Seyles artisans.

Jake indicated that he wanted to be set down by the reservoir, where it looked like Fugi and Toler were *still* arguing about the reservoir.

They ducked into nearby holes when they saw Zh'mer and Jake flying toward them.

Zh'mer set him down none too gently, though with no particular malice, saying, "Silly Kormas probably thought—well, it doesn't matter. I'd better get out of here before—"

"Challenge!" called a voice from above.

Zh'mer zipped up quickly, and the two began conversing at a speed his translator couldn't keep up with. The challenging Seyles carried two lances and definitely looked ready to fight.

Out of nervous habit, Jake looked toward the knoll where the Apothikon pit lay. He didn't think anyone knew of the gap in the woollyheads, and he wanted to keep it that way. So, as much as he had the urge to check on it, he decided to wait until—

Among the woollyheads, he saw a bright white amongst the gold-white of the flowers. An optical illusion, perhaps?

Above, the challenger sounded like he didn't care for Zh'mer's peaceful overtones and the two had floated about forty yards away from each other, aiming their lances up.

Zh'mer only had one, but Jake could not pick up from this distance if he felt any disadvantage.

Jake glanced back toward the cannon. The white blob—it was definitely there—and *moving*!

Above him, the two Seyles smashed into each other. He looked up, compelled by the violence, and couldn't make sense of what he was seeing. He knew traditionally, after the initial impact, the battle would break away from a two-dimensional opening to an outright dogfight.

He only realized the potential threat to himself when a lance came spiraling toward him. He jumped back and moved away from the aerial battle as pieces of Seyles rained down. Then another lance.

He glanced at the blob by the pit. It vanished behind the knoll.

He wanted to run toward it but worried about how conspicuous that would look. The corpse of a Seyles landed ten feet from him, and he reflexively jumped back.

Another Seyles plunged down and hovered right in front of him.

"Well, Jake Wizard, I'm off. We'll meet again, I'm sure, and you can answer all my questions." The victorious Zh'mer had a small hole in one of his wings but otherwise looked none the worse for wear.

Jake dismissed him as quickly as possible and turned his attention back toward the Apothikon pit.

Was the thing gone?

He heard a noise behind him. Looking back to the reservoir, he saw that the remains of the Seyles had been swarmed by the two Kormas, a Nock, and a bunch of Nephros who had wriggled from the fields. He even thought he saw a tiny swarm of Diptera.

Jake's stomach heaved. Now, he looked toward the Apothikon just to have something else to look at.

He had heard of the Nijins' penchant for eating each other. He had never seen it up close before. But since everyone was distracted, now was the time to make his move.

He started sprinting, arriving at the knoll where his flak cannon rested, winded and nauseated. Bending over to catch his breath, he reached in his jacket for a bottle containing Doc Blood's medicine. The pills spilled through his fingers until he steadied himself against the flak cannon and used both hands.

As they dissolved on his tongue, the question of their long-term efficacy rose once again.

They're not working, he thought. *I'm just dying slightly more slowly than I would without them.*

The spots cleared from his eyes, and he looked around. He was at Mount Olive and his base to the south on its protected plateau—the reservoir to the southeast, where the Nijin had finished feasting on the Seyles' remains.

He shuddered, not entirely from the cool breeze whipping up from the grassland to the west, where picturesque footbridges marked the wide border river. He could only vaguely make out the old roads that must have been used when there was a kingdom there.

At one point, that land had been farms, and the land beyond, too, had been developed, just as Doctor Vizgirda had said. Jake could still see the faint ghosts of the quilted pattern of farms and the skeleton outline of a Seyles town where the bamboo hadn't completely swallowed it.

No Nijins. The only lights were the soft, sleepy glow of the will-o'-wisps. The awa-vines, with their thick clusters of seed pods, also stopped at the river's edge, with no sign of anything that looked like it ate flowers.

But as he climbed down from the knoll, he noticed *another* channel of woollyheads was missing!

CHAPTER 12

BOMBUR

Jake steadied himself again. The cannon would have to be re-calibrated to allow it to rotate far enough to the left to cover this new gap. He thought of the original one as being at twelve o'clock, and the new one was at nine.

It was at least a narrower gap. The Seyles would have to fly through sideways.

Adjusting the brackets on the swivel would be easy enough, but he knew he would struggle to change the defense algorithm.

Or he could send the specs to Derek.

With his device, he scanned the area, showing the gaps. With that and the current targeting program, Derek would be able to get this done far faster than he could.

A tiny, tinny voice rang in his ear.

"The monster went over the bridge!" it said.

He looked around, not seeing anything. "What language was that?" he asked his device, which immediately responded:

DIPTERAN

"Dipteran," the tiny voice echoed the printout on his screen. "I'm Bombur. I live in the city over there. Melontikopolis."

A speck the size of a gnat appeared in front of his eye and flew toward the small-scale metropolis he had shown Dali earlier.

"But if you're a Diptera," Jake asked, "how can I understand you? I have to recalibrate my device drastically, or it just registers Dipteran voices as static."

"I'm slow," said Bombur. "And even I have to concentrate very hard to talk this slowly."

"You're still a bit faster than a Seyles if the readings on my device are accurate," Jake observed.

"You don't have to rub it in. I get enough of that back home."

Jake smiled. "That's still far faster than everyone who *isn't* a Diptera."

Bombur lazily floated in front of his face, and he had to curb his urge to clap his hands over the little creature.

"They think I'm dumb."

"You don't seem dumb to me."

"Because you're *really* dumb," Bombur said guilelessly.

Jake laughed, and Bombur tumbled in the currents.

"Is that funny?"

Still smiling, Jake headed back to his camp. "It is to me. I guess your species would consider mine very dull, but we're on *your* planet and not the other way around."

"Are you slow for a human?"

Jake said, "I guess I'm about the same speed as most humans, maybe even a little faster in some ways. Though we have people *we* consider slow. We're not always kind to them, either," he added thoughtfully.

Bombur vanished from sight, and Jake reminded himself not to brush at his hair or face, as he was wont to do when he had an itch.

"I used to think people at home were just being mean, but—I'm sorry to say this, but talking to you is very irritating," Bombur complained.

They had reached the tent and Jake said, "You're welcome in, but it will be much brighter there than you're used to."

Bombur said, "I wanna see!"

"OK." Jake nodded, and the two entered the large tent with all its equipment and sun lamps.

"Ooh," the little Dipteran buzzed. "This light is...*delicious*."

"We're kind of tethered to light and dark on my world. Even though we can make the light whatever we want, our bodies function poorly if we don't have a day that's one-half light and one-half dark. We sleep when it's dark."

Jake added, "That word, 'sleep,' isn't the same as your word, 'rest.' Sleep for us is a period of unconsciousness, during which we're largely immobile and unaware."

"Weird," said Bombur.

"We spend a quarter to a third of our lives in this state," Jake added. "If I understand the Dipteran time scale, that's about four or five of your lifetimes spent asleep."

"Weird!" exclaimed Bombur.

"So, Bombur, can you tell me about this *monster* you saw?"

"It was huge! White! Covered with...I don't know what. Sort of like you."

Jake tapped a short message ("HELP! FIX!") and sent his scans to Derek along with his current flak aiming programs and, just in case, the specs for the required energy output of the guns.

"Like me?" Jake pondered that statement. Then he grabbed a handful of his hair. "Like this?"

"Yes!" Bombur exclaimed after a pause, his voice showing annoyance. Jake realized he would have to speed up to keep Bombur's interest.

"Sorry, Bombur, I'll try not to be so slow. A creature called a 'mammal' exists on some planets." He pulled up a dense page of facts on his tent wall. "Read this and let me know—"

"Finished!" said Bombur.

Jake fumbled but clicked an even more dense page up next.

"Weird!" said Bombur. "You grow your young inside your bodies? We don't have that on Nidus. Can I...?"

Then, as Jake watched, the tiny creature bumped up against the screen, burning through the hypertext. It looked like an Earth bug smashing against a screen, but the noises from Bombur indicated that the tiny creature was reading and comprehending what he saw.

"*Mammals, reptiles, amphibians,*" he emphasized the alien words, and Jake wondered how the translator could translate them. "We don't have any of those. I've heard of things here that sound somewhat like fish, but few Diptera travel as far as the sea in their lives. My time with you here, trying to get you to understand me and talking with you, it's..."

"It's a big deal, maybe?" Jake said when Bombur trailed off. "Bombur, I believe that the Diptera are the most advanced creatures on the planet. My job here is to—"

"It's to save the Apothikon, I know. I've seen you!"

"Yes, but in the larger sense, it's to save Nidus."

"Save us from what?"

"From me, essentially. Or my kind. I try to get planets working so they can use their strengths to trade with the rest of the galaxy."

"The Seyles run the planet, and they have a poor concept of trade."

"I know that. That's why I need everyone's help. I'm worried that if we don't get them to see the light, Nidus will—" Jake stopped and grabbed a palm-sized device from his lab table.

He set it on the little storage drawer he used for a nightstand. "You read quickly," he understated, "and this is set up so you can get a sense of historic events."

The instant he set it down on his proximity mat—the flat pad he used to charge and synchronize all his devices—the little bug started bouncing off it, and the pages began to flash by at an incredible rate.

His own device bleeped. Derek had already made the changes needed for the electroflak's aimer with a "Make it something difficult next time" taunt thrown in.

For his own edification, he scrolled through the code changes Derek sent. It looked pretty easy, but such things always did *after* an expert did them.

He would have to go out to the cannon to load the new program.

Hogar had given him a program that had predicted the Apothikon pulses fairly well up till now, and his device indicated that another pulse was due soon. Or, as Georgia had pointed out, a set of pulses, like a heartbeat—systole and diastole. He'd have to stay close by.

The tiny voice was back in his ear. "Is this all true, Jake Wizard?"

Jake shook his head reflexively. "No. It's history, so it's almost all lies. But the key elements: the murder, the destruction, the chaos? Those happened. The causes are obscured, and sometimes what's reported is the opposite of what actually happened."

He took a deep breath and tried again, "Look, humans are overwhelmingly good, one to the next. But the bad ones can be really, really bad. And with billions of us, there are always enough to cause mischief."

Bombur seemed genuinely slower now like he was thinking hard. "The creatures of Nidus struggle against the Seyles and the other species, but humans..."

"We struggle against ourselves. We have yet to meet a greater threat in the entire galaxy."

The Diptera fired back, "But it's logical to assume one is out there, and just like Nidus needs to overcome its exuberant infighting, humans need to as well, or they'll end up in the same situation they put everyone else in."

"You're right," Jake replied without letting the implications sink in. He was going to have to ponder that later.

"I had better try to get this message to my people. We shall meet again, Jake Wizard."

Jake watched the speck fly away.

Just then, his device chimed. Derek again.

P.S. WAR

CHAPTER 13

JAYKAMBLER, DESTROYER OF WORLDS

"Derek! What's going on?" Jake had Q-comm'ed Derek immediately after Bombur left.

Derek, switching between devices like a maniac, managed a shrug. "The Daikhans got tired of New Helena's crap, I guess, and just launched an attack on the Azores' territory, accusing it of being a base for counter-Daikhanian activity or something."

He sighed. "Then, some parts of The Country decided that was a good time to work out some of their aggression against The City. And then other parts of The Country didn't agree with that, so there's some in-fighting going on there."

Something had gotten Derek's attention on one device, and he pounded on the keyboard. "Europe's a mess as usual, with the Caliphate in a loose alliance with the Daikhans and the Holy Empire—well, you know how that always goes. Any excuse."

"How're your people on the peninsula?" Jake asked.

"Goryeo and Joeson are still neutral, but Silla wants to break off from Goryeo and form its own country. Buyeo's making trouble with the Seven Kingdoms and rattling its saber about conquering Joeson. Again, any excuse. So far, the Middle East and the Sub-Saharan are quiet."

Jake hadn't been back to Earth in years, and it all just sounded like names out of a history book. Even places he'd been seemed unreal.

"How's XEE?" he said, referring to the Space Station he had called home for all his adult life.

"Weir's doing a good job keeping things neutral. He laid down the law on any war activity resulting in immediate expulsion, and everyone seems to agree."

"Well, that's good."

"If they weren't all lying, yeah," Derek scoffed. "The Jihadis and The Corporate will say literally *anything*. The Templars are in a low-key panic because they have vulnerable missionaries scattered everywhere, which means that they're not causing problems, but they're also not good for much else.

"*And* we're still getting hacked from every quarter."

Jake frowned sympathetically. "Hey, different topic: what have you got that can speed up my brain?"

"Dude, if I had anything that could speed up your brain, I would've given it to you years ago."

Jake laughed in spite of himself and explained the situation with the Diptera.

Derek's sudden alertness at that point told Jake had given him an interesting enough question to focus his mind on. "I'm not an expert, but as far as I know, wetware only works when it conforms to organism biology. Like, you can use it to patch brain damage or to stimulate defective systems, but trying to use it to speed an organism up is disastrous."

"Damn. I feel like I should be talking to the Diptera. Everyone else here is in the Dark Ages while the Diptera have an advanced metropolis, albeit at a fraction of human-scale."

"You need to get to Tinytown," Derek mused. "Hey, you know your grandfather has a couple of thralls running around here?"

Jake rolled his eyes. "Yeah? Still?"

"Well, you know how that technology works? You take some big-skulled lunk and plant a little chip at the cerebellum. We're not talking about some surface-level cortical neural link. It goes in deep!

"Anyway, the chip contains a personality pattern, and the master activates it when he wants to use the thrall's body. Everything's recorded, and then the recording gets returned to the master."

"One of the creepiest things I've ever seen, too. These gorillas start talking and acting like Roy—a one-hundred and twenty-year-old man." Jake shuddered when thinking of his grandfather's messages to him, delivered via thrall.

"It's creepy because Grandpa Roy uses a human as a vessel. But you could put a similar kind of chip into a small drone with your personality pattern, and it would go into Tinytown and respond at whatever rate it was interacted with. I'll send you a fabber plan.

"Gotta go, dude. If I can get this hacking under control, maybe we can grab Lefty for another game."

Derek disconnected.

Jake dropped a quick note to Jezz, realizing he hadn't heard from her in a while. "The Country" was such a mutable agglomeration of tribes and interests that he had a very poor understanding of where she was and how close to danger she might be in this war.

His missionary friend, Paul, had not responded to him in months, but according to his superiors, this was simply due to him being on a remote world, far out of touch. Jake sent him a letter anyway.

Then he fired off a quick note to his grandfather. Even with no one for light years around, he found himself mentally explaining that he meant his *mother's* dad, who had raised him. (His father's dad—whom he never referred to as "grandfather" except ironically—was the most powerful man in New Helena and the one who had tried to kidnap him back on Mars.)

Jake looked at the scant pile of his actual belongings and his *other* Q-comm, the line that went straight to his parents.

Another oddity of Q-comms was that they transmitted no location information. So, just as it was safe for Derek to call him, it would be safe to call his parents. He reminded himself of this because his caution about contacting New Helena bordered on paranoia.

With a sigh, he linked it to a projector and made the call. After several rings, his mother picked up. She looked tired and old, especially for being in her forties. His grandfather had pictures of her around when Jake was growing up, and she had once been quite beautiful.

The City lifestyle took its toll.

The City also had myriad options for "restoration"—things that made an older, badly treated body look younger—and these also left a distinctive mark. These tensions and rejuvenations had a gradually *ichthiating* effect on those who used them. In other words, while the procedures removed signs of aging like wrinkles and bags, they also made their subject increasingly look like a fish.

"Jake...baby," she said, and her voice, combined with her slightly piscine appearance, made him sadder than he expected.

"Hi, mom. I was just calling to see—I'd heard war had broken out, and I wanted to make sure you were okay."

He hoped he saw a glimmer of recognition and connection on her face, but it had to go through so many layers of other things. He conceded to himself his hope was merely wishful thinking.

"Sweet," she finally said. "You know how the Daikhans are. They took a potshot at Azores. I guess your grandfather thought it was worth mobilizing for." She grimaced a little when she said "grandfa-ther."

Then she smiled again, "Over three thousand miles away, though. Fighting never reaches The City."

She spoke breezily, somewhat woodenly, then her visage darkened, and she said, "You should come home. It's safer here."

"I'm so far out in the universe that nobody knows where I am, mom. I probably couldn't be safer."

Her face returned to normal, more like a real mother's concern appearing. "You look sick."

Just then, he coughed and silently cursed. "Just a little run-in with some bad people. I'm on the mend."

She looked unconvinced.

Dezzig barged through the tent flap, and Jake jumped out of his seat. His mother shrieked, so he quickly sat back down.

"No, it's fine, mom. It's just a...they're the... This is Dezzig. He's probably just inviting me to a party." Jake said the words that came to his mind, ridiculous though they were.

"Lord Grigg needs you. Matzhin Seyles has attacked."

To his mother, he said, "Yeah, it's just a party, mom. But I have to bring the cake, so I gotta go now."

While his mother couldn't understand what the Seyles was saying, his device translated his words into the Seyles' language.

He disconnected quickly.

Dezzig regarded him with his enormous, faceted eyes. "You should not lie to your mother, Jake Wizard."

Jake hadn't used a battlesuit since his ICF training and had wanted to try one out in a more realistic situation ever since. While fighting the Minosians and Rapticores, he longed for something with more oomph.

He wished he could enjoy putting it on now more.

The armor slipped on easily and once sealed, filled with a protective foam. Letters appeared before him on the visor.

DEXTER GENERATOR: 100%
SINISTER GENERATOR: 100%
SYSTEM FUNCTION: NORMAL
POWER LEVEL: FULL
POWER SETTING: LOW

That was going to take some getting used to. The visor screen had reticles, readouts, gauges, and warning lights—all things you learned to ignore until you needed them.

He jerked and twitched a bit as he fumbled his way out of the tent. The armor translated his body movements into its own, but it had to be trained since everyone had a different concept of what was "natural."

Probably should have given this a few trial run-throughs.

Combat specialists like his old friend, The Baron, had their own armor and personalized training programs and managed to fight while barely exerting themselves. However, the less trained you were, the more you needed to feel the force and reactive feedback.

Consequently, a less trained person actually got less force out of their suit for more effort. Jake wasn't particularly experienced in heavy armor fighting but was weakened and decreasingly inclined to exert himself. This, ironically, worked in his favor.

The armor turned his sluggish walk into a kind of hopping trot, and, encouraged by the ease of movement, he turned the trot into a run, crossing the distance toward Matzhin's kingdom along the Node Path easily, at high speed.

However, as he overlooked Valley Ridge, where the battle took place, he could find no cause for joy. The Seyles lanced each other in the air, while on the ground, the tall, thin Notos and squat Nocks traded blows with blades, bludgeons, spears, and chains.

It felt wrong. The Seyles drafted everyone into their little war games.

He decided to focus on the Seyles: they started the wars, so putting them out of commission would probably result in the quickest end to the battle.

He hesitated. His mission, to protect the Apothikon until its eclosion, had implied many things. First was that the eclosion of the Apothikon was a desirable thing. Beyond that, though, the Apothikon, which fed on the dead and the desiccated corpses of Nijins, required a steady diet to thrive and survive.

That meant if he obliterated the incoming army, he risked starving Lord Matzhin's Apothikon. Did it make sense to save one by starving another?

He retracted the blasters and fumbled through the options until he found a "blades" option. Activating it caused surprisingly thick metal blades to slide out from his armor "sleeves."

Blades with adjustable voltage, no less.

He wasn't skilled enough to fly—that was a complex ballet of balancing the jets on various parts of the suit—but he *could* jump, and once in the air, he could jet off at improbable angles.

His hardest challenge at that point became identifying Matzhin's troops from Grigg's—at least until Grigg's nearby troops wised up and fell back, leaving the fighting to him.

There was no knightly challenge of martial skills, no poetry to be sung about the Seyles who fell to Jake's blades, and any poems about Jake would probably read as horror stories.

He saw a high-flying Seyles lancing one of Matzhin's fliers and made that his first target. The targeting reticles inside his face shield picked up his eye movement and made it easy to lock on and aim.

With a mighty leap, he impaled the creature with his left, then brought his right around in an arc to slice the bug in half.

As he plummeted to the ground, he spotted another Seyles, which prepared its lance in anticipation—

A quick thrust in that direction and his blade went right down the thorax, veering off to one side before reaching the abdomen.

His sensors indicated he had been struck from behind. Without the notification, he would have felt nothing—not even have noticed it. He spun himself around with a rotating blast and clipped his attacker—but now he was spinning too fast to tell whether or not he had killed it.

He was quite a few practice sessions away from being able to fly, for sure.

An indicator suggested turning on his shields, so he did, though at minimal power. Just then, more Seyles than he could count swarmed him and bounced away, stunned by the defensive charge.

When he landed, none of the ground troops even tried engaging. A spear thrown in desperation burst into flames when it came into contact with his shield.

The nearby Seyles, vigorously jousting each other up to that point, had stilled. About half dropped down abruptly—Grigg's troops—leaving Matzhin's troops puzzled.

Jake leapt again, this time into a thick squadron, swinging carelessly and letting his shield do much of the work. He didn't even bother much with his descent, just landing, jumping again, landing, moving deeper into Matzhin's ranks as he cut a swath, leaving the remains of hundreds of Seyles (and a few other troops who got in his way when he landed) in his wake.

As he went along, Matzhin's Seyles, realizing they were powerless against him, got a lot better at getting out of the way. Once he had passed, they fervently charged into Grigg's ranks, hoping to press their advantage while Jake traveled down the rest of the line.

Seeing this, Jake retracted his blades and invoked his blasters. He cranked them as low as possible and swept back down the line the way he came, firing into every cluster of Matzhin's troops he could identify.

Injure, push back, break morale.

He couldn't hold an entire army off by himself, even if he let fully loose. He couldn't be everywhere at once.

Grigg's troops found their courage with a war god on their side, of course, rushing to fill the voids he left in his wake. Even so, Matzhin's superior numbers slowly inched forward. Pass after pass, he'd drive them back, and only his sheer demoralizing effect kept them from overwhelming Grigg's troops.

Eventually, however, the terrible power of the suit won out, and Matzhin's troops began to lose ground. Emboldened, Grigg's troops advanced further, driving the enemy up the ridge that demarcated the end of Grigg's kingdom.

It was then a message came in from his base.

ALERT: APOTHIKON PULSE

CHAPTER 14

DIVIDED LOYALTIES

Jake looked around. How far did the signal reach? According to Georgia, Seyles lords would fight over the areas of the kingdom where signals from the Apothikons overlapped. Ultimately, she theorized, the signals defined how big any particular kingdom could get.

But if that were the case, and Matzhin destroyed Grigg's Apothikon, that would mean Matzhin could only extend so far, maybe only a few miles into Grigg's kingdom. Meanwhile, to the north, Torsk would be able to expand *his* kingdom on the other side without ever having lost a troop. Torsk could then attack the weakened Matzhin.

It was all so dumb.

Before he could finish his thoughts, he noticed some injured Seyles flying upward from where they were resting, right out of the combat zone and toward his base and the Apothikon pit.

Some on Matzhin's side took off over the ridge *away* from the pit, but within a few minutes, they returned and headed right for the pit.

This meant the pulse didn't discriminate between the inhabitants of kingdoms. A signal attracted *any* diminished Seyles in reach.

Time to go.

He couldn't fly, but he had gotten better at combining a leap with a forward thrust, passing beyond the battlefield quickly, then overtaking the ensorcelled Seyles with his second jump.

He got to the Apothikon pit in minutes and found the flak cannon blazing away smoothly, except for the occasional jerk to nine o'clock and back to fill in the latest gap.

Jumping back to his tent, Jake triggered the emergency release and stepped from the armor, which collapsed into its major components behind him, crackling as the impact foam crumbled and melted away.

He grabbed his usual sidearm and a rifle.

Quickly trotting to the main gap in the shield, he watched and waited for his opportunity to get to the knoll.

The Seyles moved, from what Jake could tell, in coordinated patterns, though less like an organized battle plan and more like a savage dance to appease an insatiable god.

It reminded Jake of a childishly simple video game. The bad guys moved one way or the other, then attacked in a stream. Then, the survivors would re-group and form a new pattern, only breaking it to try another attack.

On and on, heedless of their own deaths.

Jake didn't like it, but it nauseated him less than charging through a battlefield mowing down entire legions. Through whatever means, these creatures had surrendered their agency and were threatening (however accidentally) the existence of the whole kingdom.

Presumably.

The one Seyles that had slipped through hadn't caused any damage he could see. And he wished he had had time to examine it before it vaporized itself on the shield.

He concentrated his fire on the new opening so the cannon wouldn't have to swivel in that direction as frequently. There were already more Seyles than there had been before.

It's hungrier. I've been vaporizing more of its food, so it's hungrier now and calling more loudly.

Or I'm just imagining things.

He watched the corpses creep eerily through the grass and fall into the pit, almost as if undead.

"Jake Wizard!" he heard the voice on his translator and sighed, exhausted.

He took out a pill and called back, "Bombur. What can I do for you?" When he started to drag himself back to his tent, Bombur's response was already starting before he could lift a foot.

"You lost the battle, Jake Wizard!"

Jake shrugged. "I'm here to protect the Apothi—hey, how did *you* know?"

"The Lucas, Jake Wizard! Do you not know about the Lucas?"

Jake wearily reminded himself he needed to speed up. "I've never met one in person, Bombur. I see their lights flashing, but..."

"They are very pretty, Jake Wizard, and very vacuous. They spend all their time relaying information. They never actually *do* anything."

Jake grunted. "I know the type." He turned to address Bombur and realized he couldn't really see him.

"The Lucas are also completely absent from the Apothikon pit. I just don't get it. I'd think this was news. I really should be talking to *your* people, Bombur. In Mentalikolis. I mean..."

"Melontikopolis, Jake Wizard."

"Right. So, look, I plan to visit M—your city, in the form of a... Well, it won't be me exactly, but a machine acting on my behalf."

"An angel?"

Jake couldn't help but pause. "Yes, I suppose technically, angel literally means 'messenger,' but—"

"A prophet!"

"Oh, let's just call it a messenger," Jake sighed. "It's very important to understand that I am a mortal creature, just like you. Though it would have to be greatly adapted to Dipteran physiology, our technology would make most anything I can do available to you and your kind."

Bombur said, "I will let them know. In the meantime, I wish to read more about your culture!"

Jake shrugged and set up a device with an encyclopedia and library of technical manuals so that the little Diptera could bounce through the pages. Then he sat with his head in his hands.

It's still attached, unfortunately.

His head ached, and his hands were shaking, all out of proportion to his exertions. Grabbing a hypodermic, he injected himself, which made him feel just better enough to really appreciate how bad he felt.

He wondered if he had killed Zh'mer out there. Or Matzhin himself. He wondered if Dezzig had survived and how many Nijins had just been doing their daily tasks when the troops started rolling through.

Then he wondered if anyone besides him even cared.

He was tired and sick and tired of being sick. His muscles twitched, and flashes of his time on New Helena kept intruding into his thoughts.

He had pushed it all down. Successfully, he had thought. But he'd have to tell her. When Dali returned, he'd have to tell her all he had done, and the thought made him nauseous.

A new thought occurred to him.

"Hey, Bombur, you know about the Apothikon—and you can talk about it, too? You know none of the other Nijins will talk about it with me."

"Weird!" piped the little voice absently.

"So, where are the grown Apothikons?" Jake asked.

"What do you mean 'grown?' Are you saying they get even bigger?" Bombur sounded shocked.

"I don't know. I've just been told that the cocooned Apothikons eventually break out of their shells and emerge from of the pits."

"Weird! We have no records of the Apothikons doing anything beyond just sitting there." Bombur continued flipping through the pages rapidly.

So, the Diptera didn't know much about the Apothikon, but they didn't seem to have any problem talking about it, either.

As Bombur might have said—*Weird!*

Jake reminded himself his narrative of the Apothikon's life cycle had been created by Heinrik Hogar, chief xenobiologist for the Independent Crusader Force, who based his guesses on Dr. Vizgirda's work. And as confident as Hogar was about his guesses, he warned Jake about taking any of it too seriously, given their limited knowledge.

The planet lacked any obviously interesting resources, had no compelling artisanal products, and was relatively close to other, more interesting planets, leaving it with no particular value even as a military base.

It was also near the recently quarantined Alvum, so an element of superstition may have entered into people avoiding it recently even more than usual.

The whole planet is just a big question mark.

The Dragon moon loomed so brightly to the west that Jake could see its outline through his tent until he turned that wall into a view screen showing the planet Nidus in orbit around its star.

"Hey, Bombur, what about hyper-summer and hyper-winter? What do you guys do then?"

Bombur, who might have been irritated by Jake's frequent interruptions if, for him, a whole lot of time wasn't passing between them, said, "The... I know the words but don't know what they mean together."

Jake pointed to the globe of Nidus and the longitudinal band where everything lived. "Every century or so, Nidus does a little wobble, and this band, which is normally temperate, gets either very cold or very hot. The hot part is coming up soon."

Bombur still sounded distracted as he blazed through his readings. "Never heard of it." Then his voice changed, and he said, "Wait, that sounds important."

"This isn't like the Apothikon, Bombur. We're just guessing about the Apothikon's life cycle, but this planetary wobble is *math*. It's going to happen, and fairly soon, even by Dipteran standards. Are you not preparing somehow?"

Bombur said, "Nope. We've got more immediate problems."

The little Dipteran flew out of the tent without ceremony.

He already felt bad, and his talk with Bombur hadn't improved his attitude. "What more pressing problems do you have in Mental—uh, Melon—in Tiny Town?" he grumbled.

He had enough experience to know the worst kind of problems are the ones that you're only vaguely aware of. Those were the kind that had a way of showing up when you were least able to handle them.

Not that he mistrusted Bombur, but he wondered if the Lucas could be used. His device displayed what sort of news was being flashed around the kingdom, and it was still boring and weirdly precise. It almost reminded him of his battlesuit readouts.

HUMIDITY: UP 1% TO 74%
ANTICIPATED YIELD FARM 2894: DOWN 10% TO 380U
BFrh0efUg646dL2UDImGGaNdj9OXgnn2

Always the noise, too.

However, he never had sent a signal out because he had decided the Lucas didn't have much to say. Then he saw:

EXTERMINATION OF NEPHROS IN RIDGE VALLEY COMPLETE

Just another piece of news, he thought. *What a horror show. Maybe Bombur was right about them.*

Still, it couldn't hurt to try. He sent out a signal:

GREETINGS FROM JAKE WIZARD

He waited. The readouts continued as normal until:

NILIN LUCA: GREETINGS JAKE WIZARD
SORIT LUCA: GREETINGS JAKE WIZARD

Soon, he was inundated with greetings, after which the regular readouts continued. He tried a query.

NUMBER OF CASUALTIES INFLICTED BY JAKE WIZARD AT VALLEY RIDGE?

After a brief pause, multiple numbers came back. The Lucas, too, had opinions and arguments about everything. Around 1,500 deaths, he learned.

Talk about a horror show. He tried another:

CHANCE OF MATZHIN ATTACKING BEYOND THE VALLEY RIDGE IN THE NEXT WEEK?

The answers came back fast. Close to twenty percent was the consensus. *OK*, Jake thought. *Now, a tough one.*

WHERE ARE ALL THE GROWN APOTHIKONS?

He waited and waited. There was no response, except:

oze1mAnLsnogFEVjQaFrpd6cSPSjIIt1

CHAPTER 15

THE ROYAL CARPET

He had made the now-familiar walk to Grigg's castle once again, and he stood before and below the irascible Seyles in a mood not especially suited to diplomacy. With some effort, he stood straight and tried to keep the fatigue he felt from creeping into his shoulders and bowing him down.

Mist floated down through the pergola, and Jake peevishly thought, *What a stupid roof.*

"Jake Wizard!" his translator said, turning the piercing whine and dissonant chords of the angry bug into words that almost captured the aggressiveness his own ears picked up.

"Lord Grigg," he responded firmly, though he could hear the fatigue in his own voice. He wondered if his device would translate that, too.

He found himself looking forward to a world where he could at least make the noises of the language again.

"We lost Valley Ridge, Jake Wizard! Your vaunted powers availed us naught!"

Ugh. Now the formal language. What a drama king.

"I'm sure you heard reports," Jake paused to emphasize the fact that Grigg had never left his castle during the fight. "I'm sure you heard reports of the devastation I wrought among your enemies."

"Of what use is that when the valley was lost?"

"Indeed, the only reason I didn't do more destruction was to save your own people."

"I don't care about my people, Jake Wizard! My people exist to serve me! If they must die so I may live, so be it!"

Jake didn't react to that. This wasn't an unusual sentiment in most Bug Space planets. Life was cheap.

He still found it repulsive. He didn't see Grigg as being of any greater value than Dezzig or Bombur—quite a good deal less, actually.

At the same time, Grigg might *be* more valuable in some way he couldn't perceive, maybe even having some unseen connection to the Apothikon.

In any event, succumbing to provocation would do him no good.

It's like Dali said. I need altitude, thought Jake. *You're a wizard.*

"I had to save the Apothikon, Lord Grigg. This is my mission, and it takes priority even over the loss of territory, however regrettable it may be."

However regrettable indeed.

At this point, Jake barely registered the monarch's displeasure over his public mention of the Apothikon.

The Seyles swooped down from his high perch and towered over Jake, who crooked his head up to look at him. Only a few years ago, this would have rattled him. But the Seyles were not the Lydians, who were walking weapons—each of their eight legs being like rapiers and carrying large swords called kalybuses.

But he'd killed too many Seyles to be terribly intimidated by them.

Unfortunately, his lungs began to tickle at that moment, and he started coughing. He coughed for a good ten seconds, during which he completely ignored the glowering creature.

He fetched a bottle of pills.

The only thing keeping me alive. Barely.

Grigg, already piqued, knocked the bottle of pills from his hand. The life-saving pellets dissolved shockingly quickly on the wet cobblestone.

He looked up again at Grigg with one eye, head still crooked. The beast's own enormous eyes glittered back at him.

Slowly and without breaking eye contact, Jake reached into his pocket and pulled out *another* bottle of pills, which he opened slowly and tipped into his mouth.

As if I'd only carry one bottle.

"What is it you want from me, Grigg?"

"I want you to take back the valley or destroy it, Jake Wizard! Show us your true might!"

Jake considered that as the court hummed and buzzed its approval.

"And then, I want you to go to Torsk, who, even now, amasses troops along our northern border, threatening the farms along the marshes there, and I want you to destroy his troops before they cause me any further trouble."

Jake scowled but nodded. "It will have to wait until after the next pulse," he said, "but I will remove these threats one way or another."

As a practical matter, the proximity of the foreign troops to Grigg's territory meant the Apothikon's signal would attract even more Seyles from both Torsk's kingdom and Matzhin's. And as he had been unable to determine the source of the woollyheads' destruction, the last thing he needed was more attackers on the ever-weakening shield.

Grigg seemed most pleased by his acquiescence more than the promise of any deeds to be done, so Jake let himself be dismissed and strode out of the court with his back straight and head high.

Once past the bridge, he slumped, feeling all the fatigue and a strange grief as well. The angry corona of the sun glared resentfully at him from the east while the Damsel and Dragon moons in the cool sky west danced their private tango. Newly hatched Seyles leapt from their egg clutches into the sky.

The Lucas flashed the news like distant lightning, and the thick air buzzed with the noises of life, from the Nephros roiling away in the fields to the humming wings of the Seyles.

It was like being in the middle of a big city where you didn't speak the language, and no one knew you. Crowded, but alone.

Dezzig swooped down to hover at his side. Jake offered a weak smile but little else, eager to return to his base. He was glad to see the creature alive but was too weak to figure out how to express such a sentiment to a Seyles.

At some point in their distant past, the Seyles had largely abandoned common expressions of gratitude. The translator compensated by rendering these phrases archaically, as in "Thank thee."

He thought he'd give it a try: "I give thanks thou hast survived." Then he felt foolish, realizing the translator would have done the necessary language switch for him.

"Thank thee," Dezzig said surprisingly quickly.

The curious creature floated by him quietly, with only the soft buzz of his wings accompanying their walk. The anticipation of an unasked question created an odd tension.

"Yes, Dezzig Seyles, what did you want to say?"

Dezzig's flight popped a little as if startled. Then he said, "Jake Wizard, why do you not just kill Grigg?"

Now Jake started. "Isn't that a rather dangerous question to ask?"

"Why would it be?"

"It might be interpreted as a threat?"

Dezzig floated as if pondering that. "Whether or not I *could* kill him, doing so would bring me nothing but grief. But if *you* did, you could become lord. You could probably become King of all Nidus!"

Nidus had only had genuine monarchs in legend.

Jake looked around at the swamp, felt the dank, misty air on his skin, and considered the morose eye of the sun as it rolled westward over the horizon as if trying to catch the dancing moons, and thought of a hundred insulting rejoinders.

But finally, he just sighed tiredly. "The universe is vast and full of interesting things, Dezzig Seyles. I feel no inclination to take from others."

With a short burst of cheerfulness, he added, "To be honest, Dezzig, I feel no inclination to stop anywhere even while there is space to be explored and new, interesting creatures such as yourself to meet."

Off in the distance, Jake could see Toler and Fugi in their usual slow walk around the reservoir, arguing like mad.

Dezzig broke for the sky silently, and Jake paused momentarily to watch the jeweled wings as they caught the light from the faded sun.

"Thank thee," he muttered sardonically.

He thought he might have done something similar only a few years ago. Rush off without ceremony. Conversation over. Time to go.

He never would have believed it, but he missed the little touches, the human rituals—the small talk, even—that came with being around others of his kind.

He had gone for years feeling he didn't need (and couldn't trust) anyone else. When Dali came along, he added her to his circle of needs, probably faster than a normal, healthy human would. His colleagues in the ICF, to whom he had first realized his obligation during the battle of Glashar Pass, had become comrades and even friends.

And, perhaps ironically, now he lived alone on a world of alien creatures with all the needs he had dared to need left unmet.

He found himself hungry for even Fugi and Toler's argument, which struck a chord, reminding him of his grandfather arguing with *his* old friends back on Earth.

Toler approached him first. His many-eyed fake face was livid, which, coincidentally enough, signified anger among the Nijins the same as it did with humans.

"Jake Wizard, you *must* settle this argument," Toler hissed. "We cannot delay the reservoir repairs much longer."

Fugi calmly called from the distance. He had the air of someone whose argument had prevailed, if only in his own mind. "We have plenty of time," he said. "In fact, we needn't do much of anything at all. Why, look here."

He crouched low, and Jake left Toler to join Fugi at the wall. Jake could see the mudweed growing through the mortar, as before. "Look not at the growing mud-weed, Jake Wizard, but the dead mud-weed."

Jake squinted a bit. The light was so dim, and his vision had weakened considerably.

"It's...well, it looks like it's turning into..." He finally just reached out to touch it. Thick, tacky goop coated his fingers. "It's filling in the cracks?" he ventured.

Fugi chuckled. "Exactly, Jake Wizard. It's exactly as Goni Korma the Architect said. Our repairs would actually cause more damage."

Toler hissed and whined from across the path. "No! Goni was a fool! P'khal Korma The Cautious proved that after the Great Flood of—"

Before Jake had a moment to regret the historical litany he knew was coming, Dezzig swooped from the sky and swallowed Toler whole.

Everything became still. It seemed to Jake even the reservoir waters stopped lapping against the wall. Fugi had frozen in place and so had Jake.

For that matter, so had Dezzig. His eyes scintillated, and the long maw, which had only opened for the time it took to engulf Toler, looked only slightly bigger, with just a visible bulge in one spot, and looked as perfectly sealed as if it had no opening at all.

Insectoids didn't have throats or stomachs, for that matter, and Jake found himself morbidly wondering about the biology of the bulge moving slowly down the maw, through the thorax, and then completely vanishing near the abdomen.

After a long moment—Jake would have been hard-pressed to guess how long—Dezzig turned and fixed Fugi with his glimmering, multi-faceted eyes.

In an oddly imperious tone, the Seyles said, "You will repair the reservoir according to the prescriptions laid down by P'khal Korma. Goni Korma was a fool."

Fugi whispered, "Yes, yes, Dezzig Seyles," and scuttled into the service tunnels.

Jake finally stood, regarding Dezzig in wonder.

The Seyles, who seemed to relax all at once, said, "What is it, Jake Wizard? Is something wrong?"

Chapter 16

Return of the Queen

"I'll be fine," Jake said, trying not to be too brusque with Dali. She had surprised him by entering the tent, which triggered a coughing jag. He was hunched over in his chair, and she rubbed his back.

"Doc Blood reformulated your pills," she said, handing him a small container. "Besides these, he gave me the recipe for your fabber."

"That's good," Jake said, gulping a pill down quickly, "but let's get to the important stuff." He turned around in the chair and grabbed her by the waist, pulling her into his lap. Then he noticed she had some things stuffed in her jacket.

He pulled them out slowly. They were long, white, and silky to the touch.

"Gloves?" he asked with a smile.

She rolled her eyes a little. "Princess gloves. My sister begged me to put on a show for some VIPs on Station KOR, so I did the full getup." She tried to continue talking while he kissed her on the forehead and cheeks. "I stuffed these in here when changing back into my normal clothes and forgot about them."

"I thought you were done with the princess stuff," he said, amused.

"I thought I was, too. But she guilted me into it. Then I get half a dozen factions approaching me, complaining about how she's running things." Exasperation seeped into her voice. "She shouldn't be *running* anything. Our dad—"

She stopped herself as if she had just noticed he was kissing her. She submitted briefly and then asked earnestly, "Did you think about me?"

"I thought about nothing else."

A reluctant smile threatened to break through her professional demeanor, and she rose and stepped back a little. "Jake, this is serious."

"I know! I *did* think about you."

"And?"

"Well, did you stalk a lot of guys *before* me?"

She blushed. "No! And *stalk* is a strong word!"

"Yeah, but I like it."

He pulled her in close again; she let him. "It comes down to trusting your judgment, really. This is pretty easy, normally. But now I have to believe that there's some special quality in me..."

She kissed him. "There is."

"That's a lot of pressure, princess."

She nodded and kissed him again.

"You know, we've talked about a lot of things over the years, but there are still tons of gaps in what we know about each other. For example, I have no idea how it is that you speak perfect English with such a proper accent!"

"I went to an English boarding school," she said primly.

"What? Where?"

"Victoria."

"That's on the Pacific Coast, right? One of the more stable states in The Country."

She nodded. "Lovely place. Cold. I didn't make a lot of friends. There was much more pressure to conform than I'm used to."

"None? Are you used to 'none' pressure?"

She laughed and pressed her forehead against his. "My mother sent me to another planet, hoping to straighten me out. How's that for pressure?"

"Family is complicated."

"Which brings us to you, Mr. I'm-Not-An-Ambler."

Jake flushed a little.

"Did you think I'd forgotten?"

"I assume you remember everything."

She nodded sharply. "I'll never forget our first date."

"Marooned on the *Shiva*. Some date."

"Best date ever."

"We should do it again."

"The records show—"

"You mean your memory?"

She grinned. "Exactly. The records show you rather fiercely insisted you weren't an Ambler but also pointedly omitted who you actually were. So, if you're not an Ambler, what are you?"

"My real last name is..."

She leaned in expectantly.

"Angel," Jake muttered.

"*Angel?*" Dali repeated loudly. "Your mother's family—"

Jake nodded, a little embarrassed. "Whenever I got in trouble as a kid, I'd say 'I'm a capital-a Angel, not a lowercase-a angel,' which, honestly, never helped." He always cringed when thinking of his young self.

Dali was musing on it. "Jake Ambler. Jake Angel. Angle. Angel. Wait, *Jacob* Angel?" She looked at him, startled. "Jake, are you *Jewish?*"

"I guess it depends on who you ask," he grumbled.

"I'm asking you!" She grinned.

"Then I'm not. My grandparents were, but when my grandmother died, my grandfather Yakov gave it up. He said he was too busy raising my mother alone to care what a bunch of busybodies thought."

"How did your grandmother die?"

"He never got into the details with me. But the government was involved, apparently."

"So you're from..."

"Greater Israel, that's where the farm is. Part of the Sahara Reclamation. I guess my grandfather thought that he was protecting my mother from superstition by rejecting his faith, but when my father came around..."

"The Ambler."

"Yeah. As you've noted, the Amblers are their own kind of royalty, and she was taken by—taken in by the wealth, and the glamour, and, well, all of it."

Dali clasped his hands gently. "Like you?"

Jake nodded, inhaling her fragrance. "Like me."

"I want to know it all," she said, looking into his eyes searchingly.

"You should," Jake said, becoming despondent. "You should know it all. It might change your mind."

She stroked his hair but didn't speak.

CHAPTER 17

EVEN MORE CONFESSIONS

Slowly at first, but building in pace and intensity as he began to speak of New Helena's leadership indoctrination, called the Mawla Program, Jake began to tell his story for the first time ever.

"Royal Enfield Ambler—"

"Grandpa Roy," she amended.

"*Grandpa Roy* controls The City. Many people think they know this but don't know the true extent. He isn't, for example, the President. He's never visible in Congress. He's seen as above politics—because he is.

"He controls everything just the same because he controls the education of New Helena. And the information flow. And the entertainment." Jake sighed. "The closer you get to the levers of power, the more indoctrination you must undergo to advance."

She eased him along. "Every system has to have some sort of indoctrination, right? You can't do much of anything if you don't know the basics."

Jake agreed. "One way to look at it is indoctrination narrows thinking, and that's good to a degree. You could say Grandpa Yakov indoctrinated me in feeding the chickens, which kept me from doing things like giving them candy for dinner. Again."

She giggled.

"I was five. It seemed like a nice thing at the time. New Helena's indoctrination teaches how the government works, uses its power for people's best interests, and how their interests always align with the government's. That is, *Roy's* interests.

"The Mawla Program teaches that everything has its place: information, medicine, science, art—all have their academies, and if you listen to what they say and do what they tell you, you'll never be wrong, and society will progress to its inevitable utopia. Each academy is, of course, controlled by Mawla-indoctrinated people."

Dali nodded, watching him carefully. "This is all abstract, Jake."

He smiled ruefully. "Let me build up to it. You see, Roy didn't have me selected for a position of power. He had me selected as his *replacement*."

Dali caught her breath a little bit. "But then you could do what you want, which would mean *not* doing what he wanted. I remember you saying his thrall *dared* you to take over."

"He did. It did. Whatever you call a thrall under someone else's control." He shook his head. "Anyway, New Helena has various levels of indoctrination. For The Outskirts, it's just old-fashioned propaganda. Books, news stories, and ginning up enough hate, fear, and division to drive acceptance. For the Suburbs, it's more sophisticated."

Dali said, "Diana is from The Suburbs. She said she grew up learning that the highest aspiration was to live in The City proper, but it was also probably out of her reach."

"I didn't know she was a Suburb girl," Jake said thoughtfully. "I'd never expect to find one among the Lost Girls."

Dali said, "She's remarkable, like all my crew."

Jake nodded, grateful for the momentary diversion. Diana overtly disliked him. Perhaps he had sold her short because of that.

"Basic indoctrination for The City is electrochemically enhanced. When you get to Mawla, the Leadership program, it becomes dehumanizing."

She waited, seeing how difficult it was for him to discuss.

"*Dehumanizing*," he emphasized. "It's meant to make you inhuman." He leaned back, exhausted by just thinking of it.

"My grandfather used to tell me a story about an ancient group who indoctrinated their members by knocking them out with drugs and having them wake up in a garden paradise full of wine and women. They would return to this paradise if they died in service to Allah. They then 'woke them' and gave them missions which, since they were eager to die, they were very effective at."

"Jake."

"A lot of people know that story, but they don't know how it ended. A prince was captured and brought in, but the servant assigned to drug him had been treated kindly by the prince long ago, so he prepared a much weaker sleeping draught, and the prince was sober enough not to be fooled by the fake paradise."

"Jake."

"Then, having learned the order's secrets, the prince pretended to accept a mission only to expose the group to his father, the King, who ended their tyranny forever."

She looked at him.

"Jake, do you love me?"

"More than life itself."

She waited.

He took a deep breath. "OK. After we got through basic civics, the training program became more physical. Through virtual reality—and drugs to make the events transpiring seem real—we endured a series of increasingly challenging games.

"The goal of each game is to get you used to coercing people into doing what you want. You can use charm, lies, verbal abuse, physical abuse, weaponry, police, or other enforcement crews. Whatever it takes.

"Everyone comes out of Mawla with a rank based on how far they got. You get an M-30 just for getting in. If you get through all the games, you get an M-15, which can only go down through actual service. Roy is the only M-0."

Jake detailed his journey through Mawla while she listened. Everything he had weathered, the winnowing down of his classmates—future leadership class of New Helena. Some were drawn away by pleasure, some driven away by pain, down to the remaining few who "could potentially be entrusted with power."

"The last levels were about the use of this power."

"Simulated use?" Dali asked.

"Yes. But we weren't supposed to know that. The first few levels are kind of fun. They were righteous scenarios of stopping criminals. I looked at it as a video game and didn't understand why everyone else was so rattled."

He chuckled a little. "The thought process I went through at the time went from thinking they were stupid to thinking I was special. Years later, on Mars, I realized they were heavily drugged, and I was not. Though I still don't know who altered my 'sleeping draught.'"

"None of this sounds too bad, at least for you," she commented.

He soldiered on. "After the initial levels, which are all things like arresting dangerous criminals, the scenarios start to be populated with people you *do* know. The situations tend to get much less righteous.

"Like, your local coffee shop owner refuses to pay a fine, and you can't cajole him into it. If you can't badger or threaten, then what's left?"

Dali frowned. "You could pay the fine for him."

"Not if you want to pass. The money isn't the point, not even a little. Now, what if, in a dozen of the previous scenarios, it's a man beating a woman, but instead of arresting or killing the man like you did in the past, well, it turns out he's an M-10. You're an M-15, so you have to help *him*."

Dali's frown got deeper.

"And what if the woman was your *mother*?"

Dali protested, "But you knew it wasn't real!"

"*I* did. But even so... I mean, say I printed a picture—just a *picture* of your dad. If I told you to tear it up, would that be easy for you?"

"I see your point," she said, her cheeks flushing with anger. "I could probably get to where it wouldn't bother me—I have a lot of great pictures of him. But it's the..."

"The symbolic nature of it. And that's not all of it for me. I was *angry* with my mother. And, game or not, I had become accustomed to using any means—including deadly force—to get what I wanted.

"Real life goes on during training, too, and we were required to try the tactics we've been learning outside of class, only to discover that *they work*. If I choose to, people will bend to my will—most of them without me having to do much more than present myself with authority."

Dali bit her lip. "Maybe you could use that to better people? Like, if you could convince an alcoholic to stop drinking, it would give him a chance to get a handle on it?"

"Maybe. But Mawla warps you. You know you have incredible force behind you, and you know that to avoid being subject to that force, people will not only go along with you but also convince themselves you're right and they're on your team."

"They'll turn around and start attacking people they think of as *your* enemies."

He shuddered. "You also find yourself loathing them. And you find yourself not thinking of them as human beings any longer. Ultimately, you end up loathing yourself."

She looked at him expressionlessly, sensing he had more to say. He swallowed hard.

"The last scenario I had to run through was very personal. It involved a girl I had a crush on—she had washed out early on—and was flirting with me in the scenario, but then the scenario had her flirting with everyone in my class. Mocking me. It went farther and farther until—"

He looked down. "It was meant to provoke a jealous rage, Dali. And it did. And I... I murdered them. And her."

"But you knew it wasn't real! And you were compromised! Maybe not as drugged up as everyone else, but—"

"The thing is, Dali, I would have killed her. I would've killed all of them. Whether I was compromised emotionally, physically—that doesn't matter."

"So they kicked you out then?"

"No. I passed. Technically, I'm still an M-15."

Dali's eyes widened.

"There's a paradox underlying the whole process. You're not to be tempted by this or that. You're to be incorruptible—which has a very specific meaning in The Mawla Program."

"What does it mean?"

"It means nothing can deter you from using the power entrusted to you to enforce the will of The State. At the same time, the system needs you to be corrupted—for real—because it needs leverage over you. And this tiny scrap of decency remaining in you, this sense of shame, starts you down the path of justifying your use of power.

"Do you get it, Dali? Everyone in the upper ranks of New Helena is there because they've convinced themselves of their own self-righteousness—under which lies a dread of being exposed for their shameful acts.

"Because even at the heights of power, you're still just serving Royal Enfield Ambler."

He stopped pacing. "My conscription notice showed up shortly after I passed, and I immediately ran to the recruitment office to get signed up. Somebody—maybe my dad—had my test scores changed, so it looked like I wasn't suited for anything but a desk job on Mars."

"Couldn't Roy have pulled some strings to get you out?"

"Probably. But Mars is a peculiar international effort. The war had just begun, and he might have thought it wasn't worth the risk. Mars was a safe place to store me until he was ready."

Dali smiled. "Well, at least that much worked out for you."

"Even with my awareness that nothing had really happened, I was a mess. I felt guilty. Worse, I had this unearned contempt for others. The ultimate goal of the training is to make sure you know you are above everyone else, and they live and die at your whim."

"That's abominable."

"Yes," he agreed. "It took me two years just to get out of that mindset. Coming out to Bug Space—and meeting you—are the only things that have given me back a semblance of my humanity."

He took both her hands in his.

"This is why I can't go back and just 'not do what he wants.' That...that willingness to use power over others. That's in me. If I go back and start running things, I could end up just like Roy. I would rather die."

Her lips parted slightly, and in the small exhalation that escaped, he could see that he had gotten through.

"Now you have to decide if you want to spend your life with some-one with that kind of darkness in him."

Before she could respond, his device lit, sounding a warning klaxon.

ALERT: APOTHIKON PULSE

Chapter 18

The Diastole

They swarmed so fast this time that the flak cannon could barely hold them off, even with Jake and Dali working the nine o'clock gap, which had widened *again* to Jake's exasperation.

"Why are there so many?" Dali gasped as they prepared for another wave.

"I think because Grigg lost the Valley Ridge. Matzhin moved his people in, and they're that much closer to the pulse given off by Grigg's Apothikon."

Occasionally, a red light flashed on the cannon. Dali noticed. "What's that?" she yelled in between shots.

"What's what?"

"There it is again!"

"There's what again?"

Dali was too focused to respond. Jake swapped out a battery on his gun and, in that pause, caught the flash out of the corner of his eye.

What *was* that?

"Dali! You cover the side. I'll take the front."

She moved instantly, and Jake shuffled in to take her spot. The light flashed again.

The temperature light.

Every mechanical device had a temperature indicator, of course, but it wasn't the sort of thing you paid attention to most of the time.

Until it started flashing.

There were four such lights on the defense apparatus. One reflected the state of the swivel motor, and another monitored the aimer—a surprisingly old-fashioned motorized wheel with teeth that the gun rested on at various angles. Lefty had told him that, while ancient technology, the aimer was very rugged. That light was not blinking, he realized in between shots.

The power pack itself had a heat gauge. Jake had personally experienced what happened when those went bad, back on Teila, but as far as he knew, that kind of "venting," as they called it, could only happen with sabotage since the packs were so stable. As a rule, the warning light was virtually theoretical.

The fourth light rested on the blaster generator, the fat box behind the barrel. He glanced at that just in time to catch it flash red.

At least it wasn't flashing regularly.

The generator's getting hot, he reasoned, *but we have some ways to go before it overheated.* The emitter could be a few nanometers out of whack, or it could simply be that the gun wasn't ever rated to fire this often for this long. It was probably used in some gun battery where it rotated, firing with other cannons.

If that overheated, the best case would be that it just shut down for a moment.

In the worst case, the barrel would start to melt.

Jake instinctively swapped out his gun's battery again. The Seyles were relentless and more numerous than ever.

Even if he and Dali made it through this wave, he didn't know how they'd protect the Apothikon through the next set of pulses.

Looking over at her, he saw that she had amped her blaster power up to full and put on a broad enough beam to destroy swaths of Seyles at a time, at the cost of swapping out batteries every few shots.

As he placed his used batteries in the power pack, he saw quite a few had green indicators, so he grabbed them and leapt over to stuff them in her pockets. She turned her head to give him a quick kiss, not even missing a beat between firing, swapping out one of the new batteries, and turning her blaster down a notch while widening its area of effect.

It wouldn't quite vaporize everyone she hit, but she could hit more of them hard enough to keep them away from the Apothikon.

She thinks on her feet, Jake thought, and the familiar pang that accompanied his longing for her struck again.

When they stood shoulder-to-shoulder against a foe, it seemed almost impossible that she could reject him. The current combat made it easier to push down the nagging fear that she might.

After a brief withdrawal away from the flak, the Seyles had grouped into a new attack. They formed several files, dozens of Seyles deep, at each corner just outside where the electroflak could get at them. He knew what was next: they would all charge at once.

Jake took a different approach than Dali: he set his gun beam to a narrow cone, high intensity, and tried to take out the file at one corner, reducing the amount the cannon would have to move.

Even without destroying the full file, damaging half of it was enough to scatter the remainder. Jake tried to repeat the effect on the opposite corner with some success. The flak and he split the remaining corners, defeating the organized attack before it could launch.

But the Seyles were also coming in in rather chaotic patterns right through the center. The electroflak got no break, and the light flashed more and more frequently.

It tickled his brain, somehow, these attack patterns. He couldn't deny that there was some form of intelligence at work here, but it wasn't the intelligence of the chess-playing, musical, or even martial Seyles. When Seyles in their right minds fought, there was skill. There was a high degree of quick intelligence needed to conduct a fight in three dimensions, which was a challenge even if you were used to moving and thinking in three dimensions all the time.

No, this had a kind of cunning, an instinctual feel. The Seyles weren't even acting like individuals. It was as if they were organized, wanting to get through but wanting, above all else, at least *one* of them to get through.

Jake and Dali, meanwhile, had incredible force on their side. They had advanced technology, effectively unlimited ammo, and their full intellects—all arrayed against their enemies with just one goal in mind.

Save the Apothikon.

Why, though?

Jake forced the thought out of his head. He hated that he didn't understand the why of it, but now was not the time to contemplate such things. They could ponder the philosophical implications after they had destroyed all the Seyles.

And they almost had.

Dali stopped firing, and he turned to look her way. She had completely cleared her side, and the few, more direct Seyles that acted like the shield wasn't even there were spending themselves crashing into it and plummeting to the sward below, which greedily pulled them into the pit.

Jake noticed then that when a large group attacked the shield simultaneously, a straggler often got through without much damage from the shield.

That meant *enough* Seyles could weaken the shield at least temporarily for long enough so a relatively healthy Seyles could pass through.

Swell.

A sizable crowd still arrayed themselves in front of the flak cannon, red light still flickering, but between that and Jake and now Dali, it looked like they had just about managed to fight off yet another wave of attackers.

Then the warning light went completely red. The flak stopped firing. The Seyles swooped in on each side and straight down the middle.

Jake and Dali had each taken a side and eliminated their Seyles, but a few in the squadron that came head-on got through.

Jake lunged from the cannon toward the pit and stopped at the edge, firing upward at the incoming Seyles. Six had gotten inside the bubble!

He took out the first two easily, and Dali managed to take out the one trailing the rest. She had to hold her fire since he was on the other side of the remaining three, heading straight for the pit.

One crashed into him, knocking him off balance briefly, but he had already gotten his knife out to slash at its wings.

It careened to one side, and Dali gave it a sharp kick right into the shield, where it sizzled.

He didn't even have time to register that, however, since the next one smashed into him, impaling itself on his knife. He set his foot back for balance and, dropping his gun, grabbed the beast by the pseudo-face and drew his knife through the goop-covered thorax.

Or, mostly through, because before he had gotten to the end, the third Seyles knocked him back, and he fell into the pool.

In the shadowy murk, he felt tendrils grabbing at him and could make out strange glowing shapes approaching. They covered him until he was blind from their light.

"Jake! Jake!"

He heard the voice and felt the rubbing against his body and face.

Finally, he could open his eyes, and Dali was over him, rubbing her pants all over his body. Her shirt lay off to one side, already saturated in goop.

He tried to leer at her playfully but couldn't move his face. His muscles twitched, out of his control.

He managed a smile when he realized she was wearing her princess gloves for the last time, no doubt.

"You didn't pull me out?" he asked later. Dali had helped him back to his tent, he even more naked than she since she had cut all his clothes off the instant he crawled out of the pit.

"No," she fretted. "You went in, and I shot the last Seyles first..."

He kissed her weakly. "Good girl."

"Then I ran to the pit and thought about jumping in, but if something was holding you down, I figured it would just keep me down, too."

"Sensible."

"So I put on my gloves and got down, thinking I'd pull you out."

"And?"

"I hesitated for just a moment. I looked to see—I didn't know if you were conscious. If you were okay and just needed help getting out or—"

"—or what the Apothikon fluid had done to me."

"I'm sorry, Jake."

He cupped her face gently. "Don't apologize for not getting yourself killed. I was dumb enough to fall into the pit. It seems to have had no ill effects, but if it had, and you had also gone in, we'd be in real trouble."

"You climbed out almost immediately," she recounted, pale. "But you were—I don't know what. You'd gone crazy, like you were looking at something I couldn't see, thrashing around violently. I thought you were going to crash into the shield and was thinking of shooting you in the leg to keep that from happening when you just fell over.

"That's when I started cleaning you off," she finished. "You feel okay, though? Do you really think it had no effect?"

Jake smiled. "None at all."

With that, he collapsed onto the bed, unconscious.

"No, you can't bring him back. By God, Dali, what if he has a mutated strain of foulbrood or something worse? His body's a mess from everything he's picked up over the years."

Jake, eyes closed, recognized that voice instantly. Doc Blood.

"At this point, you couldn't bring him back even if he were *healthy*. Weir's done a good job of tamping down on any overt hostility, but there's a lot of confusion around Jake. *We* know he's one of us, but many people think he's allied with New Helena. Tarkanian's trying to find a way to get him off XEE entirely."

Another voice—Leidecker.

Jake heard a slight crack in Dali's voice. In all their time together, he'd never heard it. Not when she pulled him from the hive on Alvum. Not when the Rosicrucian was torturing her.

"You have to do *something*," was all she said.

Blood said, "He's got a good fabber setup there. Take some samples and bring them back to me. I'll...I don't know what, but I'll come up with something."

The call ended, and Dali began to busy herself around the base, looking at her device and feeding data into the fabber.

He watched her through lidded eyes. He liked to watch her because she hadn't quite regained her composure, and he knew she didn't want him seeing her that way.

Few people, if any, would have noticed the slight tremble in her hand or the discrete way she wiped her eyes before any betraying moisture could pool there.

In some ways, she was his opposite. What had she said? He wore his heart on his sleeve? Dali showed people what she wanted them to see.

Did that mean she was deceptive? He pondered idly.

No, not deceptive. Creative. What Dali showed people was what she wanted to be to them. The realization brought him a profound sense of privilege: she had let her guard down with him. With others, she might have been a princess, a captain, or a pirate.

With him, she had been a woman.

"Hey," he said.

After a brief moment, she turned, and he saw a calm, almost professional demeanor with no trace of worry or weakness.

"Hey, tough guy," she smiled.

"What's up?"

"Well, I talked to Doc Blood, and he wants me to draw some blood, so I've been setting that up. When you're feeling better, I'll go back to XEE, and he can whip up a—"

"A healing potion."

She smiled but knitted her brow while he recounted his conversation with Derek.

"That *would* be handy," she agreed. She giggled a little. "You could go to Doc Blood, and he'd hook you up to a machine, and it would read '97.' He'd say, 'Well, you need three more hit-points,' and he'd give you a little pill."

"Be tough to justify seven years of medical school," Jake snickered.

Later, after she had collected everything the doctor had asked for, he said, "You were better—a lot better—than some nurses I've had."

Dali nodded. "The trick is to realize that you don't do any good by not *wanting* to hurt the patient. You do good by not *hurting* the patient."

"I don't get it."

"Sometimes you have to do something for someone's own good that might hurt them. Like, draw blood. If you're worried about hurting them, you might hesitate, tremble, or just miss, and then you hurt them much more."

"Oh, like ripping a bandage off."

"Yeah, best just to do it fast. When you're feeling a little better, I'll head back to XEE, and we'll get you fixed up."

"You should go now."

"Jake, you've been sitting on the bed for half an hour. You're not ready."

Jake stood to demonstrate his wellness, only realizing then that he was naked, and twisted around to cover himself in the bedsheets. This caused him to lose his balance and fall back onto the bed.

She hovered over him with a smile. "It's a little late for modesty between us." This brought a rush of memories of their time stranded on the *Shiva*, where they had really gotten to know each other and of them treating each other for the radiation burns they had suffered battling Telemakhos. They had already endured more than most married couples do in a lifetime.

He grinned sheepishly and pulled her down for a kiss. "Clumsiness aside, I'm doing much better. You go."

He made his case in a number of ways until she finally conceded. He even walked her to the tent flaps and leaned casually against a tent support, grateful he had sunk the poles so deep.

She clung to his hand as long as she could, and before stepping away completely, he gripped it firmly and said, "When you come back, let's get married. If you'll have me, that is."

Her eyes widened, and she smiled a big, heart-melting grin, practically running back to the *Shiva*.

CHAPTER 19

A BILLION NIGHTMARES

He wasn't *exactly* lying. He did feel better, just as he told Dali, but feeling better didn't mean he felt good. He was holding on to the tent pole, watching the *Shiva* float into the sky, barely having enough strength to return to his bed.

He collapsed and didn't bother to adjust the covers. He lost consciousness almost immediately.

Sort of.

He felt an odd awareness, like a dream state with no restfulness. He knew he was asleep but could not wake or even control what he saw. Before his mind's eye, a nightmare played out.

Then another. Then countless more.

They started familiarly: he still had nightmares about New Helena, what he had seen and done. The images blended, in the way of dreams, such that his victims became himself, or Derek, or Dali K.

Then the bugs came.

At a visceral level, he still felt a revulsion toward insectoid life. Almost as if he, as a person, had met and liked many bugs, but his body harbored its own grave reservations as to how such aliens might dissect and consume him.

Horrors it decided he needed to see just now.

He was being drained of blood by Lydians. From experience, he knew his blood was poisonous to them, but his unconscious mind did not care for such details.

Left a drained shell, he was paraded around by worshipful Cilydians, chanting his name. They paraded past a desk, where a Coleon—an Ip wearing green eyeshades—tallied the Cilydians as the procession bearing his body passed.

Then it got even weirder.

Jake broke into a sweat with visions of Myrmidons coming to destroy his hive. He dreamt he was a Seyles and swallowed a Korma, then he was a Korma, eating the remains of a Seyles. Then, he dreamed of being eaten by a Seyles.

He floated above Nidus, seeing giant glowing moths all around him in the twilight sky. Below him—from him!—it snowed, and the snow fell on the upturned faces of the Nijins, who melted away into oblivion.

Behind it all, something else. Numbers. Letters. Dates. People. Moses. Churchill. Brighthart. And Goni Korma The Architect?

Then, something else he couldn't understand at all:

bZnisbdtPk69W3M3J7hn6nnXCJpJ

Finally, he woke. His eyes popped open, and he realized he had tossed and turned himself halfway out of bed. Expecting some pain from the awkward position, he surprised himself by rising easily, without coughing, and with his muscles and bones not complaining.

When he realized he could move reasonably well, he grabbed his tools and headed for the electroflak. He had a little breathing time before the next set of pulses and decided that he better make the best of it.

As he headed for the pit, the Dragon moon provided better light than the resentful eye of the sun. He had no idea where the Damsel moon had gotten off to, but the mist in the air was nearly rain dashed lightly against him by the wind.

He found it refreshing, as if Nidus was finally going to make up its mind and have some real weather.

The actual blast generator of the gun was a simple but inviolable device. Jake couldn't take it apart or even get much visibility into it, and if it needed re-calibration, that was beyond him. He *could* tell Dali to bring a new one, and immediately after thinking of it, he fired off a request to Lefty and then a message to Derek to make sure Dali knew to get it from him.

The gun was a weak link in the chain. Luckily, it hadn't broken.

But if the gun hadn't overheated because of a defect, it had done so from overuse—actually a much more dangerous situation since it suggested a design flaw that he could not repair and which would be present in potentially every replacement he got.

Doing some quick research on his device, he saw that it was a fairly old weapon from an Earth war that had been fought and forgotten before he was born, and it had not been meant to defend against the kind of onslaughts he was dealing with.

It seemed likely that the modifications the ICF had made to make the weapon less lethal had aggravated the problem. To downscale the weapon required diffusing the blast near the tip of the barrel, where the heat would normally dissipate.

He found the insulation had burnt out, so he trotted back to his base to make more. When he returned to the knoll, he found Georgia inspecting the new woollyhead gap.

"Doctor Vizgirda," he said casually.

"Bailiff," she responded, not looking up. "I see there are some new deficiencies in the ring shield."

"Yeah. I think...well, I think I spotted what's eating them." The insulating sleeve was meant to fit snugly around the barrel, and he struggled with it. "According to an eye-witness, it might have been a—I don't know, a polar bear?"

Georgia scoffed and put her hands on her hips. "I trust you understand there couldn't be a bear on Nidus. Even if you brought one here, it would die because there's no food it would recognize as such, and it would probably poison itself on the local flora and fauna."

"As I said, a 'big white hairy monster' is all I have to go on. I think it must live somewhere beyond the river," Jake pointed, "either hiding in the forest or maybe up in the hills."

"Well, why haven't you gone looking for it? Mr. Ambler, your job here is to protect the Apothikon, not to *play with your gun.*"

Now, it was his turn not to look up. "I had planned to look for it but haven't had a chance yet."

"Well, why not?" she exclaimed.

"I've been sick," he deadpanned. "It's kind of a problem, Doc. I have to protect the Apothikon, which, on the one hand, means hunting this big, hairy monster down, and on the other, means staying close by so that it doesn't succumb to the Seyles' advances."

Finally, the sleeve went over the barrel with a satisfying snugness. "That's not all. It also means defending this kingdom against enemy invasion, which I can't do when I'm fighting direct attacks on the Apothikon. Still, when I *fail* to do it, I end up with just that many more Seyles from the invading kingdom drawn to the Apothikon pulse."

He looked sharply at Georgia. "What are *you* doing to save the Apothikon? Or what are you doing *at all*?"

She didn't flinch. "I'm a scientist, young man. I've been *investigating*. There are thousands of Apothikons, and I'm trying to visit as many as possible to see the variations and better understand what happens if they succumb to these attacks."

"Any news? Anything that might help *me*, for example?"

"I...I've found a few spots like the one over the river. Apothikons that have not made it." She shivered. "Ghost cities. Collapsing Seyles villages. Ruined Nock warrens and crumbled aqueducts."

"Not to sound dumb, but I can't see what the Nijins get from the Apothikon," Jake mused. He stepped down the knoll toward her. "Not to sound even dumber, but I guess you should know I fell into the pit."

The subsequent few minutes were not entirely pleasant for Jake, and Georgia was only partly mollified by the fact that he had been overwhelmed and knocked in by the Seyles.

Examining the pit, which she did by lying on her stomach, looking down into it, and taking readings with her device, she began to relax.

"I don't think you've done any real harm. At least, I hope you haven't. The color is good, and the root network doesn't look damaged." She stood up and brushed herself off. "I guess we'll know for sure on the next pulse. If it follows the same pattern, we're probably fine."

She re-appraised him. "You look unharmed. Any aftereffects?"

Jake shook his head. "Just some bad dreams."

"That's good." Then she volunteered, "I did observe one thing that might be useful to you, Bailiff. Besides this being the only Apothikon pit with a gap, this kingdom has far and away the largest and most advanced Diptera community I've seen."

Jake said, "Really? That's an odd coincidence."

"If it is one," she agreed. "I can't see the connection myself. Still, when we call Nidus 'feudalistic,' we're being generous. It's really quite Paleolithic for the most part. Most Dipteran communities reflect that."

"Huh. Well, I'd planned to visit anyway. Maybe I'll turn something up," Jake said.

With a determined expression, Georgia said, "I just finished a circuit through a hundred of my most frequently visited sites, and I'm about to go over them again now to see if there are any changes."

"Good luck," he said. He held out his hand. After a moment's consideration, Georgia grabbed it and shook.

"Take care, Mr. Ambler. We are very close."

He smiled. "To what?"

"Something big."

CHAPTER 20

GETTING SMALL

"How goes the war?" Jake asked with a yawn.

"Weird. Very weird," Derek looked more stressed than usual. "I'll get that replacement part you wanted for Dali if Lefty can drum up a spare."

Min-hee poked her head into the frame. "Hi, Jake! Dali's on her way back. Congratulations!"

Derek arched an eyebrow. "For what?"

"You want to tell him, Mini Kim?"

"Jake and Dali are getting married!" she said, wrapping her arms around Derek's neck and kissing him on the cheek.

Derek feigned an expression of annoyance, then said, "Oh, wow, it's about time. You're practically the last to land your Lost Girl."

"I guess so. A lot of complications when you marry into royalty." He chuckled a little.

Derek said, "Speaking of which, did you load the plans into the fabber, Prince Jake? I have to call you 'Prince' now, right?"

"I prefer 'King'. But, yes, I did load the plans and..." Jake held his device over a tiny speck on his table and zoomed in. "Printed it out."

Derek whistled. "That's a great fabber."

"The amount of raw resources needed for the filament is barely measurable. Takes a while to print, though."

"There's a lot of detail needed, dude."

"I was thinking about doing another, but I don't want to tie up my fabber. I might need to make some new meds. Also, I did the neural imprint earlier. So this flyspeck is going to, I don't know, hold my brain?"

Derek snickered. "Yeah, it could probably be a lot smaller, you're right, but all it does is hold a pattern that acts like you. Come to think of it, you probably should make a fleet of these since if it acts like you, it's probably gonna get squashed."

Jake just looked at the screen for a second, then ignored his friend's comment.

Derek went on. "It's got modified input ports, so it should be able to understand Diptera 'speech,' such as it is. It'll go do its thing, then transmit the data, and you can just lie back with some goggles on and watch it almost live."

"Except that I'm an order of magnitude slower, and I'll get further and further behind the longer it goes."

Derek shrugged. "If the model is decent, it won't matter. I mean, assuming nobody in Tinytown throws you a curve ball."

Jake laughed. "Tinytown *is* a curveball. Hey, speaking of curveballs, what did you think about that Luca noise I sent you?"

Derek shrugged. "Beats me. I ran it through several decrypting techniques. Then I took the text and looked to the underlying impulses the translator was putting into letters."

"So it is just noise?"

"Actually," Derek said, "I think we can be confident it's not. It's a little too regular. Decryption can be like numerology, though, if you're not careful."

"What does that mean, Derek? You know how I am with math."

"Give me a random number."

"Uh...sixteen?"

"OK. That's four squared. It's also the largest number you could store in four bits. It's 4PM in military time—you see, four keeps recurring here. The sixteenth letter of the Greek alphabet is *pi*, which is approximately three-point-one-four, and three plus one is four..."

"OK, even I'm not that gullible. And how do you happen to know the Greek alphabet?"

"The point is, Jake, you can see patterns everywhere. There look to be runs of this code that decode perfectly as chemical equations. I also found the Avogadro constant, a star chart, and, in fact, *pi* to a high degree of precision, but only by constantly shifting how I decoded things."

"I see. It makes sense if you make it make sense, basically."

"Exactly. Kind of like life, dude. Gotta go."

He spent the afternoon working on tuning his "psychic blocker," as he'd begun to think of it. He had done about sixty bizarre things in assembling it, at least according to the computer, and of those, fifty-eight had been disastrous. The other two, the computer labeled as "uninteresting," but Jake suspected it was because the components had never been used for anything like he was building.

He (and his computer's data model) came from a background of not believing telepathy was even possible. Naturally, the components would never have been used to block non-existent psychic powers, but he felt confident he was on the right track.

When he was young, Jake was not given to trusting his own intuition—or even listening to it—but a review of his adventures in the

ICF had slowly moved him toward an agnostic position. Right now, his inner voice was leading him to believe he had achieved his goal.

The problem was that he didn't exactly have a wellspring of psychics available to test his belief. He *had* been nursing a suspicion which, if correct, gave him the best possible subject to test it on.

He closed up his device, which was actually a matched pair of button-sized devices—and powered it on.

Acutely aware that he might be fooling himself, it still to him seemed like he could *feel* when the field they generated was live.

He set the pair down on his workbench next to his bottle of pills. He hadn't taken one in a while.

He hadn't felt the need in a while.

The little drone fluttered past him, and he said, "Bombur?" before realizing it was his own. It came to rest on the proximity mat near his chair, and he quickly linked his goggles to the data stream.

Derek had assured him VR was the best way to experience this kind of footage, but Derek sometimes had a twisted sense of humor.

Pushing aside his apprehension, he slipped on the goggles.

A wave of nausea instantly hit him.

Perspective. All wrong.

Everything swooped around, distorted as if moving away and toward him on a parabolic curve.

He barked some sharp commands at his computer to stabilize the center and correct the visual distortion, which helped. He then tried to focus as much as he could on the direct center of the image.

Eventually, he could see what lay before him.

"He" had swooped past the local ridges and the reservoir—looking quite a bit like full-sized mountains and a sea—and then past the walls of the Diptera city.

It struck him immediately as similar to one of those ancient European towns where the primitive and historical slowly gave way to newer technology. This process had been going on almost since they were first founded. There were no streets, but a complex network of bridges created the impression of a very cluttered and active cityscape.

Relatively large, flat vehicles powered by who-knows-what and stacked with crates moved between the buildings in an orderly fashion over the bridges and up-and-down elevators. There were multiple skyscrapers that at least superficially resembled human ones.

Over the tallest one, he saw a crowd of Diptera—a group large enough to be seen in the half-light—swooping around in aimless patterns.

Like every other city on Nidus he'd seen, it was dimly lit, the fascinating thing being that the lighting that Diptera *did* have was clearly powered by electricity.

Apparently, his avatar knew he'd be interested and swooped down to inspect one of the tiny lights. Incandescent, he imagined, and probably powered through a type of induction. Mesh draped along the walls suggested a possible source of power.

The drone lightly brushed against the mesh, and Jake saw its charge level rise.

Excellent, he thought. *My drone can move throughout the city at top speed and processing power by casually recharging itself on Tinytown's supply!*

Some nearby Diptera were staring at him. They weren't as majestic-looking as the Seyles, even at scale. Still, they had similar facial configurations—more human in appearance, with smaller eyes and a protuberance that was almost certainly not a nose but looked like one.

They even wore clothes, like the Seyles, though with shiny ultra-fine silk fabric and far better tailored.

"Hello," said Jake to the nearby Diptera. "I am Jake Wizard. Have you heard of me?"

One Diptera floated forward. Jake had the impression he was older and male. "We have heard of Jake Wizard. But how can you be him and also be our size?"

"I am not truly him. I'm a messenger he sent to get to know you better."

Someone else intoned, "The prophet of Comedentis!"

The drone paused. "I do not kno—"

"Nonsense. It's some kind of flying machine—a robot," said a sharp female voice. When the drone turned to look at her, Jake noticed that female Diptera had larger mouths and sharper teeth. It only belatedly registered with him that she had used some term the translator picked up as "robot."

"I am Ledalipholus. I am the Chief Scientist of the Diptera and the Technocrat of Melontikopolis."

"There's a chief scientist?" Jake cringed a little to hear his avatar speak that way while recognizing that probably was exactly what he would have said had he been there. He had known the Diptera were advanced, but he had not known *how* advanced.

Jake's surprise was not reflected in how the drone responded. "You are correct. I am a robot. I am directed by an advanced computer that tries to act the way Jake Wizard would act in the same situation."

Ledalipholus seemed impressed by this. "We would very much like to examine both the mechanism and the program running it."

"That would be agreeable. I have believed for some time that my people, the Independent Crusader Force, should be speaking with yours."

"Yes, that's cert—"

Just then, it seemed as if the whole city shrieked. He looked up and saw a Seyles, like a gargantuan hell-beast, fly over the city with its maw wide, consuming the cloud of Diptera that had been swarming around the tallest skyscraper.

The Diptera had a ritual similar to tea, except that rather than drinking it from cups, they filled a small bath with it and floated on the surface. The tub itself lay in the center of a simple room surrounded by tables containing drying fibers and crystals of what Jake suspected was sugar.

Ledalipholus had led him to Technocrat Hall, the center of government for Melontikopolis, and brought him to the tea room—a Dipteran diplomatic custom.

The Jake avatar had chosen to perch on the tub's rim, though it had collected some tea samples.

Ledalipholus had four of her six limbs skating on the surface, though she barely moved.

"Even when it's expected, it's still incredibly jarring," she said, referring to the Seyles attack.

Jake's heart was still pounding from just watching the replay, but the Jake drone had no internal reaction—an advantage of a robot body.

"It's expected?" the drone prompted for more information.

She scooped a tiny amount of liquid off the surface and sipped it into her fang-decorated mouth. "Yes. The Seyles demand sacrifices. In earlier times, we looked upon them as gods. Some historians say our first great advance was Comedentism."

"We know little about Nidus and even less about the Diptera," the drone said blandly.

"I don't know much about Comedentism myself, honestly, but the key element was the invention of a *god*—Comedentis—who ate Seyles."

"I am unaware of any creature on Nidus that can consume a live Seyles. Unless it is the Apothikon."

The real Jake gasped at that. He knew that the Apothikon, in its larval state, fed on weakened Seyles. He hadn't considered the possibility that the eclosed Apothikon might eat live, *healthy* Seyles.

"Oh, it's all superstition. But the historians claim the Comedentis—the God That Eats Seyles—allowed us to rise above fearing the Seyles."

Jake's drone said, "You worship Comedentis, but still you sacrifice your people?"

"As a society, we've evolved beyond Comedentism for the most part. But as we grew out of Comedentism, a form of worship arose called Anticomedentism. Anticomedentines *worship* Seyles. They congregate above the highest towers in our city, waiting for the Seyles to come eat them."

The drone replied, "Some Seyles seem to have a similar attraction to the Apothikon."

The expressions on Ledalipholous' face—on Diptera's faces generally—seemed to map pretty closely to human, at least in how their faces moved around their eyes. The lower parts of their faces, including their mouths, did not emote much.

Jake, on review, thought he detected a kind of satisfaction in her expression as she silently sipped her tea.

"It at least saves us from having to choose sacrifices."

The drone spoke again. "What benefit is this sacrifice for the Seyles? It can't be nutrition. Even a hundred Diptera wouldn't replace the calories used to consume them." Jake thought the drone's expression here was somewhat stilted, but of course, this had all happened in the past and was unchangeable.

Musing, Ledalipholus said, "Apparently, we have an intoxicating, hallucinatory effect on them. It can also be a way to spy on us."

The Diptera scientist rose from the tea bath, swabbed her pointy feet on a drying fiber, and headed toward a hallway. She led the drone underground, where many Diptera stood around (or hung on to the walls and ceilings) watching a box of flashing lights.

"It's a computer!" the drone said. "You really are advanced!"

"Very perceptive. If your people have devices like, well, like flying intelligent robots such as yourself, our technology must be almost unrecognizably primitive."

The drone said, "It is well ahead of any other Nijins."

Ledalipholus replied, "Indeed. This is why the Seyles eat us."

"Back up," the drone said. "Can you explain that?"

OK, that one the drone nailed, thought Jake.

"Life is short. Education is slow."

"So they eat you?"

"It's why Nijins eat each other. It is the fastest way to learn."

"It is not possible to learn by consuming," argued the drone.

Don't argue with anyone, the real Jake thought. He would have to pound that into the drone. Even if *he* would've it, it was always a mistake.

"You have reports on your world showing data transfers under similar circumstances."

Jake (the real one) thought, *We do?*

The drone said, "Those reports are not considered reliable. How did you come to be aware of them?"

She fixed her gaze on the drone's camera as if addressing Jake directly. "I believe you've already met Bombur," she said.

Oh, no, thought Jake.

"Oh, no," said the Jake drone.

It was then Dali shook him by the shoulder.

They didn't speak but kissed instead.

"I do," she whispered.

CHAPTER 21

CONTENTMENT

"How do you feel?" she asked, nuzzling his neck. The *Shiva* and all its systems hummed around them.

"Married," he murmured, smiling.

She giggled. "This was a good idea." She might have meant their marriage, their impromptu honeymoon in the *Shiva*'s lounge, or the long-delayed consummation of their relationship, and Jake agreed with all of the above.

"How did we ever keep our hands off each other the *first* time?" Jake wondered, recalling the *Shiva* being disabled outside of Alvum. They couldn't go to Alvum, but they had put themselves in a close orbit around its star, where they had once encountered the Angelis, a species of creature that appeared to be able to live in the vacuum of space.

Dali was obsessed with coming out here, hoping to see them again.

"Oh!" Jake exclaimed. "I get it now."

"Get what?" she laughed in response.

"You mentioned Diana was from The Suburbs, right?"

Dali bit his ear. "You shouldn't be thinking about other women right now. Or ever."

"Ow! But, no, look: Byron is from The Country!"

Now, she propped her head up, looking at his face. "Sir, what *are* you talking about?"

"Well, in The Country—at least the part Byron comes from—birth control is generally the responsibility of the woman. But in The City and The Suburbs, birth control is the responsibility of the man."

Dali frowned. "I still don't know what you're talking about."

"There was no reason for Diana to get pregnant *accidentally* except that she expected him to take precautions, and he expected her to do the same. So neither of them did!"

"Jake, talk to me like an alien girl who went to a British boarding school and never made any friends who talked about this stuff."

And so he did. His grandfather had had "The Talk" with him when he was a preteen, a no-nonsense, fact-based description of human reproduction. Despite having grown up on the farm and understanding the basic mechanics, Jake had cringed and flushed through the entire lecture, during which his grandpa had focused on the *repercussions* of sexual activity.

Then he'd had to sit through the same sort of lecture in The City, which was delivered via prerecorded, computer-guided videos and focused entirely on the act and its variations. Only a brief mention was given to the (temporary) sterilization process males usually underwent at maturity. The experience had somehow been even more cringe-inducing than the lecture with his Grandpa Yakov.

Dali's face lit up with understanding. She said, "Did *you* have the..."

He said quickly, "No, no, of course not. I never completely abandoned my Grandpa Yakov's ideas, and I couldn't bring myself to—"

She was grinning at him.

"Wait. Wait, does that mean..."

She grinned for a moment longer, then burst into laughter. Now, it was Jake's turn to be puzzled. He kissed her in an attempt to quiet her, and it worked when she kissed back.

Then he broke off and said, "So..."

Smiling coyly, she said, "No, on Karnata, a woman chooses whether or not to get pregnant."

"How's that again?"

"All these things you Earthlings—pardon my use of the term—do? No, on Karnata, it's basic training for girls to control all such matters."

Jake shook his head disbelievingly. "So you have telepaths and, oh, by the way, control of your autonomous bodily systems?"

Dali shrugged. "My great-great-grandfather had the idea that Earth was imprisoned by beliefs it had adopted unconsciously, and those beliefs had, in turn, shaped the reality in which everyone lived."

"I don't follow."

"It'll be more apparent when you finally visit Karnata. But even back on Earth, my people had a long tradition of being able to slow their heart rates, shift their metabolism, stop bleeding, and so on."

She giggled and added, "And then there are things boys learn to do and things girls learn to do."

Jake thought about it. "But if Earthlings knew—"

"These skills have been known on Earth for ten thousand years, Jake. Any of your—pardon me, again—Earthling doctors will explain how what I'm saying is not possible or, at best, *unreliable.*"

Lying back, she smiled more broadly, and the sight took his breath away. "I hadn't thought of it in specific terms of—well, like Byron and Diana. I'd never thought about all the hoops you have to jump through."

"I guess they hadn't, either," Jake quipped.

"But I know faith is the key to everything we do. And Earth conspires to put doubt in your heart."

"Paul has said similar things to me many times," Jake said, barely able to imagine talking to his missionary friend about the subject.

He began to kiss her again because he couldn't help it, and she didn't seem to mind. He only stopped because the light in the cabin slowly shifted from the usual stark white to a gentle aqua. For a heartbeat, the two lay there looking into each other's eyes as the color changed around them.

Then they jumped up, ran into the cockpit, and stared out the front screen.

Pressed against the screen was a face made of light, floating in the void. It had other light rays extending from it, sometimes in straight, broad beams, other times, impossibly enough, in ribbons that seemed to ripple and flow in a cosmic wind.

"Jake!" Dali said, grabbing his arm.

The Angelis mimicked Dali, mouth stretching into an "A" shape, followed by a small smile.

Jake waved.

The Angelis formed a hand out of light, perfect except for too many fingers, and then waved back. As they watched, it extended its "hand" and passed through the screen, neither harming the ship's hull nor triggering any alarm.

It was just a reaching hand.

Another hand followed it.

They both reached out instinctively, their fingers almost touching the Angelis'.

The light abruptly shifted to an angry red. Many more Angelis approached the ship and—somehow—grabbed the friendly blue creature and pulled it away, the arms extending further and further out, attempting to keep the hands where they were in the cabin.

Finally, Jake lunged and tried to grab the hand with his as if he could somehow pull the creature back.

He couldn't, of course. His skin barely registered a tingle, which he may have imagined, as his hand passed through it.

"Seeing an Angelis on your honeymoon has to be good luck," Dali said quietly.

"Is this our honeymoon?"

"The start of it, anyway."

"Let's make sure it never ends. Which reminds me, not to spoil the mood, but did Doc Blood give you some new medicine for me?"

In a gruff voice, she said, imitating the doctor: "If his situation hasn't changed, I don't have time to get into a deep analysis of his blood. Here's a bottle of the stuff that seems to be working for Peschke. I already sent him the recipe, but I'll bet he hasn't even noticed."

She nuzzled him. "Do you ever check your messages, Ambler?"

"Intermittently," he admitted.

"That's what he said you'd say, so he gave me these." She materialized a bottle of pills. "You can make more on your fabber."

At that moment, Jake's device alarm went off. He had made sure they had plenty of time to get back before the next Apothikon pulse, and the time had already slipped away.

Swallowing his disappointment, he said, "I have a new strategy for us to try with the next pulse. I'll explain on the way back. But first!"

He jumped over to his jacket and dropped the pills in one pocket while fishing through another. "I know you said it was customary to exchange tokens." He found what he was looking for and withdrew it, holding it out to her.

"You know I don't have much, but this is probably my most treasured possession."

Dali lifted it to look at it, even though she'd seen it a hundred times. A crudely but sincerely decorated medal with a tiny chunk out of the middle. "The medal Mot gave you," she smiled, almost tearing up.

"Mot had the right idea," Jake said. "He argued that you should get a medal for when you *needed* to be brave rather than after the fact. I know you've never lacked for courage—"

"It's like giving me your heart," she whispered. Then she went to her jacket and fished out a tiny item. She pressed it into his hand, and Jake's legs went rubbery.

"You know this was given by my father to another man, and I stole it back and became a pirate because that man was not worthy." She pulled him in and kissed him hard. "I give it now to you."

Jake didn't even have to look at it to know what it was.

It was the key to the *Shiva*.

Chapter 22

Will-o'-Wisp

Honeymoons may not have to end, but they cannot help but be interrupted. Dali let him drive the *Shiva* after the "stretch," a privilege historically reserved for herself and the Lost Girls.

By this time, Jake had become a sure hand at normal-space piloting, and he only veered from the direct path "home" with a little swooping arc of the forest beyond the footbridge-covered river.

"Looking for something?" Dali asked.

"A monster," he said. "Or a ghost. Maybe a polar bear."

He landed the *Shiva* near Node Path Crossroads, and the two slipped easily to the ground, snaking arms around each other and laughing as they headed to the tent.

Stopping by the Apothikon pit, Jake clucked in disappointment.

"What is it?" Dali asked.

"I built a drone to police the area in case...whatever it is...came back."

"Well, if it had come back—"

"We would've had to cut our honeymoon even shorter, so there's that."

"Can't be too upset about that," she checked his hip with hers. Her lower center of gravity was enough to unbalance him, and she leapt on him with a barrage of kisses.

He pushed her away, ineffectively mostly, until his device alarm sounded.

ALERT: APOTHIKON PULSE

"I can't tell if that's good timing or bad," Jake muttered.

After a moment's hesitation, the two broke apart. Dali headed for the knoll, and Jake headed for the tent. Minutes later, he emerged wearing his battlesuit.

The flak cannon started firing as he approached the plateau's edge overlooking the pit.

It felt like the Seyles had gotten there faster this time, but only a few so far. With a high jump straight up, Jake looked around the landscape and could see streams of the creatures headed their way.

There were enough of them that their path became visible: starting from disparate points in the city, they headed for the Callas, the enormous goop-filled flowers that bloomed around the egg clutches. From there, they streamed to Grigg's castle, where they circled until a certain number had been reached.

Then, they flew in formation toward the pit.

He could also see Matzhin's people, who now occupied the Valley Ridge area, fly upward. They singly vanished beyond the ridge. But he could see an organized attack coming back his way. He recalled his flight back from Matzhin's court and the Callas lying beyond the ridge.

Interesting. They must be bedizening there.

He and Dali had discussed their strategy: she would guard the pit inside the shield, and he would melee from the outside. She had suggested he use his blasters on light, but Jake didn't dare risk using any range weapons while she was on the ground.

It came off better than Jake could've hoped.

Dali nearly hit him several times, but the low-powered blasts would hardly have registered even if she had.

The flak cannon *did* hit him when he had leapt into its path, trying to cut through a squad before it could dive bomb. The blast registered, but its weakened force didn't drain his shields noticeably.

A late squadron flying in from Matzhin's territory got taken out by a well-launched grenade.

As Jake explained to Dali later, "I've been wanting to try these energy grenades out, and I figured the damned thing had enough food."

He had noticed a certain resentment growing within himself toward the Apothikon.

He didn't like being a tool for other humans to do their dirty work, and he sure didn't like being a handmaid to this abomination.

His temper was piqued further when, after the battle, he saw Georgia emerge from her ship with a thin smile. Jake put the suit back into the tent, set his fabber to making more grenades, and returned to the sward surrounding the pit where Dali and Georgina were in a muted conversation.

"They're very peaceful creatures," Dali was saying.

Georgia had a concerned expression. "That fits my understanding, but the stories out of Karnata have not been reliable."

Dali frowned a little. "They're so shy, humans rarely see them, even after a hundred years of living on the same world."

Georgia muttered, "False information about alien species usually means someone has bad intentions. Bailiff Ambler," she ended with a curt nod to Jake.

Trying to override his grumpiness, which wasn't, after all, Georgia's fault, he said with forced cheerfulness, "Hey, doc, how goes the studies?"

There were too many questions and a lot of speculation. As time passed, Jake grew quieter and watched the two women—who seemed indefatigable when it came to talking—and who had bonded over some indigenous but endangered species native to Karnata.

Karnata.

He wondered how much of his future would be spent there. Sure, Dali had the spirit of a privateer and had officially abdicated her title, but her eyes sparkled at the mention of children, and it wasn't as if he would argue for raising children on Earth.

It would be fine, he was sure. The strength of his ardor had only grown over time, and it was hard not to reciprocate a love that viewed him in a far more favorable light than he viewed himself.

He found himself infatuated, intoxicated even, just watching her lips as she talked, her wild black hair which seemed to come free of whatever restraint she put it in, the movements of her hands, the fluttering of her eyelashes...

Georgia must have noticed because she abruptly complained of fatigue and headed back for her ship, with Dali offering to have her share the tent. The older woman declined, concocting some excuse about needing to write up some notes before bed, and walked away.

Dali watched her walk away, then turned to look at Jake. "I guess it's just you and me, tough g—oh!" She stopped mid-sentence when she saw the intensity in Jake's eyes. Then she smiled and blushed and, after a heartbeat, broke and ran for the tent.

Jake followed slowly, inexorably behind.

"Jake? Jake!"

He heard Dali calling and fluttered his eyes open. The tent was dark but for the Damsel moon peeking through the open tent flaps.

How many times had she called before he woke up? She sounded far away. Springing up, he threw on pants and fumbled into his shirt while stumbling out of the tent. Clouds had piled up on the horizon, hiding the sun, and while it was never very dark (or light) on Nidus, it was as dark as it ever got.

"Jake!"

He sprinted toward the voice, which floated through thick, wet air from beyond Mount Olive, from the Great Marsh he had warned Dali to stay away from. In the dim distance, he saw a dark, featureless blob close to the ground and poorly directed light from a personal device, turning the features of the marsh into long-shadowed ghosts.

"Jake!"

The voice came from the blob, which, as he drew closer, resolved into more recognizable shapes.

It was Dali, crouched on the ground. Next to her, sticking out of the ground, was a human head!

It had to be Georgia, he realized. Then, a moment later, as he drew even closer, he realized Georgia had fallen into quicksand.

Dali was holding her hands and keeping her from going under completely.

"What's wrong? Can't you pull her out?" Jake gasped as he approached the two.

"No, Jake. She's not helping."

"Not helping?" he repeated, then crouched next to her.

"Hello, dear," Georgia said, angling her head somewhat toward him.

"How are you feeling, Doc?" he asked.

"Oh, fine, I guess. A little damp."

Jake positioned Dali's device, which she had set up as a light source, so that he could get a better look at Georgia. Her face wore an insipid expression as if she felt no compunction to do anything and was content to live out her days up to her neck in muck.

"We're going to get you out now," Jake said firmly.

"Well, if you think it's important."

Dali looked at him, scared. She gave one of Georgia's hands to Jake and grabbed the other with both hands.

The older woman couldn't have weighed more than one hundred thirty pounds, thought Jake, but their first attempt to extract her failed outright.

Fortunately, if strangely, their failed attempt didn't seem to bother her much.

They sought better purchase, higher up on her arms, and tried again. It seemed at first like she would be stuck forever, but then Jake felt a little snap. Then another. Then, a bunch of snaps, like tiny, breaking ropes were holding her.

The two of them walked her back to her ship, where Dali went in and cleaned her up while Jake waited outside.

A hard-headed scientist like Georgia didn't just wander into the marsh or quicksand.

Dali poked her head outside. "She's asleep."

Jake boarded the doctor's ship, the *Mendel*, which was smaller than the *Shiva*. (Of course, the first thing he wondered was how she got it. Sometimes, it seemed like everyone had a Stretch Ship but him!)

He checked the computers and found a log dated only a few hours ago. Playing it, he saw the outside of the ship. From what he could tell, it was that "night," just as the sun gave its last tired rays out.

The camera angled up, and a circular light appeared in the sky.

"Is that a Luca?" Dali asked over his shoulder.

"No, that's a will-o'-wisp."

It flitted about aimlessly. "The elletroid has a hypnotic effect on Nijins," came Vizgirda's voice from the tape. "A local explorer has nicknamed them 'will-o'-wisps'—"

"Hey! That's you!" Dali elbowed him with a laugh. He mock-shushed her.

"—and that folksy name is quite apt in some surprising ways." The camera pointed to the ground and switched to night vision. "Here is a 'snap tick.' It's a local pest that destroys crops and can also feed on hemolymph."

The creature on screen did look like an enormous tick, larger than Jake's fist, but it hopped around a little like a frog. It hopped toward the will-o'-wisp and jumped up.

The glowing ball easily eluded it, but failing to catch it repeatedly did not appear to deter the snap tick.

"I suspect the creature would exhaust itself trying to capture the elletroid." The sphere began to move away. "The snap tick will chase it across the moors, as we will see."

Silence ensued but for some huffing from the doctor as she followed the two creatures through the dim night. Dali had crouched next to Jake, a hand on his thigh. Both watched and waited.

"And finally," the voice on the tape spoke again, "we reach the target: a pit much like the Apothikon's in which the snap tick will be drowned." Sure enough, the snap tick jumped into the dark waters of the pit.

The camera focused on the will-o'-wisp, which floated to the pit and rested on the surface, the light going out.

"My first hypothesis was that the will-o'-wisp lured Nijins to their death in the pit where they were consumed by a creature living therein. Almost a poor man's version of the Apothikon, with no shield and perhaps merely drowning its victims and slowly digesting them."

She turned the camera on herself briefly. "However, no creature lives in these pits. I have scanned hundreds of them, and they're all quite empty except for extensive roots from the surrounding grasses. Do the elletroids make these kills solely for their own benefit? Or is there more to this?"

She turned the camera back around to the pit and zoomed in.

"There are more elletroids here than I've ever encountered in the past. As you can see, the surface is crawling with them, and—"

Georgia stopped as all the wisps on the surface of the pitpit's surface began to glow. As one, they rose into an enormous shimmering white light.

"Oh."

The screen was filled with white light. There was a splash, then darkness.

CHAPTER 23

BOMBUR THE PROPHET

They parted reluctantly, as always, but quickly, as Dali felt it was critical to get Georgia back to XEE and into Doc Blood's care as soon as possible.

She only hesitated for a moment. "I wasn't able to get you a replacement for the electroflak. Are you sure you'll be okay?"

Jake reassured her that he would be fine, that everything was under control, and then watched the *Shiva* take off. He returned to his tent, where he picked up his VR headset. Dali had interrupted his viewing of the recording, and he wanted to see what had happened with Bombur.

"Mmm, yes," Ledalipholus had replied. "Young Bombur went out into the world and returned Bombur The Prophet." She regarded the drone dryly. "Your doing, I presume."

The drone paused momentarily, and Jake could imagine himself stammering were he there personally. The response it did finally come up with seemed canned:

"It is customary for my people to share knowledge."

"Unfortunately, that knowledge includes things that *we* consider classified information."

The drone paused again. Ledalipholus led him out of the computer area and into a small, windowless room lit only by a few dim bulbs.

"Fortunately," she continued after the drone had not responded, "Bombur doesn't really understand any of it, and most of it is at a scale of limited applicability to Diptera."

The Jake drone said, "What area of knowledge would you consider classified?"

"Even telling you is a breach of security."

The drone said, "From your current state of advancement, I would guess you had recently formulated the theories behind atomic power."

Ledalipholus shimmered briefly, moving so quickly that even the slowed-down version looked blurry to Jake. This, he realized, was the Dipteran way of expressing surprise.

She moved in closely and, with a low voice, said, "This is precisely what can't be generally known."

"Humans were also secretive when this technology, or aspects of it, were first discovered. In humanity's case, this was to secure the position of dominance over another faction, which was also seeking the same power."

Ledalipholus spoke in a low tone. "But was that faction already of such a power that it could destroy them easily?"

The drone paused. "No. Only other humans."

She led it over to a window. In the distance, Jake could see a public square where, not far from Technocrat Hall, Bombur stood before an enthralled crowd, delivering a sermon of some sort.

"We've been monitoring him constantly." She floated away from the computer and toward a pair of Diptera listening to a speaker.

They listened in as Bombur, whose speech was painfully slow, droned on about various weird and completely acontextual things. Jake didn't understand how the normal speed Diptera could tolerate it. It was hard for him to remember the beginning of the sentence by the end of it.

Ledalipholus jumped between the speakers and pushed some buttons, which played back the last sentence at a normal speed.

Bombur said, "Mass becometh energy at the speed of light. The voice of the Lord divideth the flames of fire, and become death, destroyer of worlds!"

"Even I don't fully understand what he's saying," groused Ledalipholus.

The drone's response was more mechanical than Jake's would've been: "He's taken bits of physics and mixed it with elements of the Bhagavad Gita and the Psalms. These are religious texts of my world."

The drone then tried to sound reassuring, which Jake found unconvincing. It said, "The Seyles couldn't possibly comprehend what he's saying any more than we can."

Ledalipholus scowled. "The Seyles won't be listening to him, Jake's Drone. But they might eat him."

"Oh."

"More significantly, a number of my scientists have joined Bombur's cult."

Jake's Drone said, "None of your atomic scientists, I hope."

Ledalipholus looked squarely into the drone's camera. "None that are still alive, no. But we pride ourselves on our intelligence and education. While the rest of the planet goes around eating each other, we have managed to distill the essence of knowledge and combine it with practice so that it's useful."

Once again, the drone was bland to Jake's ear. "That's com-mendable."

"What that means, however, is that a substantial number of his followers are only a few hypotheses away from intuiting atomic energy. All the Seyles have to understand is that there's some threat from us which, if they believe it to be possible, could result in them destroying our entire civilization."

Jake's Drone floated up. "I will go talk to him."

Excusing itself, it flew out the window toward Bombur. Then the picture got blurry.

Lying in his bed, Jake tried to adjust the picture to no avail. Then he heard shouting, and the camera jerked around violently.

His drone was under attack!

Finally, the image resolved to where the drone was flying at high speed out of the city, a brief glimpse behind revealing a thick mob of Diptera swarming after him.

END OF RECORDING

Jake removed the glasses and sat up. He walked over to the proximity mat where the drone sat and realized it had reported serious damage. He ensured his base computer had fully copied the personality module and put the drone in the fabber's recycle bin.

The recording disturbed him greatly, but he couldn't help but notice that he felt pretty good physically. He stripped and show-ered and then set the device up so he could look at himself on the tent's wall.

He hadn't looked at himself in a long time. It had been far too depressing.

"Not half bad, if I say so myself. Love agrees with you," he said as his image appeared. A little skinny, sure, but well-defined musculature, good color, nice hair, except for needing a haircut and a shave. Even his scars, which often gave his skin a mottled or angry look—

He grabbed the device and held it directly to the arm Formosa's men had nearly burned off. The newly regenerated limb attached seamlessly to his shoulder without so much as a change in pigmentation!

Then he held back the device and looked at his throat. The scar there had been visible enough to see from across a large room.

It was still visible, but only faintly!

He assessed all the wounds he had received in his life, and the scars were all healed or nearly so.

He immediately looked to his workbench, where the bottle of pills Dali had given him lay unopened. Unopened because he hadn't touched a pill in days. Unopened because he'd felt excellent!

He had *easily* carried Georgia back from the pit, where he'd had trouble lifting Dali for a kiss.

Speaking of Dali, he had been—well, aggressively amorous with her, but he had just attributed that to passion.

Surely, she would have noticed his scars going away, though, if anyone would have.

On the other hand, the lighting had been very poor, and other events always interrupted them.

He knew he wasn't imagining things, though. Not with how he looked. Not with how he felt.

And how do I feel? he asked himself.

For all his time away from Earth and with all the support Dali had given him, Jake's emotions were never straightforward. He knew he should feel good because his body felt great, but his mind immediately started to ask, "Why?"

Why did he feel good?

Could it be Doc Blood's medicine kicking in finally?

A quick scan with his device ruled that out. No trace of the medicine was found. (Still, he second-guessed. Could it be that it simply had done its job and been flushed out? Unlike every other medicine the doctor had given him?)

The planet had some subtle chemical differences, he knew. Even though he wasn't eating local flora and fauna, moisture in the air doubtless carried trace elements into his body. This seemed far-fetched.

Did *love* truly cure all?

He laughed at the sentiment. It would be nice, of course, but no matter how much he loved Dali, he knew those feelings couldn't remove the scars on his back.

All this cogitation to avoid what I know to be true.

The Apothikon pit. It had cured him. Not only had it cured him, it had given him knowledge, just as the Nijins gained knowledge from eating each other.

It was a healing potion. A healing potion *plus*.

So why didn't he let himself feel good?

He knew why.

It was Alvum all over again, maybe worse.

If humans knew of a planet where they could be restored to optimum health, they would descend on it in a way that would put locusts to shame.

He had run around Nidus trying to tell the Nijins to prepare for an eventual human invasion, but that invasion would come sooner than even he had prepared for.

CHAPTER 24

TORSK

"Ah, Jake Wizard deigns to visit Torsk, does he?"

In all his time in Bug Space, Jake had never seen a fat bug. Hogar had explained it this way: insectoids stored fat poorly (perhaps explaining, in part, why none had yet been found active in very cold climates), and their exoskeletons made it impossible for their basic shape to change after they reached maturity. Exceptions applied, as some creatures continued to grow until they died, but they didn't have anything like the human propensity toward gaining weight as they got older.

Then there was Lord Torsk, the other Seyles pestering Griggs, the one on the north side of his kingdom. If it made little sense for Matzhin to take over nearby territory, it made none at all for Torsk, whose target was the same quicksand-filled marsh that had nearly swallowed up Georgia.

And in contrast to the other two would-be kings, Torsk's court looked almost human. He sat on a large throne made of sticks and covered with shiny, colorful rocks, resting his enormous thorax on the scooped-out seat while his long, segmented abdomen aggressively pushed out in front of him.

If Grigg's voice sounded like high-pitched flutes and Matzhin like a full woodwind section, Torsk was the heavy brass of an orchestra, all tubas and trombones.

The near hysteria with which Grigg regarded Jake and the glib indifference of Matzhin contrasted strongly with Torsk, who regarded Jake suspiciously, even hostilely, but never overtly aggressively.

He had tried taking an elevated tone with Torsk, an aggressive one, a friendly one, even a mildly passive one, none of which seemed to change the enormous bug's reaction in the slightest.

He had nothing else in his diplomatic toolbelt, so he had opted to wear his battle suit to Torsks's court and address him plainly. "Lord Torsk." He approached the throne slowly, hands slightly behind him, which was similar to the Seyles' stance of non-aggression.

"I've come to ask you *not* to attack Grigg's kingdom."

"I can. I must. I shall," was the only response.

"Why *must* you? What good does it do you? What do you gain?"

"Gain?" grumbled Torsk. "Must I *gain* from it? Is that how humans think?"

"Yes," Jake said, "What is the purpose of fighting and killing to grab territory of such little value?"

Torsk shifted in his seat, his abdomen flopping to one side. "Jake Wizard, our spies have seen the destruction you can cause in combat, and we have heard rumors you are holding back when you fight."

"This is truth, Lord Torsk."

"Why hold back?"

"Because I am not here to kill. I take no pleasure from it, especially when these matters could be resolved other ways."

Torsk wheezed a laugh. "This is your mistake, Jake Wizard. These matters are not barriers to resolution. They are their own reason. Seyles fight to fight."

Frustrated, Jake blurted, "And you force the Notos, the Nocks, and the Kormas to fight your battles, too!"

Torsk paused for a moment, confused. "Jake Wizard, you are powerful, but you know little. We do not force them. We *privilege* them to fight our battles."

Now Jake paused as he detected neither cunning nor malice in the statement. Torsk believed it sincerely, he was sure, and perhaps it was even true. The Coleons "fought to fight," too, but for all their casual attitude toward death, they didn't try to kill each other in war.

Life is cheap in Bug Space.

Finally, Jake said, "But if you succeed, you weaken Grigg and perhaps kill the Apothikon." Even mentioning the Apothikon was taboo, he knew, and he used the momentary silence the shock created to argue further. "There are thousands of Seyles kingdoms on Nidus, and maybe tens of thousands. But there are *millions* of kingdoms—human and otherwise—in the galaxy beyond. Instead of weakening each other, you should be trying to fortify yourselves against attacks that may come from the stars.

"You've heard some of what I can do, and that is me, by myself. A few dozen of my kind could enslave your entire species."

Torsk huffed. "If Grigg's kingdom falls, it is time for it to fall. If creatures from the stars come to destroy the Seyles, then it is time for that. Fate is beyond the control of even the Great Jake Wizard, Destroyer of Worlds."

Jake had heard Torsk was too fat to fly, and he believed it as he saw the creature heave himself off his throne and march forward, wings dragging behind him. Susurrations from the court suggested to Jake that Torsk didn't get up often.

"The Seyles do not fear their destiny," said Torsk, pushing his bug face into Jake's.

Jake didn't flinch.

"Lord Torsk, if you cross into the Great Marsh, I will not hold back as I did with Matzhin. I will destroy every Seyles, every Noto, every Nock, and even the Kormas before they ever have a chance to engage with Grigg's army.

"It will be up to you to decide whether that is so valuable a fight that it's worth being wiped out for."

With that, he stormed from the castle and leapt back to his tent.

"Well, he could be right," said Derek, listening to Jake's story. Jake had called to check on Georgia, and while Mini Kim had gone out to talk to Dali, Jake had related his encounter with Torsk.

"Yeah, believe me, I know. I'm caught in this medieval power struggle where nobody seems to want power—you know, that's what it is. It's clearly all a game, but nobody knows the rules."

Derek chuckled. "You know what it means when you're in a game and don't know the rules?"

"What?"

"It means you're a piece, not a player." Derek grinned. "You hear about Hogar and Doc Blood?"

"What about them?"

"They got into an actual fistfight. In The Lot."

Jake tried to picture that. "I could sorta see Hogar brawling if he got pushed just so. I think he was pretty scrappy in his youth. But Doc Blood? I mean, he's practically a pacifist. A sadist, maybe, but also a pacifist."

"Pacifist or no, he threw clean punches. Hogar was flailing away with haymakers. Some hard hitters!"

"You're enjoying that way too much. Do I want to know why they were fighting?"

"It was awful, but it *was* also entertaining. I'll give you one guess as to *why*."

Jake sighed. "Doc Hottie."

Derek pointed with both hands. "She wasn't even around. Whatever she's doing, it's got them both worked up. Tarkanian's ready to reassign them to different stations."

"He should reassign Lazar."

Doctor Lazar, the extremely attractive polymath who headed up the robotics/physics division on XEE, had a way about her that turned most men into thralls. Her help had been invaluable to Jake at times, and yet he seldom got over the uneasiness he felt around her.

The door opened behind Derek, and Mini Kim walked in with Dali behind her. Jake's heart skipped to see her, and he grinned himself, risking sarcastic commentary from Derek.

Derek looked over his shoulder and then smirked. "Here comes the bride."

Dali pushed him aside. "Hey, Tough Guy! How's Swamp World?"

He gave her a brief rundown of the situation and asked, "How's Georgia?"

"She was almost recovered by the time we returned to the station. I had Doc Blood look her over anyway."

"Did Tarkanian chew you out?"

Derek butted in from the side. "Tarkanian's not on XEE at the moment. I think he went to Space Station KOR—some war-related mess going on there."

Dali pushed him out of frame again. "Yeah, Walton's right." Then she turned as if seeing Derek for the first time. "How do you look like Min-hee but have a last name like Walton? Never mind. Later." To Jake, she said, "Georgia started to recover her memories on the way to XEE. Doc Blood said she was normal but for some of her body chemistry and the welts all over her."

Jake tightened his lips. "Those welts. What if there was something in the pit that drained her memories."

"That's not how memories work," Derek shouted from the back. He and Mini Kim were sitting together, mostly out of frame.

Dali said, "Jake has some...theories."

Jake, excited, said, "I think when we make a memory, it's like a bucket. The bucket gets fuller as we revisit the memory and empties over time. It's not a perfect analogy, but it explains how neural trainers work."

Derek leaned in to show Jake his *I'm skeptical* face.

"Hey, we use neural trainers, even though we're not really sure how they work. I think they make these buckets—or help make them—and then applying knowledge fills them in."

Mini Kim chimed in thoughtfully. "What if our whole lives are just chains of these training patterns, and everything we do tends to fill them up, even when we're acting tangentially—"

"Do NOT encourage him, Min-hee!" Derek interjected.

"Encourage me, Mini Kim. I need all I can get," Jake said. Then he added, "Listen, Dali, do me a favor before coming back. I need you to find someone."

CHAPTER 25

TO THE SLAUGHTER

Some days, Jake hated his job. Dezzig had woken him by poking his skeletal Seyles hand in Jake's face and whispering, "Jake Wizard? Are you alive?"

"Sleep!" he yelled at the creature groggily. "I sleep, Dezzig Seyles!"

"Oh! Yes! I remember now!" The Seyles seemed rather pleased to recall this fact about humans, even belatedly. He found the pot of coffee Jake had been keeping around for him and downed it quickly.

"Still, you cannot sleep now. Lord Grigg is... Do you know the expression 'his wings are flying to the sun, stars, and both moons?'"

"I don't, but it sounds like he's lost his marbles."

Dezzig chuckled and repeated the phrase "lost his marbles." He placed some black olive-sized objects next to the empty coffee pot. "I've been trying to make coffee from this *velda* fruit."

"How's that going?" Jake threw the pillow off his head and got up.

"I don't have the bitterness right. The velda fruit is too sweet."

Jake climbed into his armor and faced Dezzig. "Torsk is attacking, I presume."

"Jake Wizard, you are truly amazing." Jake looked closely but couldn't tell if the Seyles was being sarcastic. He wore a blank expression and stared directly at him.

Only a twitch of his four wings made Jake suspect Dezzig was having fun at his expense.

He recalled his guard drone from the Apothikon pit. He wanted to send it back to Tinytown. Megalopolis? No, it was Melontikopolis! While struggling to remember the name, he saw Dezzig's eyes tracking the drone as it drifted into the tent.

"Do *not* eat my drone, Dezzig."

"It looks like a smartbug."

"A smartbug? That's what you call the Diptera?"

"Sometimes. You eat them, you get smart. You also get crazy for a while. Full of strange ideas. Lord Grigg eats smartbugs regularly. He says that's why he's smarter than the rest of us."

Jake wondered if the Seyles he saw eating the Diptera had, in fact, been Grigg.

Interesting.

When his drone landed, Jake loaded it with his personality module, vaguely insulted at how little time it took.

"What about Kormas?" Jake said casually, sending the drone off to Melontikopolis. He knew he didn't have a good sense of how time passed for Diptera. Would this be a few days since he was last there? A week? A month?

"Huh?" Dezzig looked confused.

Jake focused on the Seyles with some asperity. "Why did you eat Toler?" he demanded.

"I can't keep track of everyone I eat!" Dezzig's voice conveyed exasperation. "You mean that aquarian?"

"That's right!"

"The Korma were unable to decide. By eating one, I was able to decide for them. The one you call 'Toler' possessed all the information needed."

"And you can recall what he knew after eating him?"

"Of course."

"But not what his name was?"

"Jake Wizard, do you not know how to learn things?"

"Dezzig Seyles, have you ever heard of *books*?"

The creature cocked its head, which was not something Jake had seen before. It struck him as almost comical. "The library is full of thousands of books. Books older than memory. But why would you read a book when you could just *eat* someone who had read a book?"

Jake did not have a response to that. In his head, he had heard Dezzig's argument before the Seyles had uttered the words.

I'm really getting to understand these creatures.

He set his fabber to create another drone guard for him, then powered up his suit. "All right. Let's go. Grigg is holding back the troops like I asked?"

Dezzig flew through the tent flaps first. "Yes, and even Torsk's Seyles are in reserve while his infantry picks through the marsh. For the most part, anyway. A few young Seyles have charged out for one-on-one battles."

He leapt toward the Marsh, surprised at how far he overshot his mark, Mount Olive. It seemed the battlesuit was struggling to recalibrate to his newfound strength.

Dezzig fell behind as he jumped, and Jake soon found himself at the edge of the Great Marsh, where Grigg's troops lazed about.

On the plus side, he thought, at least Grigg never came to the actual battles, so that was one temper tantrum he could avoid.

Torsk's foot soldiers had made it about halfway across. There were tens of thousands, just as Matzhin had used to take the valley to the south.

Jake shot upward until he could see the entire field. His core strength had improved, and after a little wobble, he managed to hover for a moment.

Pushing all power levels to full, he began launching grenades against the advancing army across its front and then going back file after file.

He wobbled and dipped crazily, but the suit was excellent at dynamically adapting his targeting, and he never missed.

Even though the grenades were small, the suit had a very limited supply, and he quickly ran out.

However, he could dial his blasters to fire large blobs of plasma. Blobs that were so hot that they exploded on contact with things like water, trees, or life forms. Just thinking about it made him wince. He fired a barrage at a phalanx of Notos, and they exploded. The fallout from this explosion was enough to take out layers of Kormas and Nocks around them.

DEXTER GENERATOR: 80%
SINISTER GENERATOR: 75%
SYSTEM FUNCTION: NORMAL
POWER LEVEL: 75%
POWER SETTING: FULL

Even as he surveyed the damage he had wrought, the levels climbed back up.

DEXTER GENERATOR: 92%
SINISTER GENERATOR: 90%
SYSTEM FUNCTION: NORMAL
POWER LEVEL: 90%

POWER SETTING: FULL

Every suit had a thin, far less powerful version of a power pack at the base of the spine, above which the main battery rested and recharged itself. This regulated the power outflowing to the suit's subsystems.

Even with big energy drains like the plasma, the suit recharged quickly.

He paused after taking out the first few rows, having literally dec-imated Torsk's troops. They couldn't advance through the burning wreckage of their compatriots, and he wanted to give them a chance to retreat.

He turned his attention to the Seyles, taking out a few tightly formed squadrons with the blobs. They quickly learned to disperse.

Jake decided then it was time to try his lance—a long, steady beam of energy used for breaching walls that could also clear-cut a forest or dig a mine.

Piercing a Seyles, as with a regular blast from a sidearm or rifle, wasn't enough to kill it. But the lance extended out and could be swept across a target or group of targets, bisecting everything in its path.

Unlike physical lances, the energy lance could extend hundreds of yards. Seyles' remains floated downward, showering the ground troops. Their spears, unused, hit the ground rather harder.

Still, the ground troops tried to advance, picking their way through flaming corpses and boiling swamp muck.

So Jake took out another few ranks. Then, a few more. Only about two-thirds remained at which point he landed back among Grigg's troops.

Dezzig looked at him with considerably more awe than before, as did all the Nijins.

"If they don't give up," Jake said, "it will be hours before they can cross the marsh—what's left of it—without dying. Go give Grigg an update."

Dezzig left without arguing, and Jake scanned the sky. A long, shadowy shape flew swiftly to the south—one of Matzhin's spies, no doubt.

Yes. Make sure that Matzhin also knows that the patience of Jake Ambler, Destroyer of Worlds, is running thin.

After confirming Torsk's withdrawal, he returned to his tent by way of the Apothikon pit.

The nine o'clock gap in the woollyheads had grown even wider.

CHAPTER 26

OLD FRIENDS

Jake stood on Mount Olive, looking through field glasses at the Great Marsh. Smoke still rose in oily black clouds, snaking upward with no motion in front of it. Hours had passed with no activity.

Torsk had learned a lesson or, more likely, had decided to regroup before trying to invade again.

He scanned to the west now, frustrated that he had once again missed the creature grazing on his woollyheads. His replacement guardian drone must have arrived just after the flower vandal had left.

As he looked for any signs of life, he felt a sensation like a giant bug crawling up his leg and back very rapidly.

Startled, he leapt to one side and spun around, only to realize *it* was on his shoulders. He quickly drew his knife and prepared to throw it off when he heard a high-pitched voice:

"It is Mot, Jaykambler!"

Jake, relieved, chuckled and sheathed his knife. "Oh, Mot, don't sneak up on me like that!"

Mot leapt off him and stood before Jake, the expressions of his spider face largely inscrutable, but his human appendage—a low-resolution imitation of a man from the waist up, in simple clothes, complete with a young man's sparse mustache bristles—was doubled up with laughter.

"He insisted!" Dali called from a little further behind. "Ran up here giggling like a maniac. 'Jaykambler will be surprised!' he said."

She climbed up the hill to greet him, and he took her hands warmly.

Mot looked at him with a stern expression on his human face. He whispered, "You should kiss your queen, Jaykambler."

Jake fumbled a little as Dali sighed impatiently, "He's right, you know."

He kissed her perfunctorily, then for real, then broke off suddenly and said, "Waitaminute. Do Lydians and Cylidans even kiss *at all*?"

Mot giggled. "No. Dali told me to say that."

Dali giggled now. "What're you doing up here, tough guy?"

Jake said, "I'm looking for—I don't even know what, but *something* keeps eating the woollyheads. It's getting harder and harder to keep the Apothikon safe."

Mot was scuttling around Jake and prodding him a little here and there. Then he climbed up to put his spider face into Jake's.

Laughing, Jake said, "You still like to do the whole close-up thing, eh?"

"Jaykambler, Mot thinks you look very strong. But there is something different about you, too, something missing—and Mot does not understand."

"Let's go back to my base," Jake said.

Mot could barely contain himself inside the tent. He pushed every button and pulled every cord he saw. Only Jake's quick reflexes stopped him before he opened all the samples Jake had collected.

"Mot has not been many places besides Teila. It is very interesting, Jaykambler and Dalikay."

Dali smiled indulgently. "Mot, you know better than to go running around poking at things. We brought you here because we think you can help us with something."

Mot scuttled up to her and leaned in with his human appendage, his head just above Dali's waist. He wrapped a fake arm around her hips and said with an earthy twang, "What's cookin', good lookin'?"

"Mot!" Dali laughed. "Who have you been hanging out with?"

"Truckers!" replied Mot in his usual voice. "And traders." Returning to his affected accent, he added, "Lydian venom, if treated properly, is mighty refreshing to Blood Spacers, I reckon."

"Blood spacers? Wow... That was what Halerd called us on Debrides. And Teila knows about it?"

Mot nodded his human appendage. Jake noticed he had gotten quite good with it and was unsure how to feel about that. The clumsier Mot of old felt more pure.

"OK," Jake said, "we have to focus. I need to ask you something, and I want you to be honest."

Returning to his regular self, Mot intoned, "The transparent web catches the most prey."

Jake paused momentarily, almost positive that expression was exactly what he didn't want, and then said, "Mot, back on XEE when you visited, and the Minosians attacked, you said you understood why I couldn't come to Teila."

"Mot remembers, Jaykambler."

"Tell me, Mot. What did you mean? What *exactly* did you understand?"

Mot looked at Dali. "If Dalikay knows, won't that cause problems?"

"It's a bit risky, but if we don't risk it here, we will definitely have trouble down the line."

"I know about...I know about the rocks, Jaykambler."

Dali looked puzzled. "The rocks?"

Jake stopped her. "You know that because you can read my mind, can't you?"

Mot giggled. "Yes."

"And you can read the spider queens' minds, too?"

Mot nodded his human head, more subdued.

"But the fact that Teila hasn't erupted into a full-scale civil war tells me that the Lydians—the spider queens can't read *your* mind."

"You understand the situation, Jaykambler."

Jake's mind reeled with the implications. Teila's house of cards was going to come tumbling down *soon*. He wanted to ask how many Cilydians were like Mot, how and when he had developed this psychic ability, and a hundred other questions, but instead, he forced himself to stay on topic.

Jake focused on the little spider. "Mot, can you tell me why I brought you here?"

It was Mot's turn to frown, which he did with his human face and all his spider eyes at once.

"I cannot," he said finally. "Jaykambler has learned a trick."

Jake reached into his pocket and switched off his electronic blocker. "What about now?"

Mot looked at him again. Then his eyes got wide—all ten of them. "Jaykambler has found...a healing potion?"

Dali, frustrated, said, "What are you two talking about?"

A long series of confessions ensued between the three of them.

Jake detailed his rejuvenation after plunging into the Apothikon pit, describing his nightmares and showing places where his scars had healed—the ones even Doc Blood couldn't get rid of.

"But Jake," Dali said, "this is wonderful! Well, maybe I'll miss some of the scars." She winked at him. "But Mot is right. I haven't seen you look this healthy—ever!"

"I haven't *been* this healthy since I left the farm," Jake confirmed.

"So, what's the problem?"

"Dali, what happens when word gets out that there is a potential 'fountain of youth' on this planet?"

Dali frowned. "I suppose...well, scientists will come and take some samples and then try replicating it in a lab."

"Maybe that's how it starts. But then what happens?"

"Jake..."

"Roy, or someone like him, gets wind of this. Roy would steal it for himself and do anything to stop someone else from getting hold of it."

Dali touched his face. "Jake, I know he's a monster. But he can't—"

"He can, and he *would*, Dali. What about the Rosicrucians? What if they were to get a hold of this stuff?"

"Darling. You're arguing for this not to get out at all. It didn't just cure the foulbrood. It cured you of whatever the Rosicrucian did to you. Imagine if it *can* be synthesized! Billions of lives could be saved!"

Mot interjected, "Jaykambler, you must tell Dalikay about the rocks."

Jake looked at Mot, then back at Dali. Finally, he spilled everything about Alvum. Everything he had held back since that fateful day on XEE when he realized the consequences were news of Alvum's natural resources to get out.

In the end, Dali looked both relieved and worried. "Oh, Jake! You've been carrying that for all this time now!"

"I'm glad I could finally tell you. I hated keeping it from you and the Lost Girls."

Mot chirped, "But Jaykambler's device works! I cannot *see* his mind when it is on. Dalikay, did you know that Jake's mind is full of you?"

Dali winked. "I did." Turning to Jake, she said, "This isn't the same situation as Alvum."

Jake nodded. "But it could go bad—in fact, it would almost certainly end up being a disaster. If I go back to XEE and people notice I'm better, that might spur them to dig into it."

Mot said, "Jaykambler is very important."

Jake laughed, embarrassed. "No, Mot, not really. But people *are* watching me."

Mot reiterated, "Jaykambler is *very* important."

Dali got a mischievous smile on her face that reminded him of when he first saw her in the V-Ring on Mars. She said, "We're not the first to want to hide the source of something we've found."

Mot giggled. "I know what Dalikay is thinking."

"I don't."

Dali said, "Jake, nobody knows you're here except me, Georgia, Mot, Tarkanian, and Leidecker. Nothing says we have to stamp your samples with a giant label reading NIDUS, longitude and latitude, and all that. Let me take Mot back—"

Mot made a pouting noise.

"—and bring Tarkanian here. I would bet the *Shiva* that he has done this sort of thing before."

Jake said, "Yeah, he might come if he gets the magnitude—the potential of what we've got here."

"What about the Apothikon pulse? Can you handle it without help if I don't return in time? Especially with the gap being widened?"

"We should have time," Jake said confidently. "The intervals between the pulse pairs are shrinking, though, so this is our best window of opportunity.

"Otherwise, I'm stuck here—forever—or until we figure it out."

They were at the *Shiva*, with Mot scrambling into the ship while Jake and Dali said their goodbyes. Before they knew it, however, he had re-emerged, scuttling down the ladder with his spider body while holding something in his arms.

"Mot has brought Jaykambler a gift," he said as he climbed down. When solidly on the ground, he handed the object to Jake, who held it up.

"It's a kalybus! Mot made it especially for Jaykambler," he exclaimed excitedly. Then he confessed, "Mot didn't make the sheath and belt because Mot doesn't know how. But since you gave Dalikay your medal, this should help make you brave!"

Jake stepped back and drew the weapon. While it retained much of the scimitar-like character of the traditional Kalybus, Mot had clearly created it for a human. "Mot, how did you get this weighted so perfectly?" Jake marveled, swinging it around.

The little spider man swelled, and then he stage-whispered conspiratorially. "Mot has a little side business with truckers. They love Mot's kalybuses, and they...give Mot things in return."

Dali looked on, amused and touched. "C'mon, big guy, we should get going. She started up the stairs.

Mot looked reluctant to follow. "Mot could stay and fight alongside Jaykambler."

Jake thought about it for a moment. Any spare hands would help, and Mot had eight of them, but then he thought better of it. He knelt down.

"This sword will help a lot, Mot, and it would be an honor to fight alongside you. But you'd also fit perfectly into a Seyles' maw."

Mot looked shocked. "They would...eat me? They're not even spider queens, Jaykambler!"

Jake nodded. "I've already seen a Seyles I consider my friend eat a Korma that I *also* considered my friend."

Mot's expression turned to defeat. "OK, Jaykambler. But—one day!—Mot and Jaykambler will get medals and then fight against a common foe!"

"I bet you're right, Mot. I bet you're right."

Chapter 27

On Georgia's Mind

"It's gotten quite out of hand," Ledalipholus said, floating in the warm tea bath, slightly below the Jake drone.

"His followers attack me on sight for some reason," the drone said.

The Technocrat—which Jake had come to realize meant something akin to President—said, "Bombur's followers think you are a machine we created to kill him."

She added sharply, "I wish we had that kind of technology."

"I thought I could entice him by telling him I had more information. I tried to get that across to his followers."

She popped out of the tea and hovered in alarm. "You wouldn't give him *more* information!"

"There are many things Bombur could be informed about that would be harmless, but perhaps sufficiently distracting—"

Ledalipholus fluttered impatiently and then settled back into the tea. "I don't think so, not at this point. We have tried bribing him with everything a Diptera wants or needs and then some. It might have worked earlier, but now I think he's got grander things in mind."

"What grander things?"

Ledalipholus immediately dismissed everyone else when bringing Jake into the tea room. Even so, she looked around.

"I think he wants to be the savior of our people. He wants to deliver the Diptera from all the evil Seyles."

"Which means?"

"For one thing, it means he's angered the Anticomedentines."

Jake's drone, being a computer, had an easy recall of who the Anticomedentines were. Still, Jake had to pause the video to give himself a chance to remember that they were the ones who *wanted* to be eaten by the Seyles and who hovered above the city waiting for it.

"I suppose they wouldn't care for calling Seyles 'evil,'" said his drone. "But your society seems stable enough to not worry about the occasional social outburst."

"Bailiff, Bombur is agitating for building missiles. Missiles with atomic warheads. He's convinced he could damage the Seyles that way." Jake had noticed that Ledalipholus had switched to using his real title. As a technologist, she doubtless found the "Wizard" title distasteful.

"He's right," the Jake drone said dispassionately. "Even a small atomic explosion could destroy Grigg's castle and the surrounding city. But given atomic fission, the greater technological issue would be delivering it."

"We're quite aware of that, Bailiff."

"At Diptera scale, it would be comparable to humans launching missiles to the other side of the Earth, which took a decade or more of concerted effort to achieve. I'm sorry, but I don't see the issue." The drone's mechanical apologies made Jake wonder if he didn't apologize enough to make a good model or if he apologized too much.

"The issue is that we're already working on such missiles. Follow me."

With twists and turns that made him dizzy, she led the drone into an underground area of impressive size, where a row of enormous missiles sat in near darkness.

These monstrous constructions rose hundreds of feet into the air or would have if the drone was at a human scale. They were probably only about a foot tall but would be deadly if they hit their marks.

Jake suddenly wondered how much of the Dipteran activity he couldn't see and how deep the city might go.

Insectoid population control tended to be savage—Jake thought of the Minosians, who sent legions of hatchlings to invade the Lydian homeland. The Lydians themselves brutally culled females to keep the hierarchy intact and let males survive only to the degree they needed workers.

On Alvum, the Myrmidons expanded, with the crust of the planet their home, and far outstripped the more sophisticated Trigonans.

There could be billions, maybe even trillions, of Diptera in this small patch of land. An entire planet's worth of life devoted to science and living at a speed at least ten times that of humans?

His drone broke up this train of thought with a simple but important question: "Ledalipholus, is your plan to destroy all the Seyles?"

She blurred again. "I can't deny our lives would be better without Grigg, and I think Torsk and Matzhin might even be worse. We've tried communicating with the Diptera in Matzhin's kingdom, but they're—stunted."

"So what can you do with these weapons?" the Jake drone queried.

"Be taken seriously. If we demonstrate our power with a sample launch in a relatively safe area—perhaps to the sunny side of the planet beyond the hills to the west—we think the Seyles will stop eating us."

"Because they won't want to die. Logical," said the drone.

Then she said, "Likewise, since a handful of them can already destroy us, we wouldn't just attack them. If any survived, they would destroy us. It's a reasonable strategy," she finished.

The Jake drone commented, "This sounds familiar."

He felt a hand on his shoulder.

"Bailiff?"

Jake removed his VR set and sat up.

"Georgia! Is everything okay?"

The older woman smiled somewhat shyly. "I decided working was my best therapy. And I have important information. Can you take a little trip with me?"

Jake agreed, and the two set off to the *Mendel*. She was a deft hand at short hops, and he found himself far removed from any part of the planet he had seen before. However, it looked remarkably similar: twilight, of course, with the humid air hanging over a few low, uneven hills, some craggy peaks here and there, bamboo forests, and lots and lots of marshy flatlands. And, of course, an Apothikon pit surrounded by woollyheads.

The *Mendel* was more modern than the *Shiva* and didn't have a drop-grav, but Dr. Vizgirda "parked" it about 20 yards away from the Apothikon pit and a few feet off the ground. With a touch of a button, the hatch opened, and stairs unfolded till they allowed for much easier disembarkation than from the *Shiva*. (Jake found himself constantly cataloging the differences between the little Stretch Ships, awaiting the day he would get one of his own.)

"These large grass patches surround all the Apothikons and, until recently, I assumed that was a simple biological requirement: the Apothikon could only implant with relatively firm ground."

"As opposed to what?" Jake wondered aloud.

"In my studies, I've had to change my presuppositions constantly. You can look down into the pit and see the vast root network that seems to be supporting the creature."

Jake blinked. "Yes. I've seen that."

"It's not just, as I originally imagined, that the plants, like the woollyheads, are reaching into the pit for nutrients. Rather, some of those tendrils extend *from* the Apothikon into the soil."

Jake followed her to the ring of woollyheads, undisturbed here, unlike his "own" Apothikon. "I guess that makes sense, really. If there aren't any woollyheads nearby, the Apothikon wouldn't survive then?" he wondered.

"Yes, perhaps. The Apothikon's possible initial state may be a package carrying all the ingredients it needs for success, and I think it goes further than that, Bailiff."

He followed her as she circled the woollyheads with her device, scanning the area.

"The Apothikon may actually drain the area around it, firming up the ground and creating this sward that they all seem to rely on."

Jake looked around. As far as he could tell, they were on the sole dry patch of land amid a marsh bigger than the Great Marsh.

"That's...interesting. I mean, that's what the Seyles do, as far as I can tell. They direct the Kormas and the Nocks to control the water, drain the excess..." He trailed off as he thought about it.

"But this is not what I wanted you to see. I don't know if you've seen any other Apothikon pits besides the one you've been guarding."

He nodded. "A few. Early on, I did a little tour. They all looked alike to me, honestly."

She said, "With you focused so strongly on the missing woolly-heads, it doesn't surprise me that you've overlooked something else. Something I only recently noticed."

He stared hard at the pit. He couldn't see much of it from this angle, so he guessed she wasn't talking about the actual Apothikon. The sward looked the same. A very vibrant, almost garish, green. *Grass without the comfort. Vaguely hostile.*

The woollyheads were lush and huge, a thick ring of shimmering yellow-white. A *complete* ring, he noted to himself.

But, come to look at it, not actually all that *thick*.

He looked at Georgia, puzzled.

"Yes, that's right, Bailiff. Here, look closer." She knelt before the ring and pulled up some stems. "These woollyheads are dead. Their tops have blown away—not been chewed off, mind you, but just decayed and carried on the wind."

"What's going on, Doc? I don't think I can protect another Apothikon. I'm spread thin as it is!"

She smiled, "No, Bailiff. I think this thinning is natural. I think when the Apothikon is about to eclose, this ring, this protective wall—starts to thin."

He blinked uncomprehendingly.

"When the wall is gone, your job is done. We're almost to the end," she said.

They returned home, and Georgia led Jake to the compromised Apothikon pit. "The upside of this vandalism is that we get much closer readings of the creature itself."

She had her device out and scanned the Apothikon as she had done the others, an air of satisfaction surrounding her. Meanwhile, he was walking around the ring, noticing for the first time that it, too, had thinned.

"By all comparable measures, our Apothikon here is doing just fine, Bailiff. Your misadventure seems to have caused no damage."

"May I ask you something?" Jake said, suppressing the urge to say, "You have *no* idea."

"Of course," she said unguardedly.

"Since your run-in with the will-o'-wisp, you seem different. Are you sure that you're completely recovered from its effects?"

She smiled and said, "I presume you mean I'm *nicer* now."

He didn't know how to respond, so he just said, "Yes."

"Bailiff—Jake, if I may call you that—it is hard to explain exactly what happened to me, especially if you've never experienced anything similar." She paused. "You haven't, have you?"

He shook his head, then nodded. Then he said, "Maybe? I don't *think* so. But then, I'm not completely sure what *you* experienced."

"My memories were taken from me." She paused and shivered. "And if you, like me, had never thought of memories as something that we literally cling to, I can promise you don't understand the pain of what it feels like to have them torn away."

He paused. "It *hurt*?"

She nodded and shuddered. "The most painful thing I've ever experienced. Like a rope, each memory or string of memories pulled through my uselessly gripping hands. By the time you got me out of the pit, I was as close to death as I ever hope to be."

The Lucas flashed in the distance like mad paparazzi. The Damsel moon sped across the sky as the rising Dragon moon lumbered after it.

"It's just that people who get hurt tend to get angrier, I think, unless—That's it!" Jake said. "It reminds me of, back on Earth, my grandfather had a friend, much older, very cranky. He died during an operation, but they brought him back. After that, he was very much changed. Almost serene."

She smiled again, and it was a warm, genuine smile. "I've seen that, but I don't know if it's quite the same. I had everything taken from me, and as it came back, I found myself looking at it from a different perspective."

She mused, "Young love. Everything is so critical, so immediate, and so fragile. But perhaps there's a difference between holding on to something because it's precious and holding on to something to use as a shield—or a wall."

"I don't understand," Jake said, but she seemed happy with her thoughts, so he didn't press the issue.

"And perhaps I'm just being foolish," she said softly. Then she pointed to the sky, where a metallic shape caught glints of the perpetually setting sun.

"The *Shiva* returns," she mumbled. "Let us greet her."

CHAPTER 28

THE TARKANIAN DOCTRINE

Dali and Jake greeted each other with some restraint—a quick embrace and a quicker separation, standing decently apart—aware of the dignified Georgia and, as always, somewhat intimidated by the bearish Tarkanian.

Then Georgia rushed from behind Jake and positively leapt into the old man's arms. He lifted her and laughed, and she kissed him enthusiastically.

"Darling Gregor!" she exclaimed.

"Georgia! What's gotten into you?" he murmured, and then, as if suddenly aware of Jake and Dali, he set her down somewhat abashedly.

Oh. Jake suddenly knew why Tarkanian had sent him here with such extravagant supplies.

"Is my man doing right by you?" he said, indicating Jake.

The scientist slipped an arm around his waist and said, "Oh, they're lovely children, Gregor. Truly splendid."

He grunted. "That one's a pain in my ass."

She tsked at him. "He's managed to keep the Apothikon from being corrupted. By my measurements, it's strong and healthy and not far from eclosion."

Tarkanian grunted again. "Well, that'll be swell." Then he looked at Jake. "But I assume you *summoned* me here for some other reason."

Georgia got on her toes and mischievously nuzzled his neck, almost getting a smile out of him.

"Dali mentioned Alvum," he said, refusing to be distracted. Georgia disengaged with a little pout.

"Let's head to the tent. Doctor Vizgirda, you might not want to be around for this. It will place a burden of secrecy on you that you might not, as a scientist, want to take on."

Georgia raised an eyebrow interestedly. "So serious," she said with a slight smile, entering the tent behind the two men and Dali.

Jake had coffee ready and handed Tarkanian, Georgia, and Dali a cup. The ladies took one sip and immediately set their cups down. Tarkanian grimaced but held on to his.

"If you should hear some of what I'm about to say and visit a world with psychic creatures—if such things existed—you could accidentally release havoc on innocent creatures."

"How are *you* all going to deal with that?"

"I've developed a device—with a lot of help, to be sure—that blocks psychic abilities. We're committed to carrying it, more or less, for the rest of our lives."

"If you know it's effective, then doesn't that mean your 'psychic creatures' aren't theoretical? All right, you know what, never mind, I've got plenty of work to do."

She left the tent with a laugh.

Dali smiled. "I'll keep her company."

When they'd left, Jake settled in to explain things to Tarkanian. He didn't know quite how to start.

"We should be prepared for major unrest on Teila," he said, deciding to start with the most minor of the issues.

Tarkanian nodded. "We have been. Lydian culture has gotten increasingly stressed, with the queens creating more males but refusing to expand their ranks at all."

"There's that, and there's the fact that some of the Cilydians can read their minds, and the Lydians don't seem to know it yet."

Tarkanian almost sputtered out his coffee. Regaining his composure, he said, "That means the males can read the female's minds *and* keep secrets from them." Then he shrugged a little and added, "It's hard to imagine the Cilydians getting up to too much. Their psychology is their biggest barrier. They would never cross their queens."

Jake nodded. "That was my thinking, too. On the other hand, do we really know what their unadulterated psychology is? Their food supply damaged their physiology. How could it *not* have also affected their psychology, like when humans are exposed to exogenous hormones?"

"You're right, or probably just right enough, anyway. The whole point of the ICF is to let native species evolve as they will. Worst case for us, as a company, is losing those resources."

Jake nodded again. "Mot seems shockingly confident about the whole situation, even for him, so perhaps there's not much to worry about."

Tarkanian grumbled, "Okay, so what's the thing you're trying to avoid?"

"Well, you saw me before I left for Nidus."

"Yeah."

"How do I look now?"

"Like a damn vagrant," Tarkanian chuckled. Then he reappraised him more carefully. "Better than when you left, I guess. Doc Blood's tuned up his snake oil."

"No. In fact, I stopped taking it."

Jake then laid out his theory of what had happened, that the fluid in the Apothikon pit had somehow healed him.

Tarkanian objected. "That's not how physiology works, Jake. It's not a hitpoint count on a silly game. Even *I* know that many complex interacting systems balance togeth—"

At that point, Jake slipped his arm out of his shirt. "This was burned down to the bone, do you remember? Doc had to regenerate it completely."

"Well, that does look—"

"Identical to the other arm, which was not regenerated. And look: where I was bitten, where I was stabbed..." He started pointing out all the areas where he had been hurt.

"Put your clothes on, son," Tarkanian said.

"And that's just the superficial," Jake continued. "Thoughts keep popping into my head. I've gotten much better at understanding the Seyles' psychology suddenly."

"That's your *job*, Ambler!"

"But I'm remembering things I've never known. Bits of Nidus history! It's fuzzy, and often I remember something without any real understanding of it, but it's there!"

"I'll have Doc Blood—"

"No! I need you to get the samples Dali brought to him back. Blood and Hogar, too—they're such scientists. Always wanting to share what they find. I hate to say it, but the ICF's philosophy might be too *open* sometimes."

Tarkanian started to consider what Jake was saying more seriously.

"You're worried that if this gets out, people will come to Nidus and drain the pits, kill the planet," Tarkanian said, thinking out loud. "The Doc's way behind these days, so he probably hasn't even looked at your samples."

"I know we've boosted security because of the war, but his treatment area's never been that locked down—"

"You don't have to worry about that, son. Your samples and Peschke's are in the high-security vault in Doctor Lazar's lab. Anything involving the Rosicrucians we keep under wraps."

Jake relaxed a little. He knew the vault Tarkanian was talking about. If the station blew up, the vault would survive, floating alone through space.

Tarkanian said, "You know we have ways of laundering artifacts to hide their origins. It's precisely for this kind of thing."

Jake nodded. "I sort of hoped we did."

"Some people will have to be in on it, though I can keep their exposure minimal. We'll make sure the samples don't get out, and we have some techniques to create a straw man so that if the samples do get out somehow, they won't lead to you."

"A straw man?"

"A fake Jake. We'll go over the details later. On top of that, almost nobody knows you went to Nidus. Currently, as far as ICF records go, you're stationed on Euphrates. Since you're familiar there—"

"I get it. Tracks covered plausibly." Jake handed his boss a sample case, saying, "There are a couple of vials of pit fluid in here. And also some gloves."

"Gloves?"

"Yeah, Dali cleaned me off after I fell in," he shrugged. "Best I could do."

Tarkanian held up a vial of the murky liquid as if he could analyze it by looking at it. "I'll tell you one thing: if it pans out, even a little bit, you'll have more than paid for your contract."

Jake smiled, "Are you trying to get rid of me, sir?"

"Maybe. Anyway, it's a long shot." He flipped through some of the data on Jake's device. "Like getting struck by a meteor."

"Which brings us to Alvum." Jake blurted out the whole story of what he had found and why he had gone to such great lengths to get the planet quarantined. Tarkanian actually sat down in the chair, slack-jawed, on hearing the story.

Softer than Jake could ever remember him speaking, he said, "Damn. Damn, son. That is..."

"I've actually loved being a bailiff," Jake said, "and my time with the ICF, but I am plagued every day by wondering if I'm making the right choices."

Tarkanian chuckled ruefully. "You and me, both."

"Sir?"

"It's the ICF's charter. 'Save the Aliens!'" He chuckled again, even more ruefully. "I used to laugh at the wide-eyed do-gooders always protesting about humans going out into the galaxy. Then I got out here, and things were sometimes far worse than even the complainers dreaming things up on their couches could imagine."

"I always felt like our philosophy made sense."

Tarkanian looked up with a faint smile. "It has generally worked out well for us and well for the aliens we work with, too. But what if..."

"What if?"

"What if I've been nursing along a species that brings down humanity? Imagine the Minosians on Earth. Or Rapticores."

Jake shuddered at the mention of Rapticores. Just because his body had healed from the scars didn't mean his mind had.

"Anyway, I'll keep far away from any mind-readers while I wargame out the Alvum situation. When the quarantine is over, the ICF will have to move in fast."

He rolled the pair of tiny discs—the final form of Jake's blockers—in his hands. "You think these work?"

Jake nodded. "I talked with Doctor Lazar before I left about the various phenomena that get lumped together as 'psychic.' She said there are most likely multiple categories. Some probably work on the same principle as the Q-comm: two tangled particles that 'know' the state of each other, not bound by time or space. Not much could be done about that."

Jake took out the two devices he now carried out of habit. "But there's a much more superficial kind of 'psychic.' It's more like seeing in the infrared band or hearing hypersonic sounds. This kind is pretty easy to interfere with. Some scientists theorize all humans have the ability to sense this type of energy innately, but the noise of our various gadgets overwhelms it."

"Let's hope so," Tarkanian said, pocketing the devices.

"One on each side," Jake reminded him, "for best effect."

Tarkanian switched one of the devices to a different pocket. "Maybe there's something to human psychic ability. I don't know. But I have trusted you at times when practicality would have dictated otherwise, and I think it's starting to pay off."

CHAPTER 29

REMEMBERING TO FORGET

The older couple had left, and the newlyweds retreated to the tent. Greedily, they recaptured the hours as husband and wife, and Jake thought, as far as honeymoons go, a planet of perpetual twilight was not the least romantic. They talked intensely and slept deeply and enjoyed an intimacy neither had felt with anyone else.

"So, Karnata sounds like a garden paradise," he said playfully. "But what if you don't like gardens?"

She smiled, "Banavasi, the city founded by my ancestors, *is* a garden paradise. It's almost built on a contradiction. We use technology to allow us to practice a simple way of life that's gone extinct."

"Extinct? Maybe one that never existed?"

She climbed on top of him, unfazed by his slightly mocking tone. "Exactly. That was my great-grandfather's goal. It was a reaction to what he saw as the Earth's ideal of a society that's shut away from nature where no one has to do anything."

Jake nodded. "The ruin of The City. Most citizens have no purpose or responsibility, so they constantly destroy things. Nobody pays attention because there's a virtual army of people and robots repairing them."

"Ooh, my mother and father used to fight fiercely about labor and responsibility. My father insisted that we girls serve a couple of hours a day with the head of some area of the castle. So, we were housemaids, scullions, gardeners—"

"Were you?" Jake smirked.

Dali nodded vigorously. "They worked us hard! My sister complained about it, and it was a bone of contention between my parents for years. But my dad won out, at least at first."

"Really? I'm impressed!"

"When we got old enough, my sister decided to work in the stables, and my mother made sure she got the nice jobs, exercising and grooming—not mucking."

"And you?"

"I liked it all. Not at first. But I grew to. Even the mucking! By the time we were old enough to work in the stables, we were strong enough from our other labors to do the job. Or I was because I had thrown myself into the hard jobs. And mucking's not so bad if you do it regularly."

Jake marveled, "I'm never gonna stop being impressed by you."

"A few other places on Karnata are similar to Banavasi. It's a fairly successful model and makes for a popular tourist attraction. People like to pretend to 'rough it.'" She smiled.

"But there are other major cities and many smaller towns designed completely differently. One city is all pagodas and temples and very primitive housing, full of aspirants for spiritual enlightenment. Karnata's home to a lot of experiments."

"That sounds not that different, really," Jake mused.

"But we also have some arcologies. Do you know those? They're self-contained cities. Domed, climate-controlled, they grow all their own food, and so on. They're very science and technology-minded. Not my favorite places, but appealing enough to draw brilliant minds who *do* like such things from all over the galaxy."

"Yeah, Derek's mentioned Karnata has made some great strides in—well, stuff I don't understand."

She laughed. "Oh, but besides Banavisi, my favorite city is called Otto. It's like nothing I've ever seen anywhere else. There are tall, beautiful buildings styled with swooping curves, wide roads, and factories that look like Gothic churches!"

"Factories?" Jake asked.

"They're mad about machines there. Not like the ones we use today. The old kind. The noisy, smelly, dangerous ones."

Jake wrinkled his nose. "And you like that?"

Sincerely, enthusiastically, Dali gushed, "It's a wonderful thing, Jake. When they're not making things—and out-producing Earth in various areas—they're racing! On the ground, in the sky, on the water.

"And the whole city is huge, the biggest on the planet in terms of area, with roads leading all over the countryside because they love going places in these ancient machines!"

He couldn't help but be charmed, which interrupted their conversing and sleeping some more before they found their way back.

"Well, I guess I have oversimplified Karnata in my mind," he admitted.

"You're still attached to Earth," she said.

"What? No. Earth is dying. It's been a slow death, a long time coming. I don't need to witness it."

He was on top of *her* now, punctuating statements with tender kisses.

"I've heard that Earth is in trouble. It's down to, what, seven billion people?"

"My grandfather used to say something called The Enlightenment was the culprit. The death of Earth began there."

Dali wrinkled her nose. "I read about the Enlightenment in school. They talked about it as though it were a good thing."

He shrugged. "There are many things you could point at to blame the death of Earth on."

"Such as?"

"A lot of people blame the blaster, for example. Especially when combined with the power pack. Gunpowder was probably the beginning of the end of traditional power structures, but blasters and power packs made it that much harder for anyone to force others to do things. It reinforced the general orneriness of the human race."

"So you blame the blaster?"

"Some people do. Not me. I think the orneriness of the human race is a good thing, which is probably Grandpa Yakov talking. Me, I think the death blow was when Kumari Kandam was found."

"You mean Atlantis? I went there once. Got a little snow globe with the ruins inside it." She smiled. "Kitschy."

He smiled back, but his tone grew serious. "Earth used to run on one idea, more than any other: that we were constantly moving forward. Haltingly, perhaps, but inexorably. Whenever evidence turned up, here and there, to refute that, we just ignored it. And there was *tons* of evidence."

"Hmmm. So when they found the remains of an internal combustion engine at Atlantis—"

"It's really Kumari Kandam. But the corporation that claimed it focus-tested a bunch of names. If you were going to use a name from Western literature, Lemuria would be more appropriate, but more people know of 'Atlantis,' so that's what they called it."

"The tour guide pointed out the boxes that looked suspiciously like viewscreens or computers, something which could've been a launch pad. Then there's the power plant. It was a fun trip!"

"The power plant, some argue, was a fusion reactor. At least ten thousand years old."

"And this," she kissed him, "is killing Earth?"

"We *still* haven't figured out fusion," Jake pointed out. "Which means we're not even the pinnacle of *Earth* progress. This lie we tell ourselves that we're on this inexorable trajectory toward immortality and enlightenment—it's nonsense, but it was nonsense we needed!" he declared, sitting upright. "Come with me."

"And be your love," she said.

"And we will all the pleasures prove," he finished. Then he added, "Or at least we'll see how Nidus is faring."

Dali leaned into him as they walked past the reservoir. He had been brooding since their talk earlier, though her presence kept his thoughts from getting too dark.

"You know I can't read your mind, right?" she said, poking him in the side.

"I know that's what you've told me," he smirked.

"Which doesn't mean I don't see through you."

He scoffed. "Oh?"

She stopped and turned him to look at her, which he didn't mind because she was beautiful and he loved her.

"Meaning, in that noggin of yours, you're wondering if maybe you can find a way to erase those memories you don't like."

He started. That was *exactly* what he had been wondering.

"You saw how happy she was, Dali."

Dali punched his shoulder. "And you're not?"

He grinned. "Of course. But I'd be happier—"

"You think that. You like stories, let me tell you one: a counselor told my father once of some monks who lived in the mountains. One of the monks went on a walk up the mountain and discovered that the side of the mountain would slide down and destroy the monastery. Naturally, he ran back to tell his brothers, who were all upset by this news. So the head of the monastery goes to the wisest, oldest monk and asks what they should do."

Jake chuckled. "And he said..."

"He said, 'Before we knew the mountain was going to crash into us, we were happy, so let us all forget this upsetting news, and we can again be happy.' So they forgot about the threat and were happy."

"Right up until the mountain slid into them."

"Exactly."

"I hope that story is made up. And I get the idea, but that's a future event. What worries me is—"

"In the past? What sense does it make to worry about things in the past? All the misery without even the possibility of affecting things."

"Well, I guess it's not *really* the past I'm worried about. I guess I'm worried about a future where I repeat the things I've done in the past."

"Ah, and everyone knows the best way to avoid repeating history is to forget it." She punched him again.

"You make me happier than I deserve."

"Hush," she said. "No more of this talk. No more of this thought. Forgetting is not the answer. Dwelling on it is *also* not the answer."

"Well, what *is* the answer, princess?"

She kissed him softly at first but with growing passion. Then she said, "Be here. Now."

"You make that an appealing prospect," he admitted. Then his device beeped, and he added, "However. There are challenges." Looking at it, he said, "My guardian drone stopped signaling."

"What does that mean?"

"I think it means that it's broken. Let's look at the last footage it sent."

He punched some buttons on the device, and soon, the screen filled with a picture of the sward around the pit. The drone had been circling the woollyheads, per Jake's commands.

Then it went black.

"Back it up a few milliseconds," she said. "I saw something."

He did, too, and for a brief blurry moment, the frame was full of large, square teeth.

He looked at her, and the two took off running.

Minutes later, the sward came into view. "There!" Jake shouted. "Do you see it?"

Dali was trailing him slightly and didn't answer immediately but then yelled back, "Yeah. It's that...white thing?"

The white thing, still too far away and creeping too low to the ground to make out any detail, vanished from sight as if it had heard them.

By the time they reached the Apothikon pit, the only trace was an interrupted path where the woollyheads had been partly eaten.

Dali grabbed him and pointed.

Jake turned just in time to see a white blob vanish into the small copse beyond the footbridges.

They took deep breaths and launched themselves toward the bamboo forest, running over the bridge. Jake pointed out the round patch of quicksand—similar to the one Georgia had been lured into—so that Dali wouldn't fall into it.

It took forever to actually reach the bamboo, Jake thought, and by the time they got there, there was no sign of any creature beyond the buzzing of tiny insects.

Still, they entered the forest quietly and cautiously, slowly drifting apart to cover more ground.

Rather abruptly, they came to the other side of the forest and looked at each other, confused. Low, rocky hills lay before them, waterfalls crashing into small pools and eventually draining into the marshlands beyond.

Dali scanned the horizon and surrounding areas. Jake just stood looking at the hills.

After a while, Dali looked at him, then up at the hills, which sloped, plateaued, sloped, and plateaued like a steppe farm. A faint quilt-like pattern reminiscent of the Nephros farms in Grigg's kingdom suggested they *had* been farms once, now dotted with white and gray rocks that had fallen from above.

As they watched, one of the white rocks near the top *moved*.

Without a word, they dashed up the side of the hill only to see a cave entrance. They approached it cautiously, hand-in-hand, and not very far in, a shiny metal strip gave off a dim gleam in the twilight.

Jake leaned in closer. Then he leaned back to look at her.

"Dali, that's a door handle. And that," he added, pointing to a square patch at the bottom, held on with hinges, "is a doggie door."

The door itself was a marvel, hanging on a frame set into the cave's stone. It was so perfectly set that any sound or light that might have been beyond didn't escape.

Dali's expression went from confusion to a cautious smile. She reached out and swung the door open.

Beyond, a large room, cozy and cluttered, and somewhat brighter than the outside, greeted them. Crates were arranged to make rustic shelves, on which sat assorted pottery, in contrast with finely crafted tables and chairs set around the room, as if guests were expected. A table covered with paper, pastels, and charcoal occupied the center.

The white blob stood on top of the table like a fat little Buddha, about four feet high and covered in white fur. It had an outrageously large nose and small dark eyes, with no sign of giant teeth until it opened its mouth in a yawn.

Jake looked at Dali, and she smiled broadly.

"Welcome," said an uncertain, unused voice.

For a brief moment, Jake thought it was the creature who had spoken until he realized further back in the room, so motionless as to blend in with the artwork, stood a tall, thin man—a human, from all appearances.

They stared at him for a long moment, and he stared back, working his mouth as though to try to figure out what to say.

"Welcome, friends. I am Noah."

CHAPTER 30

OLDER FRIENDS

Jake and Dali shot each other a look. Dali spoke first. "You said you're Noah? Noah who?"

"Can't rightly remember, ma'am. I'm an orphan, so's my last name was not a'much importance to me."

Jake looked at the willowy figure—about his height—with snow-white hair that matched the odd creature they had been chasing.

Said creature jumped from the table to the floor where a water bowl lay waiting. It lapped while regarding the intruders with a studied inattentiveness.

Noah fidgeted a little uncomfortably, looking a bit lost.

"Hello...Noah, I'm Jake, and this is my wife, Dali. Would you mind if we had a little chat?"

Noah smiled an oddly boyish smile. "I'd like that. Only don't 'spect too much on account of I hain't talked to anyone but Hippo here for quite a long time."

"You call this...*Hippo* is his name, you say? And what is Hippo, exactly?"

Noah leaned over to scritch Hippo between the ears. "Hippo? He's a capybara! Hain't you never seen a capybara 'fore?"

Jake and Dali both shook their heads.

Noah frowned. "Well, they was pretty rare back on Earth when I left. I suppose they might as gone extinct." Talking to Hippo, he said, "You hear that? You might be the last of your kind!"

If this moved the creature it all, it gave no notice.

Jake thought, *Well, I guess if you're a millimeter long, this rodent would look pretty monstrous.*

"Sir," Jake started, and the man cackled.

"'Pologies! But ain't none as called me 'sir' afore."

Dali asked, "How are you normally addressed?"

"Last time anyone was around to call me anything, it was 'Boy!'" he cackled again. "A body needed something on the ship, they'd holler 'boy!' and I'd come runnin'. Even over the comm system, they'd yell. I ken it's a satisfyin' thing."

Jake said, "We didn't know humans had been out this far. What ship was this?"

"The *Batraz*!"

Jake and Dali looked at each other again. Dali asked, "May we sit?"

Noah indicated it was all right, so they each sat on chairs. From this angle, Jake noticed that some of the crates used as shelves had "Batraz" stenciled on them.

Noah looked uncomfortable again as if he wanted the conversation to continue but didn't quite know how to prompt it.

Finally, Jake looked at him and asked, "The *Batraz*? The ship captained by Brighthart?"

Noah cackled, apparently relieved he didn't have to prompt more conversation. "Cap'n Elvis, we called him, on 'count of his first name bein' Elvis. We had been exploring space for about ten years when we got here."

He sat down, and Dali grabbed his hand tenderly. She said, "Jake, look at this."

His hand was hardly more lined and wrinkled than theirs.

"Why would they leave you behind, Noah?" she asked.

Noah blushed and said, "I like that. Hearing my name. 'Specially in a girl's voice. Been a long time." Looking at her, then looking down, he said, "You see, ma'am, I was sick. Very sick. And very contagious, at least according to the doctor. They thought I was like to die."

The capybara leapt into his lap possessively, glaring suspiciously at Dali.

"The cap'n was a good sort. I said I wanted to come down. To see one more planet 'fore I died, so he let me. All wrapped up in a sick suit."

He looked down at the capybara. "Hippo here refused to leave my side."

Jake and Dali looked at him expectantly.

"But you got better, apparently," Jake noted dryly.

"I didn't, sir, least not right away. In fact, I got worse. The *Batraz* took off, and I went into a delirium. Wandered out onto the pocosins."

Jake looked at Dali. "*Pocosins?*" he mouthed.

She just shrugged. "Then what happened?"

"It'd been raining, all lightning and thunder like you don't oft see 'round here. And when it cleared, I sees a light deep 'n the pocosins, out by the footbridges. 'N I went toward it.

"This bubble is out there, and it's flashin' light as them dragonflies was smashing into it. The ground is on fire—I think from a lightning strike—and I watch it until I pass out.

"I wake up, and I decide I'm like to see this spectacle 'fore I go to my reward. I walk out where the lightning struck, poking at the burn patch, and I sees this pit, glowin' with a pale blue light.

"So I go to look inside. And I'm tryin' to see what's down there when all o' sudden, the world around me lights up. The same flashin' I saw afore, but I'm on the *inside* now!

"It's a nightmare! Giant monsters were flinging themselves at me and burning up on this shield—terrible smell. I grabbed Hippo up so we could get out, but I was so bedazzled by it all that I fell right into a pit—Hippo with me.

"First, I thought I would drown. Then, when I escaped, I thought the liquid would kill me."

He cackled a little. "Ain't died yet. Unless yinz are angels."

Dali smiled at Jake. "He is, sort of."

Noah looked at him, then looked back at her. "'Pologies, ma'am, but you suit my idea of an angel more 'n him."

"Well, I guess I am, too," she grinned, "now that we're married."

Jake had pulled up his device and was looking some things up. *Pocosin* was an old regional term for a wetland. More importantly, however, The *Batraz* had launched on its maiden—and only!—voyage *nearly two hundred years ago!* But despite his archaic speech and manner, Noah looked like a prematurely white-haired teenager.

Something about the whole interaction made Jake feel very cautious, as if Noah were part of some faerie kingdom, a Brigadoon that might vanish were the wrong question asked.

He and Dali had many, many questions. Still, they restricted themselves to asking about Nidus and the Apothikon pit, seeing if he understood the world better than they did.

"There's two kinds of pits," he said. "The empty ones and the ones with a critter in 'em."

"Which one did you fall into?" Dali asked.

"Mine had a critter, no doubt," he said confidently. "You say Hippo's been eatin' them woollyheads?"

"That's what I think, yeah," said Jake.

The capybara had practically burrowed into Noah's lap, where it dozed under the assured attention of the "old" man's fingers.

"We try to lay low, sir, to avoid interferin' too much with the life here. But I 'spect he got bored. 'Cided to eat something."

"You mean, eat something different from your usual..." Jake stopped mid-sentence. "Wait. If you've been here for hundreds of years, you must be growing your own food. Unless—have you got a food fabber?"

Noah cackled. "No, sir. Me an' hippo? We ain't got hungry for years. Well, at least I ain't. I'd like to guess Hippo just got restless and thought them woollyheads musta tasted good. An' I guess they did, or he wouldn'a gone back.

"It does kinda 'splain why he would get upset insides, though. If yinz listen, yinz kin hear his stomach rumble." He paused for a moment, listening, apparently, to the capybara's digestion.

Jake sat back, dumbfounded. "You don't eat. You hardly age."

Dali agreed. "Your hair is white, but it's beautiful. Very thick and full."

Noah blushed, which made Dali smile warmly. "Thank 'e, ma'am," was all he could squeak out.

"May I?" Jake asked Noah, indicating paper and charcoal. Underneath the paper, he noticed the rustic low table had a surprisingly fancy silver top, very artistically engraved.

Jake began to draw a picture of the Apothikon pit for Noah and how the flowers around it grew in concentric circles. Then he added the channel that Hippo had eaten.

Noah whispered to the dozing capybara, "You did that in a right orderly fashion, Hippo."

Dali grabbed his free hand again. "Noah, you've been here a long time. You must have seen grown Apothikons?"

But the old man didn't respond. His eyes were unfocused, and the furrow in his brow deepened. Jake couldn't help but notice that it didn't seem like an old man's brow, even when furrowed.

"When I'd been here for a while, it got very hot. Then, after a long while, it got very cold. Both times, there was snow."

"Snow when it was cold *and* hot?" Jake prompted.

"Me 'n ol' Hippo used to sneak up on the Nijins such as lived on this side of the river, just to watch them work. They was terrible sick though."

Jake tried again to get information. "What did the Nijins do when it got hot or cold?"

Noah said dreamily, "There's a kind of bamboo that I use to make paper out of. Canvases. I draw a lot of pictures. Made the furniture, too."

Jake and Dali praised his furniture-building skills while looking at each other to confirm with each the suspicion that Noah's mind had not escaped the ravages of time as well as his body seemed to.

And so the conversation went: Noah was very sharp, though he had limited his exposure to the planet. Apart from some walks, he spent most of his time in his cave, mining clay and minerals from the caverns behind his home and building elaborate aquatic environs for Hippo.

He mostly ventured out to collect bamboo to turn into paper or to search for new pigments to paint with, so he had little new information. But whenever the topic of the Apothikon came up or the "hyper-summer" and "hyper-winter," as Georgia called them, he would lose focus and change the subject.

They finally gave up asking.

"How is Earth?" Noah asked them, a vague glimmer in his eyes.

Jake and Dali shrugged.

"There's a war on," Jake admitted.

Noah scoffed. "They's always havin' wars. I hope Nebraska had the good sense to stay out of this one."

"Who's Nebraska?" Dali asked.

Jake said, "It's a place not terribly far from Victoria. In The Country. It used to *be* its own country, actually."

Noah nodded. "I moved there when New Helena expanded into the Carolinas. The Carolinas and Nebraska used to be part of the United States."

Dali's face lit up. "America?"

"Yes'm."

Jake's mood had gotten darker the more the conversation went on. "Noah, would you want to stay here on Nidus?"

"Well, I've lived here so long," he replied, "but it gets a little borin' with just Hippo to talk to. No offense, Hippo," he added quickly. "You probably get bored of just me, too."

The rodent snored on, undisturbed.

Noah regarded Dali respectfully. "I wouldn't mind talking to more girls, beggin' your pardon, ma'am."

Dali giggled a little.

Jake looked him over. He made a strange picture, an old man who nonetheless moved and looked like a young man and talked like an old man—not because his voice sounded weathered or weak, but because he spoke like he had stepped out of a regional history book.

"If he went back to XEE," Jake said, thinking out loud, "the fact that he was over two hundred years old would come out, and he and Hippo would become famous."

Noah grimaced. "I wouldn't like that, sir. Not at all. Me an' Hippo's just regular folk."

"That's good," Jake said. "Because the next step would be to find out you had come from Nidus, and people would swarm here trying to find out how you had lived to be this old. Nothing good would come of it."

Dali objected, "You don't know that, Jake!"

Noah interjected, "Oh, ma'am, unless humans have changed, he's probably right. Back in my day, they harvested babies and children—beggin' yer pardon, ma'am—just to *look* slightly younger."

Now, Dali's face went blank. Rarely did Jake see her lose her poise, at least around anyone else.

"It'll be the Rosicrucians all over again," Jake mumbled.

Noah jumped up. "The Rosicrucians!" Hippo scrambled from his lap onto the table and bared his teeth, looking for whatever had alarmed his long-time companion.

Jake and Dali tried to calm him after recovering from their own shock at the violence of his reaction.

"No, it's okay, Noah. The Rosicrucians are mostly gone. We've had some bad run-ins with them, but the few still living spend most of their time hiding out in space."

"After the Civil Wars, they took over North *and* South Dakota," said Noah, settling back in his chair. Hippo regarded him warily. "Panopolis, they called it. Then, they came after Nebraska. Though the Divine Retribution took the wind out of their sails," he cackled.

"That, and people had started to kill them on sight," Jake added. "The horror stories that came out of Panopolis ensured they'd never get open control on Earth ever again. But there are always people who want to live forever and rule over others."

Noah frowned harder. "I guess I hoped that people would've changed some. You know, learned something? Brighthart tried to learn folks for years before leaving Earth. He allas said, 'The more effective

I am, the more they try to kill me.'" He screwed up his face. "I guess I remember why I left Earth in the first place."

They had a moment of silence that could have easily passed for a memorial. Then Dali brightened. "Noah, what if you came to Karnata?"

Jake smiled at that thought, too. "That could work." Dali then described Banavisi to Noah in vivid, loving detail while Noah watched her, entranced. Maybe as much as half of that due to what she was saying, Jake thought. "After Brighthart, many people left Earth to make their own worlds, and Karnata is one of the most successful. You could sell your art, too, if you liked."

"People'd be interested in this junk?" Noah laughed.

Jake said, "Maybe not," which deflated Noah somewhat. "Oh, I didn't mean it wasn't good, Noah. I meant maybe we shouldn't be taking back pictures that show the two moons and the eclipsed sun and the flying bugs—someone, at some point, might recognize them."

"I guess that's fair," said Noah. He seemed to be thinking hard about something. "Dali?" he asked shyly.

"What, Noah?"

"It's old-fashioned, I suppose, it was even back in my day. But does Karnata have—"

Dali leaned in expectantly. "Have what, Noah?"

"Cars?" he finally spit out.

"Cars?"

"Automobiles?" He looked away and then back. "You see, ma'am, I used to love—we used to—Brighthart and the whole crew used to love taking old cars and racing them around and fixing them up to go faster." His excited speech gave way to a little sadness. "I don't suppose anyone uses those anymore. They just fly around in spaceships."

Dali looked about to explode. Gently, she said, "Noah, I know just the place for you."

They agreed, then, that Noah would go to Karnata. While Dali ran back to get the *Shiva*, Jake and Noah packed up his belongings, deciding what was safe and what wasn't.

The paintings really were extraordinary, Jake realized. "Let's try to store the ones that are too obviously Nidus. Maybe someday we can come back for them."

This elicited a muted acknowledgment from Noah. Besides the art he had on display, he had many more canvases, all made from bamboo and large bamboo tubes stuffed with the art he wasn't displaying. A whole section of the cave was full of them.

The pigments were unique, too. Noah had found some minerals in the cave, and had foraged some plants.

Then there were the pottery and furniture. On inspection, Jake could see that Noah had even reinforced and decorated the old crates from the Batraz that he used as shelves. He had been busy in his time on Nidus.

Jake mused, "I wonder what would happen if someone—I don't know why anyone would do this—but what if someone analyzed these paintings for DNA? Could it be traced to Nidus, I wonder?"

Noah stood there looking at the cave for a long moment. "You know what, Jake," he said. "Let me get shed of it all. I'll just keep some of my souvenirs from the *Batraz*..."

"Which your great-great-great-grandfather..."

"...my namesake, outfitted 'fore it went on its voyage. Easy." Then Noah's face brightened. "Oh! One thing, maybe you should take," he said, returning to the main cabin. "I found this when I first got here. I worked on it like a Sunday crossword puzzle. Do they still have those?"

Handing him the large silver disc that Jake had thought was just part of the tabletop, he added, "I allas thought as it might be important."

Jake ran his fingers over the engravings on the plate. It wasn't made of silver. It was something harder and lighter. The disc was round and very thin, with a little give, but the edges weren't sharp.

"Noah, this is writing," Jake said.

"That's what I thought," Noah agreed.

"And you *found* it?"

"Yessir, while digging around in the cave in my first decade or so. Never found anything else like it."

"I think you're right, Noah. This could be *very* important."

CHAPTER 31

EVERYTHING PUT TOGETHER

They agreed that Noah should be evacuated to Karnata as soon as possible and were both surprised at how quickly he recognized some of the equipment on the *Shiva*.

"We had a couple of Stretch Shuttles like this on the *Batraz*—according to my grandpa," he added slyly. Jake hoped he would get subtler with his tells over time. "What's the doohickey on the bottom do?"

"That's the drop-grav," Dali replied. "It gives us normal gravity when we fly. Kind of archaic."

Noah squinted at her, "Cap'n Elvis had plans for something like that. But he couldn't never get the drop to be less than a mile long, which was impractible."

"These days, Noah, they can put them *inside* the ship, which I confess I don't understand," she commented.

"I allas kinda liked zero-gee, myself. But I guess that's impractible, too."

Dali gave Jake a chaste kiss, and Noah looked away, embarrassed, so Dali gave him a much less chaste one and murmured, "Hyper-summer is about four days from now, right?"

Jake nodded. "I'm guessing we'll get the next big Apothikon pulse around then, too."

"I'll be back in two, in time to get there and back, plus a little time to help Noah get situated. I know a guy in Otto, very discrete, who will take him in."

They broke apart. It was as hard as ever, but powered at least by the motivation to reunite soon, and Jake found himself alone again, watching the winking stars as the *Shiva* vanished into the darkening sky. Or was it lightening? It was so hard to tell on Nidus.

His device chirped.

DUDE, YOU'RE GONNA WANNA SEE THIS.

Jake suspected that message portended something more sinister than its casual nature would belie, but he went back to his tent and projected Derek on his big wall.

Derek looked into the camera briefly and then pointed his device at a wall of flame-licked smoke. "Check it out, Jake. The fire controls on XEE are amazing."

Jake looked, and it was impressive to see smoke roiling behind a transparent wall, with flickers of light and occasional flare-ups, while people watched with excitement—but without fear—close by.

He'd heard the fire safety measures on space stations were expensive and robust, which seemed ironic when there never was any fire to speak of. He couldn't even remember if the flamethrower used to clean up some Minosians a few months back had triggered the system.

Derek said, "Check this out." He tilted his camera so Jake could see black scorch marks on the floor. It must have been an astoundingly forceful blast to have gotten that far before being contained. People were toeing the liquid sprayed on it to put it out.

"An explosion? Where?" Jake still couldn't orient himself to where this was on XEE.

"Dr. Lazar's lab," said Derek.

Derek, of course, had not led with the most pertinent information first.

The fire, as it turned out, was *extremely* hot—beyond what one would expect from a "normal" lab fire, and enough to obliterate the contents of the lab almost entirely. Hot enough to burn through metal boxes where other flammable chemicals were kept, thus ensuring a difficult fire to extinguish fully.

The room had to be completely depressurized and airless until the chemicals had "settled down," in Derek's words.

The secure vault where some of the most sensitive artifacts the ICF had discovered in Bug Space had survived intact—but also had apparently been left open, so its contents were destroyed.

The loss was incalculable. The scheduled annual inventory had been delayed over months, and had finally been set for the following week, so figuring out what had actually been lost would take a while.

"Where's Doctor Lazar," asked Jake, not even as a question, but as something he felt he knew the answer to.

Derek, who had returned to his room, where Min-hee immediately made him change his clothes, said, "Nobody knows. At first, we thought she might have been killed in the explosion."

"That would explain why the vault was open," Jake said blandly. "Because she'd never leave the lab with the vault open."

Derek said, "Yeah. Hogar's working with the custodial staff to scoop up every trace of ash or burnt stuff. He says even with the high heat, he can probably tell if she was in there by the amount of her genetic material in the remains." A little less casually, Derek added, "It's not impossible that she was forced to open the vault and then kept in the room while someone set up explosives."

Jake nodded. "Yeah. I guess." He had a hard time imagining it. It was a gruesome possibility but not the worst one he could think of.

Which, ultimately, the two didn't talk about.

It could be that the brilliant and beautiful Doctor Lazar had been a mole sent by one of ICF's rivals to throw a wrench in the ICF's works.

After all, she managed to create acrimony between Hogar and Doc Blood, the ICF's top scientists in Bug Space. And whose division had caused Jake so much trouble on Alvum.

It was hard, in retrospect, not to notice all the mayhem that surrounded her at critical times.

Jake didn't like that idea much. He had grown to regard the older woman as a valuable resource—her advice had saved him and Dali from Telemakhos, after all. He liked her even if she did make him uncomfortable.

Jake could tell she was crafty, but he had felt sincerity when she talked about the horrors of her early career as an indentured servant for the Rosicrucians.

How horrible for Doc Blood and Hogar, too. Either they had been fighting over a woman who was merely manipulating them or a woman who had died, possibly murdered at the hands of war criminals.

ALERT: APOTHIKON PULSE

"Wait, what?" he said out loud. He checked again, then he checked his device. "It's way too soon," he protested to no one. He double-checked the detectors, then went outside and climbed up the crag.

Over Grigg's castle, a squadron had already formed.

"It's way too soon!" he yelled at them.

Cursing under his breath, he slid back down and ran to his battle armor, donning the pieces quickly and feeling the now familiar cushioning foam fill the spaces.

He couldn't afford to take any chances. He set his audio outputs to blast a message of warning. Then, fretting over whether that would be effective, he thought of the Lucas.

He had his device send a message to them:

EMERGENCY REQUEST: BROADCAST THE FOLLOW-ING MESSAGE FOR THE NEXT HOUR.

WARNING! ALL SEYLES MUST LEAVE THE AREA OF JAKE WIZARD'S HOME OR BE IMMEDIATELY DE-STROYED.

He waited for a moment, watching as the Luca readouts switched from crop yields and weather reports to his warning message.

They might be empty-headed but the Lucas could be useful. Then there was this irritant mixed in:

CEIoAfXZ0suKs35YOpbF6SwzpoTb
imWrkxlIT7eUuWt7dtQvRc9ztyOS

Shrugging it off, he bounded over to Mount Olive. From there, he could see the Seyles streaming from all over Grigg's kingdom, first to the Callas and then coalescing briefly over Grigg's castle. When a few scores had collected there, they dove straight toward the pit.

Jake began firing at everything in the sky. Grenades turned the first incoming squad to flames, and Jake already wished he had a lot more.

He used his second set of grenades on the new squad forming over the castle. Perhaps a giant fireball over his head would teach Grigg a little about the power of Jake Wizard.

As if they had already learned, the squads had dispersed and formed loose "clouds" that rolled toward him like a fog.

Grimly, he switched to his lance and began sweeping through the clouds—much less effective than grenades, of course, but until they re-grouped, he didn't have much choice.

The firing of the flak cannon alerted him to more proximal enemies. It thwumped away with a vengeance, and Jake switched to full-power blasters to take the ones at the cannon's nine o'clock.

The woollyhead ring around the circle had thinned dramatically, and the squads of Seyles thickened in equal measure. He couldn't play nice. He had to vaporize as many as he could.

He didn't spare the grenades, and when he ran out of those, he switched between the blasters and the lance, depending on which would quickly allow him to take more out.

Even then, inside the perfectly controlled environment of the suit, he began to sweat. There seemed to be no end to the beasts.

He had slowly worked his way into the ring and positioned himself right in front of the pit. He wished he had mastered the controls well enough to hover directly over the pit, but remembering his crazy flight patterns fighting Torsk, he would settle.

The flak turned to its nine as Jake obliterated the swarms at twelve o'clock, finally rewarded with seeing a thinning of the Seyles' ranks.

The grass roiled underneath him, the Apothikon sweeping in the assailants' remains—sometimes only ash. The pit pulsed with a nervous energy and a flickering blue light that Jake found unsettling.

The cannon stopped firing. It had overheated.

We're almost done here, Jake thought, not panicking.

The remaining Seyles rushed in from all sides. Of a dozen, nine were destroyed by the Apothikon's shield, littering their smoking remains over the sward.

Jake switched to his electric blades on both arms and waited, watching the battlesuit's target reticles dance dizzyingly around.

Two Seyles dove straight at him.

He had a strange confidence: he realized he knew how they would attack. For one thing, he'd been watching them for months at this point, and he didn't understand it but felt something else at play.

Kadzak Seyles, the Tactician, had said, "If your goal is beyond the opponent, feint to make the opponent respond one way, then go around!"

Good advice, if your opponent doesn't know you're going to do that, thought Jake.

Instead of thrusting straight out, he jumped backward to land on the far side of the pit. The Seyles had bobbed up, expecting him to stab forward, only to impale themselves when they bobbed back down onto his waiting blades.

He tossed them to either side into the energy shield.

The third one had waited above the pit until Jake was occupied, and plummeted straight down.

Twisting around, Jake fell backward, using his armored body to cover the central portion of the opening, skewering the last Seyles on one blade.

He quickly sliced it into thin pieces with the other blade as though he were preparing sushi. He was breathing hard.

Breathing hard, yes, but it felt good.

Getting up without falling into the pit might be tricky. Jake would probably have to roll over and away, but for the moment, he locked the armor in place to give himself a little rest, opened his face mask, and breathed deeply.

All around, parts of Seyles crept toward him as the grass pulled toward the insatiable Apothikon. A big chunk of abdomen got lodged between himself and the pit's edge, so he unlocked his armor and rolled from the opening.

He had done well, he thought, *alone and surprised*.

But this was the systole. The diastole would be far more intense. And Jake could no longer tell when it would come, given how this one had surprised him.

He did a quick inspection of the cannon. It had already cooled, which was good. One of the refrigeration units had burnt out—an easy fix. He could probably squeeze another unit in with some clever arranging.

Then he checked the ring of woollyheads. Before, he had dreaded seeing the paths that Hippo had cleared. Now, he just wanted the ring to die out.

Wasn't that what Georgia had told him?

"When the ring is gone, you've done your job and no longer have to defend it."

Now, frustratingly, it looked the same thickness as before.

Wait, no.

He did a quick count of flowers in the ring at several positions.

It wasn't even a dozen thick at the thickest spot. Initially, there had been at least two dozen.

He headed back to his tent, shed the armor, thanked the Lucas for their help, and set his fabber up to build a few more refrigeration packs.

Then he fretted for a moment. Why had it seemed so urgent to send Noah to Karnata? He'd waited centuries.

Of course, they'd thought they had plenty of time, and it seemed cruel to make the old young man wait.

Unfortunately, he couldn't just call Dali back. He could only call Derek. Then Derek could call Dali and tell her to hurry back. He activated his Q-comm with XEE.

Nobody picked up.

His drone drifted in and landed softly on the proximity mat.

Chapter 32

All Creatures Great and Small

"Bombur," the Jake-drone said to the "slow" Diptera, who was surrounded by throngs of adoring worshippers.

Jake found it comical. The followers were walking around in slow motion, speaking hardly at all and only very slowly when they did.

A line of females were feeding him drops of nectar (each had one drop in one of her hands), apparently quite happily.

But Bombur didn't even recognize him, which Jake realized made sense since he'd only ever seen him as a human.

However, he did look somewhat offended to be addressed in such a familiar manner.

"Bombur, it is I, Jake Wizard," the drone said. (Jake wondered again why the drone did the occasional weirdly formal or stilted line.)

"You? You're an impostor! I have spoken with the *real* Jake Wizard. I regard him as a friend. I should have you crushed. In fact, I think I shall."

A few of the Dipterans responded to the implicit command, but the new drone the fabber built had a bit more armor and a lot more speed.

"You are correct, Bombur," the drone said while effortlessly dodg-
ing. "It is not Jake Wizard in person, but a messenger of Jake Wizard,
who has come to ask his friend a favor."

Bombur ordered the attackers to halt and said suspiciously, "Where
do you grow your young, Angel of Jake Wizard?"

Jake cringed at Bombur's use of the word "angel."

"As a messenger, I do not have young. But Jake Wizard's species,
humans, gestate their babies inside their bodies."

Bombur sprung up excitedly. "How wondrous! It is you!"

He floated over to the drone and looked closely at it. "You're speaking at exactly my speed, too!"

The drone replied, "Jake Wizard alerted me to your differences
from the other Diptera. Tell me, why are the others around us moving
so slowly?"

Bombur chuckled and dismissed everyone from the room. "The
knowledge that Jake Wizard allowed me to absorb has made me divine
among my people. They worship and emulate me."

"Not all of them," the drone noted. Jake found the computer imitation of him uncanny at times.

Bombur fluttered his wings indifferently. "Oh, there are the jealous, but I haven't time to worry about them. My followers grasp my
greatness, and I've taught them they must slow down, slower than me,
even, to comprehend my wisdom."

The drone commented, "Is your wisdom not just the information
you got from Jake's device?"

"They don't know that!" Bombur wheezed through all his spiracles
at once, overtaken with mirth.

"But they'll probably find it out, Bombur."

Bombur scrunched his face up. "Oh, don't tell them, Jake Wizard!
I'm finally getting the respect I deserve!"

The drone paused for a moment. "I've already told Ledalipholus, but she seems to prefer to keep the information secret. It is not in my nature to hide things—"

OK, that's the drone speaking for itself, Jake thought.

"—but I have no desire to disrupt your society further."

Bombur seemed pleased with that response.

"I must warn you that Ledalipholus is not amused by your activities."

Bombur moved in very close, apparently having grown quite comfortable with the flying robot.

"Jake Wizard, she's not important right now. I've realized that even though we are just a fraction of the size of the Seyles, we could use some of your technology to strike back at them."

He hesitated. "I'll give up the followers. I'll tell everyone the truth, but right now, I need them!"

"For?"

Conspiratorially, the Diptera got very, very close and whispered, "To launch atomic bombs."

Jake sat up. Even if he managed to protect the Apothikon, it was hard for him to picture Grigg's kingdom surviving the events of the coming days.

The Diptera had not said he was going to "make" bombs. He had said he was going to "launch" them, which suggested to Jake that he knew about Ledalipholus' secret missile cache.

Ledalipholus' plan to threaten the Seyles or to demonstrate her power could be quickly short-circuited—with a push of a button.

It took him a heartbeat to realize that Dezzig had stuck his head in the tent.

"Dezzig Seyles," he said. "What are you doing here?"

"Jake Wizard, I have come to ask for help."

Jake rose quickly and said, "I'll be right out. Take the coffee if you want it."

He donned his battle armor quickly. He'd gotten good at it, and he had a lot of visits to make today—no time for casual strolls.

He had set his tent screen to a countdown, thinking it would relax him: "Only this many more hours before the wobble, and Dali will be back, and then I can get out of here."

But watching the seconds count down, he realized what a bad idea that had been. Instead of "this long to get past it," it read more like "this long till it all blows up."

He found himself reluctant to turn it off anyway.

He left the tent. Dezzig rested at the edge of his plateau and not, Jake noticed immediately, on one of the high crags that dotted the surrounding area. He was sipping thoughtfully from Jake's big pot.

His wings, normally extended (even when standing on the ground), were folded back almost timidly. He was leaning back slightly on his abdomen, which he had tucked behind him and formed a despondent-looking "S" shape.

"Dezzig Seyles? What is it?"

Dezzig twisted around to look at him. He paused, started to say something, then paused again.

Finally: "Jake Wizard, I am thinking of bedizening."

"W-What?" Jake stammered, walking toward him. "I didn't think that you could choose to bedizen. I thought it just came over you!"

Dezzig buzzed his wings listlessly. "It is what we tell ourselves, and I think it is usually so. But if a Seyles decides to end things, it's a way to hide that." He looked ruefully at Jake, his eyes taking on a deep blue. "It is ironic, is it not, that we hold life so cheaply, but suicide is considered dishonorable?"

Jake didn't answer because he didn't know how to unwrap that.

"But Dezzig Seyles, you have a good life, do you not? You fight, you feed, you probably have many offspring..."

"It becomes tiring after a while. Do you know the only thing I've found to interest me as of late?"

"What's that?"

"I've been collecting the *velda* fruit from the place over there at different stages of ripeness." He pointed to Mount Olive. "I'm trying to make coffee. I think the young, unripe ones work best."

But then he sagged and walked along the plateau edge, dragging his wings behind him. "Torsk is amassing more troops to the north. Matzhin will probably attack within hours, and our armies and air force will fall."

"I've destroyed legions of Torsk and Matzhin's troops at no cost to Grigg and will continue to do so. How is it they can keep overwhelming him?"

The creature sighed and slumped. "Our land is poor. We have fewer damsels. Our clutches are smaller and sicklier."

Then he admitted the truth. "And Grigg is simply terrible at what he does. He cannot correctly balance our people. We have too many Kormas and not enough Nocks, so we never get things built. If the food isn't rotting because we have too many Nephros, we're starving because we have too few."

Jake considered how difficult balancing even a simple economy would be and almost felt pity for Grigg.

"Then there's that!" Dezzig exclaimed.

Jake tried to figure out what he meant. "Melontikopolis? Tiny-town? I mean, the smartbug city?"

"It's huge. It's a monstrosity. That land could be used for clutches and more farms."

A slow realization crept in on Jake. "Dezzig, why is there a wall around the city? Is it to keep the Diptera safe?"

Dezzig wheezed a laugh. "Jake Wizard, it is to keep the Diptera from spreading across the entire kingdom, starving us all out!"

Jake remembered what Georgia had said: all kingdoms had Diptera populations, but none as big as Grigg's. And hadn't Ledalipholus been disgusted by how primitive the other Diptera were?

"But you could easily wipe them all out!" protested Jake.

"Grigg would kill anyone who tried. He and his court are addicted to them. They eat them and scheme and issue orders and get crazier and crazier. You have done well defending this kingdom, Jake Wizard, but it will not survive much longer."

"So you'll sacrifice yourself to the Apothikon?" Jake found this distressing.

A wry expression distorted Dezzig's enormous eyes. "By now, you know my people do not think of the thing in the pit. I was like them. I found it hard even to concentrate on."

"But since you have arrived, it's become easier and easier. And if I can get past you, I think it won't be a sacrifice after all."

Jake considered this. He had some idea of the effect of the Apothikon on his own physiology, but this gave him no insight into what it might do to a Seyles. It might have the magic spoken of in legend—or it might just kill him.

It was too much to think about just now, so he said the only thing he could think of. "You'd make me kill you? Dezzig, that is an unfriendly thing."

"Consider it an honor," Dezzig replied. "Have you got any more coffee?"

"You've gotten much better," Jake said, knocking Matzhin's king over.

Matzhin lounged regally in a seat he seemed to have commissioned for the sole purpose of making it comfortable to play chess.

"I forced my aides to learn and play it," he chortled. "It's a gross abuse of my authority, but what is the point of authority if not to grossly abuse it now and then?"

Jake's humanity made it hard for him to forget that the Seyles lord had consigned thousands of his own and Grigg's people to death for no apparent reason—apparently *not* an abuse of authority. At the same time, he was so much more charming and likable than Grigg.

"What is it, Jake Wizard? Here you sit in your omnipotence, yet you are unhappy." Matzhin leaned in conspiratorially. "Can it be that winning the battle is not as much fun as fighting the battle?"

"I wouldn't know, Lord Matzhin. I have so many battles going on sometimes. It's just not clear which ones I'm winning or losing."

"A most disagreeable circumstance," Matzhin said sympathetically. "Is it not better to live a short, glorious life and die in battle than to struggle with all the mystery and confusion you are steeped in?"

Jake started. "What?"

Matzhin said, "You and I have played many games of chess, but the more we play the less you enjoy it. Do not be surprised that I know this, Jake Wizard, for while your powers are beyond my ken, your emotions are as obvious as the Damsel moon."

He began setting up the pieces on the board.

"You cannot enjoy a nice game of chess because you want to convince me not to attack Grigg. You want, in essence, to change the nature of what I am."

Jake watched numbly as the creature set up the pawns. He noticed the Seyles put the back rows up first and the pawns last and seemed to enjoy doing both sides.

"But we do what we must. The same thing that drives you to try to save lives drives me to take them, to waste them in the cause of taking more. It is no less survival for us than your passions are for you."

Jake let that thought sink in and watched the Seyles open with a knight. Jake moved a pawn out to see if he could bait Matzhin into taking a pawn at the loss of a knight.

"Couldn't there be," Jake finally said, "an objective way to measure good and evil? A way that removes our prejudices and passions from our decision-making?"

Matzhin wheezed with laughter. "Why on Nidus would you wish to do that?"

"Because I would want a world where all Nijins could live out their natural lives, fulfilling their dreams and ambitions in a way that suits them and in a way that benefits all Nijins! A way that this rigid, brutal caste system does not."

Matzhin stopped laughing, finally, and grew still. "Jake Wizard, I am concerned with the soundness of your mind. The Nocks, the Notos, the Nephros, and even the Seyles are all just part of me. What you say is as silly as me saying you should free your hair. Yes, it's like me saying you should set your hair free to pursue its dreams."

Jake thought of the Trigonans, who had a similar point of view regarding the bees that composed their "body."

He knew it would be pointless to argue about it, so he said, "Would you, then, just as a favor to me, delay your invasion for three or so days?"

Matzhin touched Jake's hands with his hard, cold claws and, leaning in to look at him closely, said, "No."

CHAPTER 33

THE CORRECT THING TO DO

It had gone even worse with Torsk, unsurprisingly. It appeared that the corpulent Seyles had learned of Matzhin's plans and had decided the best time for *his* attack was just after Matzhin struck.

The injudicious Grigg, Torsk reasoned, would send all his troops to defend against Matzhin's attack, and nothing Jake could say would dissuade him.

The obvious threat—that Jake would *tell* Grigg of Torsk's plans—fazed the lord not at all. Grigg would then split his troops, assuming he would even listen to Jake's counsel.

Grigg's foolish irascibility made him very weak and rather predictable.

Jake pointed out that he could, once again, destroy Torsk's *and* Matzhin's forces, but even that didn't phase the Seyles lord.

"Because," he said smugly, "even wizards cannot be in two places at the same time."

Exasperated, Jake threatened to blow up Torsk's kingdom right then and there; nothing.

"I do not know your motives, Jake Wizard. But if you had such inclinations as to destroy Seyles' kingdoms, it seems to me that you could have done so long ago. Certainly, I would have done so in your position."

Jake briefly contemplated the prospect of destroying Torsk's king-dom, or at least his court. Still, he realized any action he took on that scale that might endanger Torsk's Apothikon could result in failing his mission in actuality while succeeding in the letter of it.

He accepted defeat again and returned to Grigg's kingdom. He didn't jump straight to his base, preferring to walk and ponder his situation.

He saw Fugi working hard along the base of the reservoir wall—the first time he'd ever seen Fugi do anything approximating work—and strode over to the Korma to investigate.

Fugi jumped back in fear.

"Fugi Korma! It's Jake Wizard! Sorry to have startled you. I forgot you've never seen me in my battlesuit."

"Jake Wizard? Oh! Yes, I see your face in there. What remarkable armor!" He held in his hands something that looked like shears and a trowel. He removed several triangular bricks where water trickled over the side as he went along.

"Why are you releasing the water, Fugi Korma?"

Fugi looked at him as if he were stupid. "Because it's time, Jake Wizard."

Jake indicated the tools. "Well, are you going forward with Toler Korma's plans to maintain the reservoir?"

"Oh, not at all!" said Fugi enthusiastically.

"You aren't? Aren't you worried about what Dezzig Seyles might do?"

Fugi shuffled over to Jake and said, "The Seyles don't know any-thing about engineering, Jake Wizard. Would you listen if they told you how to fly your ships or fire your guns? Come, let me show you something."

He tugged on Jake's arm.

"What if Dezzig finds out?"

Fugi awkwardly tilted his head back, still pulling Jake toward the wall. "Jake Wizard, the Seyles issue many, many commands to the Korma, but they seldom remember what those commands were. If Dezzig Seyles challenges me, I will simply explain that I'm doing what he told me."

Jake thought about it. "They all seem to believe whatever the last person told them." Or what the last person they *ate* believed, he didn't add.

"Exactly. As long as one is performatively subservient, the Seyles do not deign to understand the work of their lessers."

The Korma pointed to the wall, which, Jake had to admit, looked much better than it had previously. "You've trimmed some of the mudweed, and that's allowed the seed pods to grow more."

"Exactly! And when the seed pods break open, the hulls will mix with the existing mortar and strengthen the reservoir."

Reaching out to touch the pods and realizing he couldn't feel anything, Jake had his armor scan the plants. "Well," he said, "it seems stronger. But might not the cold from the pods damage the walls?"

Fugi got exasperated. "Oh, you sound just like Toler Korma The Stubborn! It will be fine, Jake Wizard, you'll see. It's the correct thing to do." He looked at Jake with a certain disregard. "I suppose wizards can't know everything."

"Can't know everything," Jake repeated, "and can't be in two places at once."

"Eh?" Fugi had already returned to his duties, and Jake didn't really want to interrupt again, so he headed back to his tent, mulling over the idea that "even Jake Wizard couldn't be in two places at once."

Because, after all, he *had* been in two places at once. Or at least his drone avatar had acted as a reasonable surrogate.

Could he have it fight for him?

Even if it acted as he would in the same situation, the tiny drone couldn't pack much of a punch outside of the Dipteran world.

But the drone wouldn't have to carry any firepower if it *were* the firepower. And if it had a lot of friends.

With a little research, he discovered that explosives could be quite small and, if clustered together, could create an effect similar to the flak at full power. Attach a propulsion unit to it along with a simple guidance system he could control from his device, and it was possible.

Programming his order into the fabber—including the massive quantities he wanted—resulted in the extruder issuing a warning to his device.

"Praseodymium? What on Nidus is Praseodymium?" He scrolled through the description and saw pictures of silvery-looking rocks. He had seen similar rocks in the hills near Mount Olive.

He rummaged through the odds and ends he kept at the far corner of the tent. Bits of bamboo, some rocks—nothing like what he needed, unfortunately—the grate and plate he had initially used to try to close up the pit during Apothikon attacks, scraps of chitin, and finally, his stash of scavenger sacks.

For those times when you want to combine "scientist on an alien world" with "space looter," he thought.

He was going to need a lot of this rock. He grabbed a big sack.

Hours later, he was back and in a great mood. He had found tons of the rocks, which he confirmed with his device had the desired praseodymium, and his muscles were loose with exertion and pleasantly fatigued.

He had forgotten how good it felt to use his body without pain or punishment, and he resolved never to forget again.

He fed the rocks into the extruder input bin, and it got to work, separating all the component parts the fabber needed. It would be a while before it could create enough filament for the fabber to get going, but once it started, he had enough for an entire fleet of drones.

He sat down and checked his device.

A message from Derek had come in.

I CAN'T REACH DALI. SORRY, DUDE.

CHAPTER 34

A CRY FOR HELP

"How can you, of all people, not be able to get through to her?" Jake was nearly yelling at Derek.

"Dude, just because I can do things you can't doesn't mean I can do *everything* you need me to do exactly when you need them!" Derek responded, exasperated. "The war's got us locked down. Karnata's not even *in* the war, and their comms are strictly limited."

"Why?" demanded Jake, rather unfairly.

"I don't know. I guess they don't want to get dragged into it. Karnatans come from all different places on Earth. There could easily be people there trying to form alliances involving the planet or parts of it."

"Well, who would have the authority to shut it down? Dali's sister?"

Derek asked, "No, the monarchy has nothing to do with it. And why are *you* grilling *me*?"

Quietly, Jake admitted, "Because I don't know what else to do."

Derek, mollified, said, "Hang on a second." He punched some keys, swept his hands across some kind of tablet, and said, "OK, it looks like there's only a single orbital comms provider on Karnata, some guy named Talon, and he's controlling incoming and outgoing info."

"He doesn't answer to the king?"

Derek shook his head, "You know nothing about that place, do you?"

"That's what I keep telling Dali."

"OK, look, it's a monarchy, but the monarch's power is more...theoretical."

"How does *that* work?"

"Pretty well, most of the time. But apparently, the satellite guy is denying requests from Dali's sister and brother-in-law."

"Setting up a competing network should be easy, though, right? We do it on every planet we visit, out here in Bug Space, light years away from Earth," Jake argued.

"It's a piece of cake. Except for the whole war thing. You have to take a certain number of steps, and a well-placed bomb can easily short-circuit any of them or—honestly, just paperwork, which seems to have tripled since the war started."

Jake looked over at his fabber. It had churned out piles of dumb drones fairly quickly, but he would need thousands—tens of thousands, even—to make an impact on the incoming armies.

"I need help, or I'm going to be crushed. Within days. Or maybe hours." He looked at his back wall where the timer was counting down. *I should turn that off*, he thought.

But he didn't.

Derek leaned in as if that made their conversation more private and said, "Hey... You know those mercs that have been hanging out on the station?"

Jake did. They had cleaned up the Minosians who had invaded the XEE a while back. "Yeah, the...Bloody Fists?"

Derek smirked. "The Red Hands. Listen, they've been after me to do some tech stuff for them, and I've been putting them off because I'm really busy. Also, I don't like or trust them at all, but I could probably do a few easy-for-me tasks in exchange for them being fire support for you."

Jake, once again, found himself impressed by Derek's willingness to stick his neck out for him. "I appreciate that, man. A lot. But I can't let anyone know where I am."

Derek scoffed. "Dude, you're not *that* important. I think most of the people who were interested in you redeployed to Earth on war missions weeks ago."

Jake sighed. "Well, that's a relief. But it's not about me, exactly, anymore. It would be better for everyone if I died here rather than it getting out where I am."

"What, like Alvum? Dude, you're some kind of apocalypse magnet."

"Jake Ambler, Destroyer of Worlds," Jake chuckled ruefully.

They sat in a heavy silence for a moment.

"Wait. Wait, I know! Karnata is a major stop for several pleasure cruise lines." Derek began typing furiously now. "Yeah, yeah, yeah, three ships are stopping at various Karnata vacation spots in the next 24 hours. Two of those ships have friends of mine on them."

"Two!" Jake exclaimed. "What are the odds?"

Distractedly, Derek said, "About 60%. The cruise liners pay big money and hire the best guys. Min-hee's been saying I should get a job with them when my contract with the ICF is up." He grinned.

"Would you do that?"

"What?" Derek replied. "And let someone else have all this fun?" He chuckled and slapped a key hard. "OK, we probably couldn't smuggle any contraband in, but once the ship-to-shore shuttles get inside Karnatan air space, they can access the Karnatan global network. We could send a message that way."

Jake thought for a moment, "What should I say?"

Derek said, "Try this."

On Jake's screen:

JAKE NEEDS YOU TO SAVE HIS BUTT AGAIN. RIGHT
AWAY.

He winced a little, but he couldn't deny it was true.

"Send it."

"The ship will be there in a few hours. The shuttles down to Karnata will follow sometime after. I don't know how plugged in Dali is,
so it may take her some time to get the message."

"Ah, hell, that's—she went incognito."

Derek said, "We've done all we can at this point. What's your back-
up plan?"

Jake looked over at the pile that had formed under the fabber. He
quickly explained his idea to Derek, who, somewhat to Jake's surprise,
approved of it.

"How's it going?" Derek asked.

"Slower than I'd like."

Derek said, "Not to slow you down further, but for every five
hundred to a thousand dumb drones, make another Jake drone."

Jake sighed. "Can't the one drone handle a lot?"

Derek said, "Sure, it could probably handle fifty or a hundred
thousand. But what if it gets damaged or destroyed? You're gonna have
a bunch of dumb flying bombs running around with no leadership."

Jake sighed again. "Yeah, you're right. Again. Thanks."

Derek looked genuinely worried. "Hang in there, man. If I know
you, you'll come out of this smelling like a rose."

"I have no idea what you're talking about," Jake wanted to say. But
instead, he just said, "Thanks, Derek. See you...soon, I hope."

Jake signed off and sat awhile, listening to the drones plop out of the fabber. Every few seconds, one would fall onto the proximity mat, which he had moved from his desk.

Every five hundred would form a little squad and fly to the top of the tent, waiting for instructions. If they had been gnats, he could have really ruined a picnic with them.

He was making about a thousand an hour. Adding smart drones would cut that down significantly.

He would let it run for a while before adding smart drones to the cycle. If he slowed down the bomb drone production much to make more smart drones, he would end up with a very smart but useless force.

"Jake!" he heard his device say in a distinctive, high-pitched voice.

"Bombur?" he said, guessing.

"Jake, they're trying to kill me!"

Jake picked up his device and saw the Diptera had landed on it. "Well, what did you *think* would happen, Bombur? You could've gone back and shared the knowledge—and where you got it from—but you chose to buffalo everyone instead."

"You don't understand what it was like, Jake, being the outcast, a pariah... Hey, wait a minute. You're...you're not slow anymore!"

Jake realized it was true. He had modulated himself to be at Bombur's speed without even trying.

Another curious development.

"A lot of how you Nijins operate has become clearer to me over time, Bombur. And I *do* understand what you've been through, in a way. Still, you took advantage of me to exploit your fellows."

"And I know that was wrong, and I'll never do it again, for sure," Bombur pleaded. "But I don't deserve to die for it."

"Well, I'm not going to kill you for it."

"Ledalipholus is!"

Jake nodded. "Yeah, she's a hardass. You're probably safer out here with me."

Bombur whimpered. "I don't wanna be an exile, Jake. Exiles have very short lives!"

"What can *I* do?" Jake asked half-heartedly.

"You could kill *her*!" Bombur exclaimed. "We're friends, right, Jake?"

"I thought so, but I'm always suspicious of friendship that's contingent on murder."

"Okay, okay, I didn't really mean it, anyway. You could threaten, though. Ledalipholus wouldn't need to know you wouldn't go through with it."

Jake shook his head. "I don't like it for a lot of reasons, not the least of which is she might call my bluff. Then what?"

"All right," Bombur said, acceding quickly. "But what if you just talked to her? She might listen to you."

"Unlikely, but since I'm just marking time, we can give it a try."

Melontikopolis rose over the horizon as they flew low to the containing wall, and Jake realized he had acquired the capacity, somehow, to keep up with the proceedings, or nearly so. He probably could have even controlled the drone directly had he chosen to, but the thought made him nervous.

It would scale up to full Diptera speed when dealing with anyone but Bombur, and he didn't know if he could do that.

Instead, he watched and waited.

From his normal scale, the activity in the city would've looked like little more than gnats swarming in mindless patterns.

At Diptera scale, the violence was horrific, with Diptera smashing into Diptera with all manner of assorted sticks and clubs. A few even managed to have torches, which Jake really wanted to get a closer look at, not even sure what a flame would look like at that size. The flames were bluish and intensely bright like they were burning a type of metal.

However, his drone decided to avoid the mob and scooted around the bridges and buildings along the inside wall.

The drone led Bombur to Technocrat Hall, where Ledalipholus' office was. Bombur waited quietly as the Jake drone announced himself and asked to see the Technocrat.

She appeared almost immediately, and Bombur thrust himself forward. "Ledalipholus...do—do—don't have me killed! P-p-please!"

Jake cringed a little to hear Bombur, who was trying to speed himself up and stuttering as a result.

She bade them to follow her into her tea room, but Bombur refused. "D-d-d-don't kill me!" he screamed.

Jake's drone approached the terrified Diptera. "Bombur, she is only offering you tea. I have analyzed it myself, and it contains nothing toxic."

Jake was unaware that the drone had done any analysis, but it didn't surprise him.

"Jake Wizard, you don't understand. She wants me d-d-d-dead!"

"Of course I understand. That's why we're here, to prevent that if possible."

"If p—p-possible?"

Ledalipholus had floated closer, apparently concerned by the outburst. A crowd had formed in the lobby. Outside, the mobs continued their clash, floating slowly toward Technocrat Hall.

"No one wishes for your death, Bombur," she said, not very reassuringly. Jake noted a distinct coldness to her tone. "But your actions could bring death to us all!" She spoke softly so the crowd couldn't hear her.

But if discretion were her goal, Bombur did not share it. Instead, he popped backward and held up a tape player. It played his voice, but he had sped it up to match full Dipteran speed.

"Traitor!" the voice came out of the speaker—much louder than Jake had expected. "Ledalipholus has had the means to destroy our tormentors, the Seyles, for ages and yet she refuses to use it!"

The Technocrat made some sign, and Bombur found himself swarmed on all sides by Dipteran police, but he kept the player away from them.

"Hidden in a silo not far from here are weapons powerful enough to wipe out the Seyles, but Ledalipholus prefers to *negotiate* with our oppreso—"

Someone had knocked the device out of his hand and it smashed into the floor, silenced. Bombur yelled out, "T-Traitor!"

Jake wondered what Ledalipholus would do now. She presented herself as someone who abhorred violence but also someone who didn't shy from using it.

Would she put him on trial? Find a way to publicly humiliate him as a fool to "debunk" the idea that she had weapons?

He never knew because, at that moment, the mobs outside burst in, and a riot commenced. The police were overwhelmed. He lost sight of Ledalipholus almost immediately, and the Jake Drone got dragged down from all sides and smashed, ending the signal.

He sat up in his bed, heart pounding.

He hated wasting another smart drone but had to keep track of what was happening in Melontikoplis.

"Watch the city from a distance, and alert me if anything flies out of there that isn't a Diptera," he instructed the drone.

If Bombur managed to get those missiles launched, everyone in the kingdom—including himself and anyone who might be with him at the time—could end up dead.

With the short flight times the missiles were probably programmed for, they'd all die within minutes.

Chapter 35

Bedlam

"Can you see my countdown clock?" Jake said to his device. The fabber had been running constantly for hours now. Even though he had made over ten thousand drones by this point, they just made it look like he hadn't dusted the tent ceiling in a while.

Still, he was feeding more raw material into the extruder. "Too many" was not a concept in play here.

Meanwhile, he had called Dr. Vizgirda.

"Yes. That is accurate. The hyper-summer should begin in about eighteen hours."

"What do you think? Will that be about the same time the wool-lyheads vanish?"

"They're thinning out all over the planet. It seems impossible that it could be a coincidence."

"And when they're gone?"

"When they're gone, we can assume that the Apothikons no longer need protecting."

Jake, mildly annoyed, asked, "Which means what?"

"I can think of a number of possibilities. For example, the grown Apothikon may be able to defend itself actively."

"That sounds like something we should be prepared for."

"Quite. I plan to be far above the activity in the *Mendel*."

How lucky for you, Jake thought.

"Another possibility is that it loses its appeal to the Seyles. Perhaps the pits will cave in."

"I don't think so, Doc. I think the will-o'-wisp pits are defunct Apothikon pits."

"How did you come to that conclusion?" she demanded.

Jake thought of Noah. "A local told me."

Georgia stammered, "Who? Was it a Korma? Or did you get it from your Diptera drone?"

"Neither. Look, it's a long story, and we're short on time, Doc. Do you have any idea how hot it's going to get?"

"Rather hot. Over fifty degrees."

Celsius, Jake thought. "We used to get that on the farm sometimes. How long?"

"A few hours."

The tent climate controls could handle that easily, as could the suit. Even in the worst case, a few hours of 120-plus degrees wasn't a huge threat. He could jump into the reservoir if desperate.

Jake chuckled to himself when he realized he had trained himself to think of worst-case scenarios after a few years in the ICF.

"What if...the tent fails...and the suit fails...and...I can't jump in the reservoir because it's frozen. Dali's right: I do worry about dumb things." Jake said aloud.

"What's that?" asked Georgia.

"Nothing important," replied Jake. "Thank you for the information, doc. I'll call back closer to the zero hour."

He disconnected and considered how he'd handle these final pulses. He'd be in his suit, without question. The damned thing wouldn't starve in the remaining few hours, so he was prepared to unleash everything he had against all attackers.

The possibility of Melontikopolis launching an atomic weapon while he was distracted added an unwanted wrinkle.

"I was just worried about the reservoir freezing somehow but brush off atomic warfare as a 'wrinkle.'" He said it out loud so he could hear how dumb it sounded.

Chuckling, he ran diagnostics on his armor and checked the joints and surfaces for mold or any irregularity. The modern battlesuit was a marvel: it looked brand new, in full repair, and only in need of a refill for the safety foam charge.

He mainly regretted he couldn't turn the fabber to pumping out grenades.

The tent lights had been dimming. His "night" was coming. He noticed that he had needed much less sleep over the past few weeks but decided to take the opportunity to give his circadian rhythms a chance to normalize.

It would be his last chance for a while, he figured. So Jake slept.

Dezzig poked his head in, waking him.

He looked at his wall clock: ten hours, forty-three minutes to go.

Jake said, "I'll be right out."

His device chimed. Derek had left a message, so he put it up while getting his suit on.

"Dude... Jake. Don't worry too much, but Dali hasn't responded to our messages."

Jake froze and looked at the screen.

"I know you're already freaking out, but don't. Some fighting broke out on Karnata, near some place called Otto. The rumor was that Dali was there for some reason, but I don't have any details."

Even as he said it, Derek looked like he realized how awful it sounded. "I'm sure she's fine, dude. The only reason I even bothered to call was that I'm not sure she got your message, and, well, yeah. She might be delayed getting back to you."

He fidgeted briefly with his hands. "I can still try to get those mercs to help. Let me know, and I'll figure out where you are." Then he just shrugged, and the message ended.

He could suit up in under a minute now and soon joined Dezzig at the high crag above his base.

She's fine. She's fine. I'm not going to get distracted.

The sheer number of times he had repeated this to himself made him less convinced of its truth.

Jake focused on Dezzig and noticed he had bedizened himself with the sparkly goop from the Callas. The Seyles noticed that Jake had noticed.

"I'm mostly kidding," he said in his hard-to-read deadpan. "Matzhin amasses his troops at the edge of the Valley Ridge territory," he said.

Jake looked in the opposite direction. "And it looks like Torsk isn't even going to wait. His infantry is already picking its way through the Great Marsh. That's somewhat easier now as my earlier assault hardened a lot of the ground."

Dezzig nodded. "Torsk's air force will hang back until his infantry has a chance to strike meaningfully."

A thought occurred to Jake. "Dezzig, when the enemy troops—well, *if* they reach this far into the territory, what will they do?"

Dezzig said, "They'll kill everyone, of course, just as Matzhin did with Valley Ridge."

Even as Dezzig said it, Jake heard it echoed in his head and said it with him: "And if they come across any reservoirs, they'll destroy them."

Dezzig turned to face him. "Jake Wizard, you seem less stupid than before. Have you been eating people?"

Jake was too numb to be insulted or amused.

She's fine.

"They'll drown the land. That will kill the Nephros, the Kormas, and any underground Nocks." Jake recited as if reading from a book.

My greatest fear at this point, Jake thought, *is that I'm never going to understand what's going on. It will all end, and I'll be just as confused as when I started.*

You mean your second greatest fear.

"What will you do, Jake Wizard?"

"I'm going to start by setting the Great Marsh on fire. Then I'll go back and sweep through the Valley Ridge with my lances. If all goes well, I can wipe out Matzhin's troops before Torsk's army can make it through."

Dezzig buzzed appreciatively.

"If I get too preoccupied with one side and the other makes ground, I'll unleash my own air force."

"Amazing. This plan sounds—"

ALERT: APOTHIKON PULSE

The two of them looked toward Grigg's castle. Already, a cloud of Seyles had risen over the city and streamed in a line toward the Callas.

Then they looked to the south and saw Seyles swooping off over the ridge—toward Matzhin's Callas.

Turning to the north, they saw a similar pattern. Jake didn't even know where Torsk's Callas were, but he had no doubt that's where the Seyles were heading.

"Three points of attack, Jake Wizard. Much more challenging to deal with, no? *Now* what will you do?"

Jake looked at Dezzig, whose eyes were sparkling with fascination.

Jake, whose mind was barely holding off his violent thoughts, replied grimly.

"Something ugly."

CHAPTER 36

STOPS PULLED

He needed to buy time, a delay. And he didn't have a lot of time to buy that delay.

After a moment of reflection, he turned toward Valley Ridge. Then, he set the dispersal on his left arm blaster just wide enough to catch the advancing army and about a third of the Seyles in the sky.

Then he turned it to maximum power.

Then, he raised it beyond maximum power. The whole inside of the suit turned red.

PROBABILITY OF DESTROYING SINISTER BLASTER: 90%

PROBABILITY OF SYSTEM SAFETY SHUTDOWN: 50%

PROBABILITY OF SUIT DESTRUCTION: 10%

He read the warnings. Then, lacking any alternatives he could see, he leapt upward into the sky, aimed, and fired.

As hard as the Nijins had hit him in the suit, he had never felt it, thanks to his shields, the safety foam, and the sophisticated inertial compensators.

But he felt this—a massive discharge of power that vibrated the whole suit and made his teeth rattle. He could feel the safety foam crumbling around him. (It would still work, he was pretty sure. He hoped.)

He didn't even have time to assess the devastation before his controls went dark, and he plummeted to the ground.

The world spun around him. The Dragon and Damsel moons and the lethargic sun rolling indifferently along the horizon, catastrophic flaming wreckage was on the Node Path—and then a pair of giant, scintillating eyes filled his view.

He could tell his descent was slowing. Dezzig must be trying to catch him. As he fell toward his base camp, the Seyles tried several approaches: catching him in his arms and trying to float him upward, getting under him and pushing, and finally pulling up on his arms.

Dezzig managed to slow the fall, but the weight was too much for the Seyles to stop him entirely.

PREDICTED DAMAGE FROM IMPACT: MINIMAL

"Dezzig, you did it! Thank thee!" he said.

"Thou art welcome!" Dezzig replied, dropping him completely.

He landed on his back, smashing into the crag above his base with a jolt and then, slowly but inexorably, sliding down the side of the crag, crashing once again into the rocky plateau under his base.

He was in the dark, except for the light coming through his faceplate and some dim but angry warning lights. One of the lights indicated a connection break from the generator to the main battery.

He remembered a drill from training where the units replaced each other's batteries. The only trick was to make sure the battery was snugly up against the generator.

He speculated he might have hit the rocks just right to slightly lever that out. It was a long shot, but at least it was something that could be fixed.

It could also be that he'd hit it just right to break the cradle. That was game over.

"Dezzig!" he yelled out.

The giant eyes filled his faceplate as Dezzig floated down. Jake jumped inside the suit.

"Yes, Jake Wizard?"

"Look at my back and tell me what you see!"

Dezzig hovered to the other side of him, then back. "What am I looking for?"

"Damage. Does anything look off?"

"Not really," Dezzig said. "Just a little..." Jake felt a powerful vibrating pulse at his back. He fought to stay upright as the Seyles beat against the back of the suit.

The lights in his suit went on.

POWER LEVEL: 15%

Dezzig floated in front of him again. "Did that help, Jake Wizard?"

Jake replied it had, and the Seyles floated out of sight again. Whatever battles were going on was more interesting than seeing Jake limp around in a broken battlesuit.

He felt the foam melt and reform around him in a disturbingly intimate way and did a quick diagnostic to confirm the suit was still usable.

Not *quite* broken.

His left blaster was burnt out. His safety systems had worked but were demanding recalibration. The whole suit was asking for a thorough detail strip—a complete disassembly with diagnostics run on all the parts individually.

But it was still working.

Now, he adjusted his right blaster beyond the safe maximum. He just had to get off one shot at Torsk and probably wouldn't get a second chance.

PROBABILITY OF DESTROYING DEXTER BLASTER: 99%
PROBABILITY OF SYSTEM SAFETY SHUTDOWN: 80%
PROBABILITY OF SUIT DESTRUCTION: 40%

He paused. He really didn't want to kill the suit. He still had the Apothikon pulse to deal with.

"What is Grigg up to, Dezzig?"

"He's deployed his troops against Matzhin, Jake Wizard," Dezzig replied from above.

"Didn't I take them out?"

"You did an impressive amount of damage," Dezzig confirmed. "More importantly, Matzhin's troops seem to be stunned. Demoralized. Unwilling to travel the Node Path, which is molten rock at this point."

"So, why on earth would Grigg devote his resources there? *How* would he even do it if the road's on fire?"

Dezzig said, "Speculating, I would say he wants revenge and sees a chance to reclaim the Valley Ridge." Then, in a disapproving tone, the Seyles added, "As for how? He simply orders them to find their way through the lava. The Seyles don't even want to fly over it, it's so hot."

"And he's ordering this while Torsk's forces destroy him from the Great Marsh?"

Dezzig landed just so he could shrug with all four wings. "As we have discussed, Grigg is an idiot."

"Well, my luck's been bad up till now. Maybe the tide will turn," Jake said, leaping up and firing toward the Great Marsh. A horrendous energy gout spewed forth, and the suit went black again.

He hit the ground standing up, the barely powered armor and cushioning still robust enough to prevent any damage to him, and ejected immediately onto the plateau of his base. Below, he could see the flak cannon already firing and jerking between the two gaps.

But the woollyhead ring was still intact, meaning he still had to protect it. He ran to the tent and pulled out the grate he had used early on to cover the pit.

Dezzig was watching him curiously.

"Hey," said Jake. "What are you doing?"

"Just observing, Jake Wizard. I've seen many battles, and they've begun to bore me. You act in novel and amusing ways."

Jake asked, "Are you willing to carry some stuff for me?"

"Certainly."

Jake gave him the grate and said, "Drop that down by the Apothikon. Don't get too close, and above all, watch the cannon and don't get in front of the gaps, or you'll get shot."

Without acknowledgment, the Seyles picked up the grate and flew it over the plateau rim while Jake ran down the path leading to the pit.

"Thanks," he called out over the buzz and blaster noises.

"Thou art welcome again," said Dezzig.

Jake grabbed most of his weapons from his tent: his sidearm, his rifle, his knuckles, his knife, and even strapped on the kalybus Mot had made him. Then he plunged down the side of his plateau to where Dezzig, who perched watching quietly, had dropped the grate.

Jake picked up the grate with one hand and dragged it behind him. The flak cannon had shifted to the nine o'clock position, so Jake ran in at the twelve.

"OK," he said, running to the pit, "However much you hate it, we're going to have to make this work for your sake and mine."

He dragged the grate over the pit, and immediately, the movement of the grass pushed it aside.

"I know you're not even hatched yet, but could you stop acting like a baby?" he said, exasperated. He smelled smoke—the cannon.

He couldn't tell if it was from Seyles remains, mold, overheating, or something else, so when the gun shifted back to twelve o'clock, he got on the knoll and fired his rifle to clear the nine o'clock, hoping to relieve some of its burden.

He blasted at full power and area and swapped out batteries like mad, only breaking to drop used batteries into the base's charging slots and pulling charged ones out.

He had things under control.

Except the attacks weren't stopping.

The supply of Seyles didn't even slow down. He had used every battery in the base and was cycling back through his original batteries, which were only partially charged.

He growled and looked at the grate lying to one side of the pit.

Clenching his jaw, he ran back to the pit and threw the grate over it, standing atop it. He slipped on his knuckles and waited. The grate rumbled and protested beneath him.

He didn't have to wait long. While the flak cannon blazed away in one direction, a few bold Seyles charged through the other gap.

One dive-bombed him, and he punched upwards, sending it into the flickering shield, where it burst into flames.

Two came at him at once, and with a pivot, he landed one good cross on each. They careened into the shield.

He was moving fast, anticipating their attacks and responding before they could react. The grass rumbled hungrily and tried to cast the grate off, but with Jake standing on it, it could only slightly imbalance him.

Three more got in. One sailed over the flak cannon right toward him while the other two came at him from either side.

He crouched and delivered a cross, which punched straight through the enormous maw and drove into the thorax, all the way to the abdomen. As he flung the dead creature off, he saw the other two grabbing at the grate and trying to pull him off.

He wobbled as he stood and drew his kalybus, which he used to bisect the creature on his left. He turned and looked at the one on his right, kalybus raised in warning.

It showed no sign of consciousness, no reaction to his threat.

He plunged the sword down and through, ripping it back up for good measure.

Looking at the electroflak, he could see the battery charger lights had turned green, so he sheathed his sword, leapt from the grate, and grabbed some batteries to pack into his long gun.

He'd felt so good for so long at this point that he'd practically forgotten that even he, Jake Ambler, could grow fatigued.

He almost panicked when the cannon stopped firing before he realized the attack had ended.

Behind him, the grate had been cast off. The pit roiled angrily, grass pulling in from around an unending stream of smoking corpses.

CHAPTER 37

THE MADNESS OF LORD GRIGG

"Jake Wizard! Jake Wizard!"

Jake had extracted himself from the sward after a quick check of the cannon and trotted around the ring of woollyheads. It had gotten much, much thinner.

But it was still there.

This meant he still had to protect it and, to some extent, still had to care what the insane Lord Grigg had to say.

Except at this point, not only would he just as soon see Grigg dead, but it was only sheer pigheadedness keeping him on the mission at all. If anything happened to Dali because he had been stuck here, he'd launch Ledalipholus' atomic missiles himself.

He had returned to his base to check out the battlesuit. He found it had powered up, fortunately, and in a frantic mode of running self-diagnostics. He checked the back and saw the freakishly precise hit on the connector between the generator and the battery. It seemed relatively secure now.

The blasters would need complete replacement. At least the electric blades still worked. The climate control was compromised; he couldn't tell how badly.

It was this focused train of thought that Grigg, finally deigning to descend from his castle, interrupted.

The monarch swooped from the crossroads and landed on the high crag overlooking Jake's tent. Many of his court followed. Jake could see a phalanx of Notos had come down from the castle and was waiting at the bottom of the path leading from his base.

Rather than respond, Jake stepped into the armor. Then he stepped out again and went into his tent for a safety foam recharge pack.

The doomsday clock on the wall said six hours to go. The fabber had continued plopping out drones. The tent ceiling was blackened with them. It suited Jake's mood.

Six hours or no, the diastole was coming, Jake realized. He could feel it.

The next wave was soon, and it would be the biggest to date, he realized, emerging from the tent.

Grigg froze. He had seen Jake cheerful, helpful, weakened, resentful—but never *indifferent*. Never impudently careless of Grigg's wishes.

Jake could see the notion scared him, and his only thought was: *good*.

The Seyles perched on the crag, shaking with greater and greater intensity as Jake loaded the safety foam pack and re-entered the suit. The foam oozed comfortingly around him.

"Jake Wizard! We're under attack!"

Jake regarded the Seyles critically. The stupid crown he wore on his head looked about to fall off, and Jake toyed with the idea of trying to knock it off, just as Grigg had once knocked the medicine out of his hand.

"Did you not see the destruction I wreaked upon your enemies?"

"Yes, I did," Seyles said without changing his tone.

"And that was *while* being preoccupied with protecting the pit."

"But some remain!" wheedled Grigg.

"*Lord* Grigg, you have an army and an air force which Jake Wizard has not attacked. Split your forces and send half to the north and half to the south. You should be able to fight off your enemies that way."

Grigg continued to whine and cajole him. "That's what I *am* doing. And what is Jake Wizard doing? Nothing! Have you grown tired and *old* in your time on Nidus, human creature? Are you out of power at last?"

Jake made a face the Seyles couldn't see. There was a small amount of truth to it. Even though it had kept Grigg's kingdom from being completely overwhelmed by burning out his suit blasters, he had been robbed not just of those weapons but also his plasma and his lance, as all the energy weapons ran off the same subsystems.

His fabber had been too tied up for grenades.

He was pretty sure he had limited jump power, at best.

Not to mention, the climate control barely worked, and he was already sweating profusely.

He marched down from his base to the Node Path crossroads, the Notos parting to make way for him. He had destroyed the south-bound path with his attack on Matzhin and the northbound path the first time he bombed the Great Marsh.

The westbound path ended at the river.

The eastbound path led to another kingdom over an area he vaguely remembered being called the Endless Marsh, which was vast enough to prevent trouble from the kingdom beyond it.

As Jake stood at the crossroads, considering what it all meant, Grigg had not ceased his haranguing, swooping down to yell at him up close.

He ran the suit through its physical diagnostics: arm extension, leg extension, hands on hips. The crowd that had started to form bubbled with amusement at his activities while Grigg escalated his shrill rant.

He thinks that because I haven't killed him, I'm not to be feared. He thinks this despite everything!

The crowd stood watching the strange tableau: a nine-foot-tall dragonfly haranguing an impassive golem. Jake regarded the stocky, stiff Nocks, the stick bodies of the Notos, the furtive Kormas bobbing their giant heads, and the hovering Seyles, all focused on him and Grigg.

Even a few Nephros had poked their impassive faces out of the dirt to observe the spectacle.

"Well? What are you going to do, Jake Wizard?" All the creature's spiracles wheezing at once was unpleasant, even filtered through the translator.

Focus. Don't take the bait. Don't think about Grigg being alive while Dali is...

Jake whipped his left hand out and snatched Grigg under his "nose." The crowd gasped. Jake issued a command from his device to his drones with his right hand. The sky grew black over his head.

His personal storm cloud.

"Well, *Lord* Grigg," he said. "My plan *was* to take *my* air force—each one of which can kill a dozen Seyles—and split them between your enemies.

"This would have saved you from your incompetence, yet again." The Seyles shook in his hand. "But I'm not going to do that. Do you know why?"

The Seyles was trembling too hard to answer.

"I asked, *do you know why?*"

The wheezing from Grigg's spiracles confounded the translator. His device blared:

ALERT: APOTHIKON PULSE

Jake pointed toward the Apothikon pit and then threw Grigg into the crowd, which gasped. Then he turned and walked toward the pit. A few Seyles had already peeled off to bedizen.

Behind him, a shrill voice called out, "Kill him! Kill Jake Wizard!"

In his reverse-view-screens, he saw a few spears crash impotently into his back. The suit turned on its defense shield, which still partly worked but made it even hotter inside, and Jake ignored them as he proceeded to the pit, a cloud of deadly drones following behind.

The woollyhead ring was only a few flowers thick all the way around.

He landed the drones in a blanket at the base of the steep hill under the plateau. He didn't want to use them until he absolutely had to, and he didn't know how intense things might get.

Very, he suspected.

Grabbing the grate from where he left it leaning against the flak cannon, he stomped over the sward and threw it down on the pit. Then he stood on top of the grate and waited.

The grass complained.

"Shut up. You've eaten enough, you glutton."

With that, he extended his blades and waited.

The electroflak had started firing and kept firing. Then it stopped. Then, after a few minutes, it started firing again. Then it stopped.

Must be overheating, then cooling off, then overheating again, Jake guessed.

Jake had to speculate because he couldn't see clearly. Frenzied Seyles swarmed him on all sides as the gun couldn't keep up with the massive numbers. His blades flashed, dissecting them as quickly as they came and piling up their bodies around him. His armor bounced the ones he missed back into the Apothikon shield.

It was ugly and unpleasant, but it was working.

Every strike he made and every one against him caused his power levels to drop a tiny amount. He even began personally registering the occasional hit as the suit's inertial compensators were overwhelmed.

Was it time?

He took a breath and reduced the power on his blades and shield, hoping to stretch his energy reserves out. He had gotten better at moving the suit with less force and had brought his emotions under control so that his movements were more like a gently flowing kata than aggressive shadowboxing.

He was sweating profusely nonetheless. At the lowest setting, the suit's climate control focused on balancing oxygen and carbon dioxide levels.

He only really started to worry when the power was down to the barest sliver of red on the gauges, and it became harder and harder to move the suit arms.

If only he could see better.

The flak stopped firing again.

Time to launch the drones. I'm not going to make it.

Then he thought, *Let's see how bad it is.*

With a grand sweep of his right arm to one side and his left to another, he threw the carcasses of Seyles off him completely.

The sky, while filled with smoke, was otherwise clear.

The pulse was over.

He kicked away the bodies, clearing a path. The flak cannon, while smoking and surrounded by wreckage, looked functional.

He opened his faceplate to freshen the air in the suit and, assaulted by the smell of ozone and burning carapace, closed it right back up.

The grass had thrown off the grate to draw the bodies to the pit, and he trudged through the gap—the woollyhead circle now down to three or even two flowers in places—and toward the Node Path.

The mob had grown. It filled the narrow passage leading from the lowland where the pit lay up to the crossroads; from what Jake could see, it spilled out far beyond.

He approached the subdued mob, thinking, "Maybe I'll get some respect from—"

The large rock dropped from a high altitude, knocking him on the helmet and preventing him from finishing that particular thought.

CHAPTER 38

LAST STANDS

Well, this would certainly be a *dumb* way to die.

He rose slowly as the mob, emboldened by the attack, surrounded him. The Nijins threw rocks at him, and a few poked him with their spears, even as enemy armies pushed toward the crossroads from the north and the south.

The suit's power regeneration had stalled, and the levels remained at the dangerous low they had reached after the last pulse.

And with only about an hour to go.

He felt a sense of shame that he was going to let Dali down. He had made promises to her.

And, deep down, he wondered if those feelings were just a way of denying that something might have already happened to her.

He looked up at Grigg, who had perched once again on the crag, and yelled, "I just saved you!"

He tried a jump. He broke free of the crowd, but the suit stuttered and only made it about halfway up the cliff face, rebounding and landing next to the crossroads. The crowd cleared so they weren't squashed, but not as far back as Jake would've liked.

At least he landed on his feet.

Grigg shouted from his perch. "Kill Jake Wizard!"

But as angry as the crowd was, Jake detected hesitancy. Maybe he could talk his way out of this after all.

"Grigg! Even now, your armies struggle to preserve your kingdom. Why divert your energy to me, the one who has already saved your kingdom over and over?"

"DIE!" yelled Grigg.

He saw the Seyles with the rock this time and managed to almost get out of its way, the sluggish response of the suit resulting in the rock clipping him on the back. He felt it, but it hadn't hurt.

His shields were well under one percent, barely registering. The inertial compensators were also out completely, but he'd realized that after the first rock knocked him silly. Even the safety foam had crumbled into an irritating sand.

"I don't want to have to kill you," he warned the crowd half-heartedly as it began to overcome its trepidation and approached him.

Swarmed him.

The battery should have been charging his subsystems, but the generator had stopped feeding it.

Temporarily overwhelmed? Or completely burnt out?

Nocks surrounded him while Notos jabbed at him with spears. Seyles circled above or perched to watch.

His battery was so drained that the suit had switched all its power to climate control.

He wouldn't suffocate while they beat him to death.

He didn't know he could fix any problems with the suit under the best of circumstances, much less while being lynched.

Out of morbid curiosity and with the idea that suffocating would probably be better than dying of internal bleeding, he overrode the climate controls long enough to do a diagnostic.

The air immediately got thick. Jake realized he had been panting heavily and focused on slowing his breathing.

The dimly lit controls showed what he expected. Low power, blasters burnt out, shields and compensators out.

Oddly, the generator reported being both in good repair and *idle*. Then Jake saw the generator-battery connection must have broken again. He immediately switched the power back to emergency climate control.

Dezzig had managed to beat the battery back into place. Maybe he could do the same.

It's a long shot, but if I fall backward—or jump and land on my back—I might be able to fix that connection—at least long enough to give myself a little juice.

He did a short hop, curling up his legs and falling backward. He felt a squish. There was a bug underneath him, cushioning his fall.

The crowd grew more enraged.

He barely fell at all on his second attempt. The crowd mostly shoved him back up again.

Jake had to laugh. They were going to be able to kill him by preventing him from falling over!

Another rock hit the back of his head.

Nocks and Notos began climbing on him, up to his shoulders and head. As light as they were, he began to feel the weight.

Static on his translator sounded like the Kormas arguing: "Trebawly Notos the Pugnacious admonished us to go for the legs," one said, while another claimed, "Kradnal Seyles the Conqueror said head shots were best."

The final indignity: to be killed amid a meaningless argument.

But if Dali were dead, he didn't really want to live, anyway.

A call came in:

"Jake, can you hear me?"

"Doctor Vizgirda? I'm a little busy—actually, you know what, I've got all the time in the world. What is it?" They had driven him down to one knee.

The expression on his face may have concerned her but she burst out in excited talk. "Jake, I've made a mistake."

"I've made a few myself." They had driven him down to both knees. The remaining readouts in his suit, already dimmed, began to flicker off, one by one. Only the comm connection (which was just a bridge between the suit and his personal device) still worked.

She said, "I've gotten it backward. I thought the eclosion was the Apothikon hatching, that it had been gestating under the ground for decades, but that's not the case!"

He was on his hands and knees. The impacts were registering significantly now, with the low shield power protecting him just well enough to allow him to enjoy his battering.

He endured, watching the flow of water underneath him.

"It was time," Fugi had said when he removed some bricks from the reservoir.

Georgia carried on: "And the Apothikon pulses aren't like heartbeats! They're more like a combination of death throes—and *contractions!* We're not seeing the Apothikon coming into its maturity. We're seeing it die! Its final act will be to reproduce!"

"That's...interesting," Jake said, though he had little energy to expend. He could feel himself being smashed from every angle, and only the physical strength of the armor and the Nijins' poor understanding of human anatomy kept them from killing him now.

Then he thought of the drones. They were always there in the corner of his mind. He could fly them into this mob. Blow everyone up, including himself. Talk about a dumb way to die.

He *could* instruct the smart drones to try clearing the area around him without blasting him. He'd be like the girl the knife-thrower tries to miss in a show.

Except this knife-thrower would be hucking bundles of TNT at him.

And if it saved him here, he'd be empty-handed for the next Apothikon pulse. With a barely functioning suit, bigger swarms of Seyles than ever, and alone.

The buffeting from the crowd escalated. A Nock with a stick used his helmet as a drum. The clatter around him grew.

He said in a low voice, "Georgia, tell Dali I love her." He liked this aspect at least: he could die believing Dali was still alive.

Georgia yelled back, "What? Jake? What's going on?"

Ignoring her, he began to explain what he wanted to his device, interrupted many times by the battering he was taking.

"Override safety protocols. Destroy the Nijins that are—" Jake stopped. Ten feet? Twenty? Too close, the bombs would kill *him*. Too far, the Nijins might not scatter.

"Twenty-five fe—"

The next sound Jake heard was different but familiar, like the thwump of the flak, only more profound—bone-rattling and followed by some impressive explosions.

The Nijins crawling on him stepped away for a moment in shock, and he seized his chance, immediately jumping to his feet and right onto his back.

As he impacted the ground, all the panels lit up at once. His power levels stayed squarely in the red, but they were there.

"Good enough," he thought, extending his blades.

Another call came in on his screen. "How you doin', tough guy? Nijins giving you a hard time?"

"Never better, princess!" he gasped out, "but I do appreciate the hand! Where have you been? I was worried!" He started slashing his arms out viciously, blades extended, driving away the murderous mob.

A little power and a little hope were all it took to turn things around sometimes. As sure as he was that he would die before, Dali's presence made him feel practically immortal.

"Rebels had me pinned down on Karnata!" she answered. "I got lured into a trap—it's a long story. Do you want me to do more crowd control?"

The Nijins had suddenly remembered why they feared Jake, and scattered quickly. Even Grigg had jetted back to the castle when the *Shiva* had started firing.

"I think we're good, princess. Land that beauty and join me at the tent—"

ALERT: APOTHIKON PULSE

"Join me at the pit—"

WARNING: LAUNCH DETECTED

Oh, now what?

He had forgotten Melontikopolis.

"Oh, no," Jake said. He played back the video from the drone watching the city. Melontikopolis was burning, plumes of smoke rising from its buildings. The riots must have kept going—it had been the equivalent of days for the Dipterans, and Ledalipholus must not have been able to get Bombur and his followers under control.

"Dali, do you see anything being launched from the Diptera city?"

There was a pause.

"Very small missiles! Are they dangerous? The Shiva says they'll hit points north and south—and one's gonna land really close. It's aimed at the castle! Jake, I'm getting a radiation reading!"

Torsk, Matzhin, and Grigg. All wiped out. Mission spectacularly failed.

"Dali, those weapons have atomic warheads!"

"Can I shoot 'em in the air?" she said.

"Better not. Filling the air with radiation might seriously mess things up. Drag them out to space."

"OK. That'll take a while!"

ALERT: APOTHIKON PULSE

Jake groaned. Was that a repeat warning? Or was there another pulse? Looking around, he saw a sky filled with Seyles, darkening the moons and sun.

"Do it quick, and then get to the pit as soon as you can! This pulse is practically drawing every Seyles on the planet!"

"Got it!" She immediately steered the *Shiva* toward the Dipteran city on her mission.

He stood on the grate in his battlesuit, stubbornly ignoring the protests of the grass beneath him and the warnings of low power in his suit. It was bobbing at just above critical, but he felt like he could stand against the whole damnable planet with just his bare hands at this point.

He had his blades out, waiting as the flak cannon started blazing away.

The cannon was already taxed, still hot from the previous assault. The crowds in the sky grew thicker.

A bright flash in space—one of Ledalipholus' atomic warheads—turned the twilight to high noon. All the Seyles immediately turned toward the unusual light, giving him a moment's breathing room. Then, eerily, as the light faded, they all turned back as one.

ALERT: APOTHIKON PULSE

The Apothikon was sending out pulses faster and faster. He disabled the warnings. One way or another, he wasn't leaving this spot until it was all over.

A second flash came. All the Seyles stopped once again and turned toward the light. The flak cannon had a group in its sights and blasted them into oblivion while they hovered, mesmerized.

Then they all turned back once again.

The third flash was much further away—it must have been the one targeting Torsk.

This one didn't get the Seyles' attention, unfortunately.

"Good girl, Dali," Jake muttered. That was one iron out of the fire, at least.

He had his blades out and dissected an incoming Seyles. The sky crawled and bubbled with them, and he was already exhausted.

He kept glancing at the woollyheads. There was still a ring, but barely. They had thinned rapidly. As he watched, the flowers seemed to be wilting, just not fast enough.

The bubble lit up blindingly as about a hundred Seyles crashed into the shield simultaneously. As long as Jake stood on the grate, he just had to wait for the Seyles to fall into his blades.

Still, their numbers hadn't thinned appreciably.

Georgia reconnected, "Jake, are you okay?"

"Yes, Georgia. How are you?" he said as if he hadn't just tossed a Seyles into the shield.

"I'm in the troposphere, far away from the madness. But I'm watching."

Swell.

"And it seems to me," she continued, "that the Apothikon where you are is unique. Most of the pits around the world are under siege right now and are still being deflected, even by the thinning shields."

Swell.

"The siege over your head looks to be an order of magnitude heavier than any other pit I'm monitoring."

The sky lit up once again, this time with fireballs. The *Shiva* swooped in, blasters on rapid fire. The sky rained charred Seyles.

"Looks like you have a guardian angel, Jake."

Dali Angel.

He liked the sound of that.

This was the first time he had seen the bedizened Seyles truly disrupted. Their instinctual patterns and grouped attacks gave way to utter chaos, as they had no system for dealing with this gargantuan, death-dealing creature in their midst.

The Comedentine, Jake thought grimly. *Maybe the ancient Diptera were on to something.*

A few tried to crash into the *Shiva*. They couldn't even get close enough to be noticeable.

Their attacks on the shield got more frantic, too, and the flak cannon easily picked them off.

Jake took a deep breath.

They were going to make it.

He looked at the ring as the final woollyheads started dying off. The shield was down.

CHAPTER 39

FAILING BIOLOGY

Jake froze. Then he called up Dr. Vizgirda.

"Georgia! The shield went down, but... Is it over? Can I get out of here?"

"What color is the Apothikon pit?"

Jake looked down. "What do you mean, what color is it? It's the same color it always is, a kind of pale blue!"

"No, that's not right. The Apothikons all over Nidus are changing, and they've all shifted from blue to pink, almost red, right before the last woollyhead dies."

Jake stood there, the grate rattling under his feet.

"It's blue. It's the same color it always has been! What do I do?"

"Stay calm, Jake. You've almost certainly had some unnatural effect on it. Is it able to feed?"

"No, I've got the grate over it."

"Jake, you're going to have to let it feed. You're going to have to get off the grate, but don't let any healthy Seyles through just yet."

Jake looked around, surrounded by Seyles, who, too, seemed to pause in shock, awareness that the shield—the Apothikon's teeth—might be gone. The flak cannon fired in the same two areas it had been firing, and the Seyles immediately moved out of those ranges.

The cannon fell quiet.

"That may not be easy."

It's time to bring out the cavalry.

He used his device to address his smart drones after carefully canceling the pending order to blow up everything around him.

"Drones to destroy all Seyles surrounding the Apothikon pit!" he said. Then shouted, "Wait! Except Dezzig Seyles!"

The drones rose behind him and didn't immediately attack. The "Jake" drones were marshaling them in complex attack patterns. Patterns he couldn't have grasped even if he wasn't currently being dive-bombed.

As he slashed his way clear, he saw a line of fire in the sky. Thousands of the circling beasts combusted and even fell to the ground or flew around, spreading the flame and throwing the rest into confusion.

They looked around for something to attack, but there was nothing, of course—just a sea of chaos and their flaming brethren.

Jake, meanwhile, had become a whirling dervish, fighting off every Seyles that still had enough drive to try to get past him. He stayed anchored to the grate.

"You're not getting in yet!" he grunted.

The flak cannon sat idly. He wished he had a moment to program it for attacks in a three-hundred-and-sixty-degree arc, but Jake couldn't move away.

A massive cloud had formed at two o'clock and began to drive toward him. He wouldn't be able to fight off all of them.

Then, a circle of flame appeared, extending out on both sides as a narrow cone. Seyles corpses flamed and rained down on the landscape.

Many were killed, but more importantly, the drones disrupted the attack—except for the six very fast Seyles who struck Jake in the chest in rapid succession. He tried to use the suit's jets to push down, but it just didn't have enough power.

One foot came off the grate.

He went to one knee and raised his blades in a cross shape. Incoming Seyles sliced themselves, trying to get through.

He killed more than he could count, piles of bodies forming walls around him, but there were still enough to assail him effectively with brute force.

He could see scattered explosions in the air as the drones took the Seyles out wherever they were foolish enough to clump. He could also still see more streams of the creatures coming from over the Great Marsh.

The attackers had adapted, moving to hit him on the side and back now, smashing through the piled-up bodies, so he rose up and started slashing at them again.

Another squad battered him in front.

His lead foot started to move off the grate. The soles of his boot had caught on the holes, and the impacts were causing the grate to rise with the hits.

"No, no, no...still not time..."

The pit stayed infuriatingly blue. In the brief time, the grate had lifted, and the grass on the sward had pushed a pile of corpses in.

Near the river, in between the footbridges, the *Shiva* landed. Dali slid down the ladder quickly and brought out the batons favored in the type of Karnatan martial art she knew. They had juiced those weapons up for their battle with Telemakhos, and once again, she wielded them with devastating effect.

She rushed to the sward, which had slowly become more crowded as the Nocks and Notos migrated down from the crossroads. Initial resistance was met with sharp raps of the batons, and a path quickly cleared for her.

She stepped through the area where the gap had been and ran to Jake. "Dali," Jake yelled, patching her into his call with Georgia, "the shield is down. Be careful!"

She ran past the electroflak and smashed a Seyles that had designs on trying to knock Jake off the grate. "If the shield's down," she asked, "why are we still fighting?"

"We're waiting for the pit's color to change," he replied, looking at the circling Seyles.

"Jake, look down!"

He did and saw the pit had shifted to a light pink. "It's happened, Doc! The color changed. What does that mean?"

"The Apothikon is ready to be fertilized."

"Fertilized?" Jake and Dali said together.

"Yes, fertilized," Georgia affirmed. "The Apothikon will be fertilized—you'll see once you let one of the bedizened Seyles in."

He staggered back off the grate, and the grass quickly tossed it aside, now forcing the carnage back.

Done feeding, I guess.

A Seyles dive-bombed the pit.

"Here we go…" said Jake.

Before it could complete its journey, something sped through the air and knocked it to one side, viciously torn through by a spear.

Jake and Dali both followed the blur, confused. When the creature turned, they gasped.

"Dezzig?"

"Sorry about that, Jake Wizard." He shouted to the Seyles floating above the pit in confusion, "None of you are worthy." Jake's coffee pot dangled from his claw, and he pointed at his fellow Seyles accusingly.

The walls of the pit began to collapse slowly, opening it wider. The grass was pushing the corpses away further and further.

Jake saw Grigg land on the crag above the pit. So did Dezzig.

"Not you either, Lord Grigg."

This seemed to pique the arrogant Seyles, who Jake was pretty sure didn't actually want to go into the pit anyway until he noticed the insane monarch had bedizened.

Dali whispered, "Jake, the other kingdoms' armies are at the crossroads. We might want to get out of here."

Jake finally noticed that many Seyles were attacking targets in the distance. He could hear the clash of battle.

That's why you want in the pit, Jake thought. *You know your time is up, and you think this will give you some kind of immortality.*

"You dare deny me? This will mean your execution!" Grigg shouted at Dezzig, who just sighed.

"Grigg, you are a fool. None of us will survive Matzhin and Torsk."

Georgia called in again. "Jake, what's going on? Why hasn't any Seyles gone into the pit yet?"

"Beats me," whispered Jake hoarsely. He was feeling completely drained. It was over. Maybe.

"A Seyles with nectar from the Callas is the catalyst—the final step! And yours is the only one that hasn't received a Seyles yet!"

Mine, Jake thought ruefully.

"Dezzig, someone's gotta get in there. And it's gotta be someone with the goop." Jake spoke calmly to the Seyles.

"I'll go," said Dezzig.

"It's sure death, you realize."

"Grigg's going to kill me anyway. This could be interesting. Goodbye, Jake Wizard. Perhaps there is a world we can share coffee—"

From Grigg, on his crag, they heard, "Kill them all!"

In the confusion and chaos following the mass slaughter at the pit and the three armies clashing at the crossroads, Grigg didn't have much pull.

Furthermore, the Nijins no longer knew what "them" meant.

Grigg floated down from his perch and landed on the sward, directing his wrath at all the Nijins. "Kill them all!" he screamed again.

A few Seyles descended on Jake, Dali, and Dezzig. Jake and Dali quickly dispatched theirs while Dezzig struggled, smashing his unarmed opponent with Jake's coffee pot.

Grigg screeched and charged at Jake, who put his blades out in anticipation.

But the crafty Grigg veered at the last moment and plunged into the pool.

Immediately, the pit sealed up, enclosing itself in a clear, waxy shell. The ground began to heave. Jake stumbled backward, Dali joining him outside where the woollyheads had been. Dezzig and his antagonist stopped fighting.

Several of his smart drones had survived the onslaught and were taking images of the area, which Jake was sending to Dr. Vizgirda.

"Yes, Jake, you've done it! It's in God's hands now."

It struck Jake's ear funny. Far from the human homeworld on a planet where the only known god was the Seyles-eating Comedentine, evoking the idea of a loving deity in whose trustworthy hands everything rested seemed incongruous.

Paul would have chided him that God was never incongruous, of course. Jake hoped Paul was alive and delivering his message out there somewhere. He couldn't claim to be a believer but took comfort in Paul's faith anyway.

Jake held Dali with his armored arms, and she grabbed them as if they were real. In his head, he was trying to compile what he needed to do before leaving—he fiercely wanted to be off Nidus—but it was hard to focus on anything but the egg.

The pit had bubbled up more of the waxy substance, forming a kind of cradle for it as the liquid around it drained away. They could hear a sound reminiscent of water being forced too fast through too-small pipes.

Inside the egg, a worm thrashed around.

As they watched, the worm changed shape, lengthening and coiling. Then it got fatter, and as it got fatter, it got darker and darker.

Finally, it lay still, completely opaque.

The planet held its breath.

Then the egg cracked, allowing a bit of a large, glowing blob to stick out.

The egg increasingly cracked, revealing an enormous but rather disappointing (to Jake's eyes) blob of a bug, like a fat caterpillar but with no legs, no eyes, no arms, and no wings.

The only point of visual interest was the appearance of glowing seams along the body, hinting at a more complex anatomy than the blob revealed.

Jake was about to tell Dali they should start packing up when the pit started rumbling again. The base of the waxy shell began to bubble—and then the worm shot high into the air!

Chapter 40

Eclosion

The Apothikon shot into the air, slowly rotating as it rose, and as it did so, the lit seams revealed themselves to be wings, slowly unpeeling from its body. Two wings emerged opposite each other on the softly conical form, then two others evenly spaced between the first two.

At first, they stayed curled closely into the core, then one set of wings unfolded completely, giving the impression of a great purple butterfly. Then, the other pair spread out.

The four-winged moth seemed an impossibly un-aerodynamic form, but then it split into two, and each of the two new Apothikons repeated the same dance.

Those two split again, and there were four. Then sixteen. Then, an uncountable swarm. The sky filled with moths as they watched, each unfurling their wings in a rhythmic dance.

The pattern on the wings combined with the circular flights of the moths had an almost hypnotic look to them—Jake checked himself. Not *almost*. He looked around, and every Notos, Nock, and Korma stood watching the thing in complete silence. The Seyles had landed and were equally mesmerized. Even Dezzig looked up vacantly.

The sounds of distant combat had ceased.

He wondered if the Nephros had stopped tilling and if the Diptera in their tiny-huge cities were also staring upward. All around, the landscape flickered with the lights of the Lucas flashing in unison.

Even Dali stood there, enchanted, though she did grab his arm tightly.

"Jake…It's beautiful."

"I don't like it," Jake grumbled. He didn't want to ruin the experience for her, but he'd grown to hate the Apothikon. In his head, it was responsible for all the suffering he had seen on Nidus.

"Mmmm-hmmm."

He looked at her, alarmed. She was still staring upward. Jake followed her gaze up to where the Apothikons were twirling in the sky, glowing brighter and brighter.

"Will-o'-wisp. That's all this is. A giant will-o'-wisp!"

As he said it, tiny glowing lights—very much like *actual* will-o'-wisps—began to float down from the moths. The moths spun faster and faster, and more and more of the lights began to fall.

Soon, the sky was full of flickering lights, which floated softly downward to blanket Grigg's kingdom.

Like snow.

Jake found himself mesmerized, too. He'd had a dream about this, hadn't he?

In the distance, he could see Mount Olive covered with Nijins, and he zoomed in to make out the Notos standing at the top of the hill, looking more like bamboo than ever with their upturned faces.

The little lights landed on them and immediately dissolved.

Something inside him screamed in protest.

"Dali…Dali, let's get inside."

The lights were coming closer. It was so hard to move.

"I don't think we should be—we don't know what these things will do to us. We don't know what they're doing to anyone! Let's go!"

Dali sighed a little. "I don't want to, Jake. I want to watch."

He turned the heavy armor toward the tent and, after a brief hesitation, picked her up bodily. He swiveled around and ran hard up the path to get to his tent.

She should have laughed or gotten angry. She should've complained, at least, but she did nothing but crane her head to look at the lights in the sky.

The will-o'-wisps were everywhere. On him, on her, the whole countryside was blanketed with tiny lights.

He stuck the armor's arms (with Dali) inside the tent and activated the emergency release. As it crumpled to pieces behind him, he leapt out of it and grabbed her as she fell.

She had a vacant look on her face.

He went to brush off the will-o'-wisps with a towel, but they were all gone.

He slapped her face gently.

"Dali? Dali, are you okay? Dali!"

Slowly, her eyes came into focus, and she smiled at him. Relieved, he hugged her and kissed her face. "Oh, thank God."

She smiled bigger and said, "Who are you?"

He leaned back to look her in the eyes. "Don't kid around, Dali."

"You know me? Only my father calls me 'Dali.'"

"I'm your husband!"

She blushed and pushed away gently. Looking around, she said, "I can only presume I married for love, then. You must be quite persuasive—besides being handsome."

"We don't *live* here. This is a field trip of sorts."

"Oh? Is our home nicer?"

"Well. Uh. It's on a space station."

She lit up at that.

"Which one?"

Jake stammered a little. "Eks-eeh-eeh?" He spelled it out slowly.

Her eyes widened, "Bug space!" She looked at the doomsday clock on his wall. "Your counter is done."

Sure enough, it read zero hours, zero minutes, and zero seconds.

The beginning of hyper-summer.

He checked outside again. The glowing lights had all settled and dissolved, and the land was quiet and dark again, the Lucas still pulsing in sync.

The readout was all gibberish:

nI2Tc3aBQENAr5MfDWhLOMse3dqa

nI2Tc3aBQENAr5MfDWhLOMse3dqa

nI2Tc3aBQENAr5MfDWhLOMse3dqa

nI2Tc3aBQENAr5MfDWhLOMse3dqa

As he watched, the Lucas stopped pulsing and held solid.

Once again, the planet held its breath.

The horizon continued to brighten. Yellows and oranges began to break through the seemingly invincible purples to the west. He grabbed his device and sent his remaining smart drones to see what was happening.

Beyond Grigg's kingdom and beyond the wilderness where Noah had once lived, the hot edge of the planet crept forward. As it did, the marshy lands began to change, to dry out, and to crack with the heat. As the land dried out, Jake saw motion.

From the cracked, rapidly drying ground, creatures arose. Thousands of creatures shaking off the sand the heat had turned their homes into.

"Princess, we gotta go."

"Go where?" she said.

"The *Shiva*. Now."

"The *Shiva*!" she exclaimed in excitement.

He didn't think he had time to explain, so he helped her up and led her from the tent. Outside, Jake saw the seed pods cracking open. A white mist escaped from inside.

Dali reached out, but Jake grabbed her hand. "The *Shiva*!" he yelled. "Now!"

Her eyes wide, she took off toward the ship, and he followed close behind, trying to ensure his device was synced with the data servers in the tent to preserve as much data as possible.

The temperature, which had been getting warmer, was becoming much cooler, fast.

In fact, it was getting downright cold. His feet started sticking to the quickly freezing water on the ground.

"It's time, Jake Wizard," Fugi had said to him when releasing the water. It was like a dream where Fugi's face melted into Toler. He was falling asleep on his feet.

He began to slow his approach to the *Shiva*. He saw Dali's concerned face as she looked back, but it didn't worry him anymore. He'd just lay down for a bit—

She grabbed him by both arms and helped him up the ladder, pulling him inside the ship with all her might. The door shut behind them.

As Jake regained himself, fully awakening, he realized he was lying on top of her, and she wasn't sure who he was. They both blushed and stood up.

She said, "Now what?"

"Fly us up above the Apothikons so we can watch. Head westward."

For the first time since he'd been on Nidus—and for the first time in about two hundred years, if their math was correct—the sleepy fiery wheel of the setting sun bobbed upward, escaping for a brief moment the eclipsing shadow of Nidus itself.

The sand creatures he had seen marched from the increasingly warm west. A long line of them marching into the Seyles'—or the Apothikon's—kingdoms. They had squat bodies, like toads with triangular heads that sat atop, neckless.

They also had two giant eyes, one on each side of their skulls, and they dragged themselves forward on poorly articulated legs, mouths unhinged and scooping up everything in their paths.

The two watched, aghast. Dali even took Jake's hand as the mud creatures began to consume everything in front of them indiscriminately. They swallowed the rocks and stones like everything else, but Jake suspected they had some alimentary sorting system that allowed non-food to pass right through them.

They only ate around things that didn't fit into their mouths, like the bamboo.

The heat pushed forward ahead of them, and Jake wondered how the water-based Nijins would react. But the white mist from the awa-vines continued to flow forth, creating a thick, foggy layer. Every corner of the twilight ring they could see revealed the mist slowly building up enough even to creep up the hills.

"What are they doing?" asked Dali, awestruck.

"Just eating. Look, some are starting to retreat already. They've eaten enough." He looked at her, her hair hanging wildly over her shoulders, struck by her beauty and stung that she didn't remember him.

The area to the immediate west of Grigg's kingdom—the one with no Apothikon—offered no barrier to the encroaching devourers, and sure enough, they crossed the river—some over the pretty little footbridges and others right through the water. They reached the pit around which Jake had centered his life over the past months, which had already begun filling with swamp water.

As the invaders entered Grigg's kingdom and traveled up the Node Path, their skin came into contact with the wet but quick-freezing stones, locking them into place.

When a creature fully stopped, one of its brethren climbed over it and continued the advance. Soon, they were walking over a path paved entirely of their own kind.

The sand creatures slowed more now as the fog overwhelmed them. It spread more and more from the Nephros fields, and Jake and Dali could no longer see the advancing, ravenous army.

"Once they've eaten enough, they'll go back to where they came from. I'll bet they spawn and hibernate, all in preparation for two hundred years from now when they do it again."

"What an odd life!" Dali said innocently.

It was odd. The whole drama he had lived in was odd, what with the wars and civil wars and arguments over every detail.

Hundreds of thousands of creatures living out personal dramas, completely unaware that nothing they did mattered in the slightest to the organism they were barely aware that they were linked to.

But then, he supposed that wasn't exactly true. How the Seyles ran their kingdoms mattered a lot. Grigg's Apothikon was at risk due to his manner of running things. And the Dipteras came very close to a level of technology where they might have escaped their on-rails existence.

Bug Space had gotten to him again. He had just gotten around to grasping the potential upside to life being cheap, only to stumble on a world where life was not just cheap but *also* meaningless, a pantomime acted out at the behest of an invisible puppeteer.

As they watched, the light-line began to recede, and the creatures that had not retreated from the twilight band began a frantic reverse charge back to the mud where they hibernated.

At those places, the sand was churning, and Jake didn't know (and didn't want to know) whether they were digging back in or spawning or what.

Not all of the creatures made it back. The mist had kept them from laying waste to the kingdoms by slowing them down or, with the water, freezing them in place. The kingdoms on the east side of the twilight band hadn't even been touched.

Jake supposed their time would come when the hyper-winter arrived a century or so from now.

Below, the Nijins—the ones who had survived, anyway—were stirring from their Apothikon-induced slumber, and they fell upon the now helpless invaders.

Eating them, Jake presumed, feeling queasy.

He became aware she was watching him.

He looked her in the eyes.

"Jake," she said.

He waited expectantly.

"Kiss me."

He did. He put his heart and soul into one deep kiss, breaking only reluctantly.

"Did that help?" he asked.

"No," she smiled. "But I liked it."

Jake knew he had to get her back to XEE.

Chapter 41

Wreckage

Just as with Georgia, only rather more slowly, Dali began to recover her memory. She was calling him "dear" and "darling" and even "husband," but Jake wasn't sold.

He only felt a glimmer of hope when he said he had to leave.

"I've gotta get back to...the planet," he said to her while Doc Blood was setting up her recovery program—an interesting mixture of VR therapy and some bad-smelling nutritional concoction. "I need to get my stuff and see what happened...after."

"That seems dangerous," she said. Her former insouciance had given way to a somewhat fearful conservatism—understandable given the huge gaps in her memory.

She was worried for him even if she didn't remember him well. She turned over Mot's medal in her hand somewhat nervously, fingering the gouge. She hadn't understood why he was so poor that he had given her a crudely fashioned medal as a wedding ring.

"Don't worry, princess. They don't scare me."

"Go get 'em, tough guy."

He smiled. It was the first time Dali had called him that since the eclosion.

Now for the real challenge: finishing the job on Nidus without being completely distracted worrying over her—a challenge made all the tougher after reviewing her logs from her trip to Karnata.

She had finished getting Noah situated when she received a message through some of her closest connections that they had urgent news that couldn't be trusted through the public network.

She'd already gotten Jake's message and rushed to the secluded site—a seldom used family home in the country—thinking whatever it was could be related and important.

What followed was an attempt on her life, followed by a firefight where rebels tried to talk her into surrendering to them.

Jake's heart hurt to see the old Dali as she said the exact words he was thinking, "Rebels? What is there to rebel against on Karnata?"

Over the next few days, she logged the results of her research. The rebels had cut her off from the outside network, but the house itself was a planetary data mirror so she had most recent events at her fingertips—as long as it happened before she got there. She combed through it to try to unravel her predicament.

"Jake, it looks like some of my father's court is very unhappy with my sister. And with the way Karnata is run generally."

He found himself charmed all over again as he realized that many of the logs were addressed to him—some as letters and some as if he were there.

"I guess I abdicated and married you at the right time," she winked at the screen as if knowing he would see it someday.

Another log:

"Who are these people? What do they want with me? Jake, what would you say?" She smiled mischievously. "You'd probably say they're after you!"

"Knowing you, you'd be right, too," she laughed nervously. "I'm sorry I acted so foolishly, my darling. I never thought I could get trapped or I'd be there with you now. Karnata can take care of itself."

Her logs got increasingly urgent. At one point, she looked right at the camera and said, "Hang in there, tough guy. I'll get there in time."

Jake had to shut it off. She'd gotten there in time, all right. And he'd let *her* down.

The tent was still there. Placing it on a relatively high rocky ground had paid off. Jake started to pack things up.

Tarkanian hadn't given him any actual orders to decamp, he realized. He also realized he didn't care. He was done with Nidus and needed to be on XEE for Dali.

Rather than packing it up, he took a moment to wipe down his battlesuit and check the diagnostics. It was still complaining about needing a refit, but when he cleaned and repositioned the battery over the generator, the power levels went to normal quickly.

Slipping it on, he stacked everything on his bed and carried the whole load to the *Shiva*. Feeling rather pleased with himself that he could control the suit well enough to get everything there without dropping it or launching it into orbit by accident, he set it all down in the cargo hold.

"That looks like an old McClean Model A cargo hold!" he had gushed.

"It hauls plenty of stuff," Dali had replied warily. She had always been so unguarded with him, except when he first saw the *Shiva*. He had been uncharacteristically over-the-top.

He had been saving up ever since for his own ship. And what nobody knew, except for a little Ip on Debrides, is that he almost had enough money due to a very fortuitous set of investments. He hoped to surprise Dali with a key like the one she had given him.

It would mean little if she didn't remember him.

He kicked himself mentally as he recalled their discussion about the value of being able to forget. *What a dummy*, he thought. *How insulting to Dali to pick apart the road that—for all its bumps—had brought them together.*

He sighed and stepped out of the armor, leaving it locked in the standing position. When he stepped out of the hold, he saw the *Mendel*. He must have overlooked it when he was carrying everything.

He tried to reach the doctor, but his device pleaded ignorance as to her location. Then he remembered it had been keyed to the Q-comm in his tent, which he had packed up.

He trotted along the base of the hills leading to Mount Olive and hiked up. He grabbed some of the velda fruit along the way. For some reason, he had never taken samples of them. He just recalled Dezzig's commentary.

His eye was immediately drawn to the site of Melontikopolis.

The *former* site.

Only a blackened patch remained. Even the walls were gone. Water had begun to seep up, and shoots of green peeked up on the charred surface.

He played the last video his smart drones had taken of the city. It was too far away to know the fates of any individuals, but apparently, the riots had calmed down after the intercepted missile launch. Fires were put out with moderate damage to several buildings.

Then he saw the Nocks come, with their squat little bodies and large hammers, and they hammered down the wall. When the walls came down, they hammered into the city, too. In the sky, Seyles alternated between consuming the terrified Diptera and knocking down buildings.

The remains were set on fire.

From Melontikopolis, he looked to Grigg's castle. A few Seyles circled aimlessly. Sometimes, fights and other mid-air activities broke out.

Occasionally, he saw groups of Seyles approach a loner, who either joined them or was killed.

Along the reservoir road, a pair of Kormas inspected the wall.

It could be Fugi and—well, it couldn't be Toler. He looked to the crossroads. Still very visible to the east and west, he saw the southern path—where he had melted it—under repair by a squad of Nocks.

He checked the northbound segment, which led through the Great Marshes. The Node Path was under repair there, too.

And picking her way through them, toward Mount Olive, he saw Dr. Vizgirda.

CHAPTER 42

RESET

They met at the pit, now covered with el-letroids—will-o'-wisps. Jake had knelt to collect a few samples from the pit by the time she arrived, but they were so murky that he doubted they retained much of the "healing potion" quality.

Georgia found him examining the little pinholes that covered the inside walls of the pit. He looked up at her, but she immediately dropped to her knees to join him.

"It's just a completely different kind of organism, isn't it?" he asked her, the exasperation in his voice probably more due to Dali's condition than anything.

She gave him a genuinely sympathetic smile. "I believe it is. We kept trying to create familiar analogies for it. The shield was like teeth, for example. And it was, but it was also like a skull."

"So the pit is the brain?"

"It might not even be the whole brain. For example, the Lucas acted like a nervous system."

Jake had that dizzying feeling of the world being upside-down and trying to right itself. "That would mean— The crop news, the weather reports... that was the noise, then! The not-really-random letters were the actual messages going out?"

"Perhaps so. Our bodies constantly send chemical messages back and forth, and our translators would be useless in decoding those as well. They're not anything like words.

"It will take a lifetime to sort out all the details. Every time I think I've figured it out—well, for example, those tiny holes. I thought those were for roots!"

"Aren't they?"

"Some of them, at first. But the Apothikon gets most of its food from things falling into its pit. These are more like nerves."

"Nerves? Doing what? Going where?"

"This was the thing that helped me the most, Bailiff, when I realized it. The Apothikon is not the thing in the pit. It's *everything*—what we've been calling the kingdom, including the Nijins, the plants, the farms, the reservoir, and even the shape and extent of the land."

He sat on his butt. The ground squished beneath him. The sward was dying out, having served its purpose.

"So...the Seyles are...?"

"A little like white blood cells. They fight off infection. The Nephros are sort of like a stomach or perhaps the whole digestive system. The Nocks—well, the analogies fail me here. They build things, so they're sort of like bone marrow, and the Korma have functionality like a hypothalamus—"

"OK, stop, my head is already hurting," Jake said in a friendly tone. "I'll read your paper when it's done."

"It'll be a while," she said. "The tendrils—I'm going to try to stop using analogs—" she added apologetically. "The tendrils run from the Apothikon pit to the elletroid—that is, the will-o'-wisp pits. The Apothikon draws things into those pits to learn about them."

"So, it's more like a nose?" Jake struggled. "The Apothikons die, and their old homes become noses just waiting for—"

"It's a way to get information," she said. "The awa-vines, mean-while, may also have some sensory value but primarily serve as a de-fense mechanism. This is what keeps the Nijins from being annihilated by the hyper-summer and the sand creatures. But the entire organism, what we call a kingdom, is a biome. It's comprised of these symbiotes, parasites, and completely independent flora and fauna."

Jake nodded, thinking of the complexity of the human biome, with all its diverse microorganisms, which raised another question in his mind. "What's the analog for the Diptera in all this?"

"If we were using analogs—which we're going to try *not* to do in the future," she said pointedly, "the Diptera would be something akin to a disease. Like cancer."

Georgia seemed to be formulating her theory as she talked. "At the rate they live, they had the equivalent of twelve or thirteen hundred years to advance out of the Stone Age. Unlike the rest of the Nijins, they served themselves and not some unknown larger force."

She added, "They grow out of control, from the Apothikon's per-spective, and they also pervert the Seyles, acting as a kind of hallucino-gen."

"I'm trying to put something together in my head," Jake said. "The knowledge of Nidus—it's all in the fluid that the Apothikon sits in. But this knowledge is...incidental?"

"The Apothikon has the blueprint for its entire biome, just like our bodies have blueprints for our blood, brain, and other organs. This is by design. But the culture of Nidus, the music and the language and the rituals—yes, these are carried incidentally with the data the Apothikon truly needs."

She smiled and rose, and he popped up next to her.

"And not to analogize," she said, "but imagine if your liver and brain started to conceive of themselves as independent creatures with their own goals in life. Your blood cells running around carrying oxygen, but dreaming of doing something else, perhaps."

They walked up the Node Path from the pit to where their ships were parked.

"What about the taboo against speaking about it? And not just taboo, it seems like it completely wiped memories of its existence out," Jake said, not mentioning Noah.

He didn't know why he should be so cautious but had been mentally cataloging what he had told Dr. Lazar over the years and wondering if something he had said carelessly might come back to haunt him.

"Plain old evolution, I imagine. And again, not to analogize—" Georgia laughed a little given how much analogizing she had done since she'd sworn off it "—but if human blood and organs were capable of living independently of the brain, the brain that best survived might be the one that found a way to eliminate knowledge of itself from every other part of the body.

"Especially," she added, "should if those organs came to an awareness that many of the things they thought were aspirations were just rationalizations over what they had been born to do."

Jake nodded, not sure he understood how it all worked. "The legends surrounding the pits, like that they had magical powers. Or of Seyles emerging from it with great wisdom might be true, then?"

"On our devices," she said, waving hers, "we have most of the knowledge of thousands of years of history. Probably things that could have helped us in this little adventure. But it didn't, did it?"

"Not much," Jake admitted.

"The Nijins are mad about data, piling it up like treasure, but they seldom know how to use it. The Apothikons probably have all that and more. Someone who emerged from the pit with the knowledge that he knew how to apply and to change the world?"

She winked at him. "That person would seem pretty wizardly, wouldn't he?"

Jake nodded. "Yes, he would. But could the pit make them giant, like in the legends?"

The doctor looked skeptically off into the distance. "The thing is, Jake, I think the pit is full of memories, both as you and I understand the word and, in a more organic sense, like how your DNA 'remembers' how your body should be. Could there be a creative element in there as well? I suppose there would have to be." She sounded like she had talked herself into it.

"So *maybe* it could change them but you *are* confident it could at least strengthen them, restore them to their full health?"

The older woman scrutinized him, and he realized how different he must look now. He'd shaved, stood up straight, and showed no sign of sickness. "Perhaps you should tell *me*, Bailiff."

He had hemmed and hawed, and she gracefully, if somewhat teasingly, let him off the hook, explaining she had many stops to make and that her job had only gotten busier now, as she had limited time to analyze all the changes since the hyper-summer.

According to her, among the new Apothikons, those who best managed to capture the remains of the previous generation's kingdoms would most likely thrive in the latest generation.

Jake remembered his discussion with Dezzig about mothers. The eclosed Apothikon was mother to thousands and fed them off her own remains. Dezzig was part of those remains, morbidly enough.

Before he left, Jake had to see if anyone had taken up residence in Grigg's castle.

All across Nidus, the old kingdoms had broken up, and new ones were being formed—all with an Apothikon egg at their base. These kingdoms would expand and destroy their rivals for decades.

When they reached the final phase of their life, the woollyheads grew, and the Apothikons became toxic to each other—a poison pill against their overly aggressive kin. If destroyed at this phase, something like the wilderness where Noah lived resulted.

Georgia had yet to isolate what the toxin was or how long it would last.

Jake suggested at least two hundred years, thinking of Noah and the lightning strike that probably ended that Apothikon.

As Jake walked the Node Path north to Grigg's castle, he could see two tribes in the Nephros fields. The Seyles stood watch as the Kormas directed the Nocks in some basic tasks.

One set of Nocks had set up channels around an area of land to drain the water off. The Kormas appeared to be debating how to do that best. Somewhere in that area, Georgia had assured him, was an Apothikon egg.

She had gotten out her device and showed him a video of the eclosion. If he ignored the mesmerizing lights, he could see dark ovoids plunging to earth.

As the castle neared, he noticed some of these ovoids on the road, smashed open and revealing a network of complex strands. He prodded at one with his foot, and a little gray lump fell out.

Sort of like seeds or eggs, but we're not analogizing.

Some were fortunate enough to land on marshy ground, sink to just the right depth, and begin whatever process it was: electrical, chemical, or something else that drew in the Nijins to do the necessary work.

Whatever they thought they were doing, however they rationalized it, the Nijins were doing what the Apothikon wanted.

The idea hit close to home and made Jake uncomfortable.

Strangely nervous, he found himself on the bridge at the foot of Grigg's castle.

It was rather chaotic, with Seyles dogfights breaking out overhead and the thin, tough Notos pushing Nocks and Kormas around. Across the city, some of the towers had fallen, and beyond that, the Callas lay unperturbed by anything that had passed.

There were no Seyles eggs yet, only the cracked and blackened remains of shells. The sky, however, did not want for Seyles in heart-shaped embraces. The kingdoms would be replenished soon.

And they would fight, again.

Entering the castle, he saw a chair being assembled by some Nocks, with spear-wielding Notos on either side. Whether to monitor the Nocks or just look menacing, he did not know.

He looked around for a "lord" and didn't see anyone who stood out. He was about to leave when he heard a familiar voice.

"We don't get a lot of wizards around these parts."

He turned and exclaimed, "Dezzig! You made it!"

The Seyles shrugged. "You've got me mistaken for someone else. They call me Jadakma. Lord Jadakma. I'm in charge around here. Not that there's much to do, especially once we've routed out the upstarts."

Jake smiled, though his heart was conflicted. He had liked Dezzig and wondered if that person still existed.

He took some of the velda fruit he had grabbed as samples and held them out to the new lord.

"What's this? Velda fruit?"

Jake nodded. "Try boiling it in water and making a drink out of it. You might like it. I understand they're best when not ripe."

The former Dezzig gave him the deadpan stare he remembered and said, "This is a great gift, wizardly one. Thank thee." He rattled his wings just a little, and Jake wondered, amused, if the new monarch was mocking him.

When he trod the path he had taken so many times to the castle and around the reservoir before this newly emerging world, he was somehow not surprised to see a pair of Kormas arguing.

One was trying to replace the triangle bricks Fugi had removed. He was gesticulating with it while yelling at his partner.

Fugi?

It was Fugi, with the same scary Seyles head image on his giant alligator head.

"Greetings," said Jake. "I am Jake Wizard. Are you arguing about the maintenance of the reservoir?"

They bobbed enthusiastically. Fugi said, "I am Peret Korma, and this is my foolish friend Taka Korma, who believes that we can just leave the reservoir as it is, that there is no danger from the decaying seed pods."

Taka objected, "A simple look at history, the works of Metmet the Fecund, shows that the awa-vines and seed pods constantly reinforce the bricks—"

"Toler the Stubborn knew well the folly of your casual attitude," Fugi said stridently.

"Wait," Jake said. "You're...*Peret* Korma? And you're on Toler Korma the Stubborn's side?"

"I am on the side of truth, *sir*," proclaimed Fugi. "What know you of our history?"

Jake paused thoughtfully. "Well, I considered Toler a kind of friend."

"You knew him?" Taka said in awe.

"Well...yes. And I also knew his friend Fugi Korma, who would have agreed with you, Taka."

"Aha!" exclaimed Fugi victoriously. "Fugi Korma the Lazy was renowned for his carelessness in maintaining the reservoir!"

Jake left them arguing, of course, because that's what they were born to do.

CHAPTER 43

THE PERSISTENCE OF MEMORY

"What does Doc Blood say? Will she be okay?"

Tarkanian sat at his desk as Leidecker slouched nearby. Jake had missed a lot while on Nidus. The war had taken its toll.

Jake replied, "They're using a similar amnesia protocol on her they used on Dr. Vizgirda. They recreate your life virtually from the point where your memory ends, and you relive it. There are some physical exercises and supplements as well that Doc Blood says to facilitate the process. Dali has a relatively well-documented life."

Leidecker sputtered a little. "Wouldn't that leave holes where your more...personal...moments were?"

Nodding, Jake said, "They use an inference engine to fill in the blanks."

"That's what Ge—Dr. Vizgirda told me," Tarkanian said. "Wouldn't that give you false memories?"

Jake smiled wanly. "The doc gave me a pretty good lecture about it. In the old days, they had a device that just hammered in fake memories, as I think you're both imagining."

"But this is played like an interactive movie or a video game. The idea is that the patient sees the parts that are right, and then when the wrong parts come up, they notice and correct them. Over time, they can reconstruct things properly and with incredible detail. Some say it actually improves memory."

Tarkanian nodded. "The key thing is, the memories are still there, but you have to refresh them."

Jake breathed a sigh. "It looks that way. Dali had already corrected a bunch of stuff when I left. And it goes faster the more you do it."

Leidecker clapped his hands, "That is excellent news!"

Tarkanian, relieved, lapsed back into his more usual irascibility. "Meanwhile, the laundering of the—well, we're trying out a bunch of different names for it, currently *Elan Regen*—is testing well. What did you call it, Jake? A healing potion? We've managed to heal some very wealthy, very sick people with just a few drops from your samples.

"And sure enough, our competitors discovered that we were the source. Nobody knows how we got it. We're going with 'invented it in a lab.'"

Leidecker held up a tiny patch of fabric. "In other subterfuge, the labs reworked your psychic blocker. ICF clothing will be made of this fabric going forward."

Tarkanian smiled like a shark. "The beauty of this approach is that the Lydians will only know they can't read our minds anymore, but the troops never knew that they could in the first place. The spider queens will never ask, and even if they did, our boys couldn't answer."

"So I could go back to Teila?" Jake asked, wondering if that was even a good idea.

Leidecker asked, "Do you think that's a good idea?"

Tarkanian said, "That's not the point. It's a small galaxy. You might run across one of those spider queens or who knows what else. And *this* will keep an accidental encounter from automatically being a catastrophe."

Tarkanian stood up and extended his hand. "Still, Jake, hell of a job."

Jake shook his hand, then Leidecker's, conscious of the strength that flowed through him. "Can you synthesize more of the...*Elan Regen*?"

"We're trying. There are a lot of variables, not the least of which is you."

"Did you test those samples I sent back with Dali?"

Leidecker said, "No, they were...in Doctor Lazar's vault." After a brief pause where questions hung in the air unanswered, he added, "This actually works out since nobody saw those samples, and we can launder any future ones we need from you."

Tarkanian added, "Also, I might be able to coax Geo—Dr. Vizgirda into swiping some more, although she's telling me the Apothikons stay hidden until their final phase of life, so it's a good ninety years."

Jake, who found himself not caring very much, made a perfunctory pitch: "An argument can be made that we should be trying to reach the Apothikons, not the other Nijins."

Leidecker looked a little surprised by that notion. "Interesting," was all he said.

"So, Doc V got what she needed?" asked Jake. He didn't add, "Since that's why you sent me down—to help out your old flame."

Tarkanian spoke more warmly than usual. "Doc V said she learned more in a couple of hours than she had the rest of her time on that planet. And she attributes a lot of that to you, Jake."

Jake tried to smile. "I don't know that I did anything except delay the Seyles for a while."

"Georgia says if you hadn't, the Apothikon would've eclosed prematurely, and its defenses would've been spent before the hyper-summer. The sand things that wake up every two hundred years—she says she's going to call them Gregordians—" He coughed a little. "They would've wiped out all life in the kingdom. She even speculates that had they gotten that far, they might have pressed through to the cold side of the planet. Enough to bisect the twilight ring, which—well, who even knows what that would've resulted in."

Jake nodded, anxious to get back to Dali. "Great. Sounds like it's all under control."

Tarkanian reached into his desk and handed Jake a box. "I don't know how you got the money for this, but if you want to sell it back—"

"What's my next mission?" Jake said abruptly, taking the box and putting it in his jacket.

Tarkanian laughed. "Take a little time, son. Maybe go on a honeymoon. With the war, things are up in the air, so we're expanding cautiously right now."

Jake just nodded again, excused himself, and went back to his quarters.

They had somewhat restored his old room, except that everything but his old dresser and the bed was piled high with boxes.

Dali had re-arranged some of the crates into an impromptu chair and sat reviewing missing parts of her life. Her face was wet.

She slid the goggles down around her neck and smiled timidly. Jake found some tissue in a drawer and handed it to her.

"My father died," she said, wiping her face.

He smiled sadly.

"It's the third time I've gone through it today, and I've cried every time."

Cautiously, he took a step toward her and held out his hand. She grabbed it and laughed through a sob, "I'm a mess."

"You're beautiful," he said.

The expression on her face was pained. Waving the goggles, she laughed a little nervously. "I'm glad this is on a private feedback loop. I've gotten very detailed."

"So, you remember...everything?"

She released a little laugh but with warmth underneath, and Jake felt better than he had in a while. "I think I probably remember things better now. Jake, our time together—that's what got me through this." She indicated the goggles.

"I knew," she grabbed his other hand and pulled him closer. "I knew that when I got through all the bad stuff in my life, you were waiting at the end. It made it so much easier."

He smiled, internally relieved. It felt like Dali again. "If I can be that little bit of happiness you count on, that's all I would ask."

Her expression grew melancholy.

"What is it?" he sat next to her, and she clung to him. It felt good. Normal. Natural.

"Jake, we have to go home."

Chapter 44

Circles

Jake marveled at how he could feel so physically fit, so well, and not sick or poisoned or weak for the first time in a long time, and simultaneously have every cell in his body suffused with despair.

She was gone. Again. And maybe for good.

He walked along the second-floor promenade of XEE, which ended abruptly in a cul-de-sac with a hastily constructed guardrail. Nobody wanted to invest in the station while the war was on.

The human population of the station had dropped significantly. Too many people rushed back to wherever home was.

Too many wanted to be killed in the right place.

We have to go home, Jake.

That's what she had said.

I'll come to Karnata with you!

A simple assertion.

No. You have to go to Earth.

He didn't buy it. Not at all. He wanted to be with her. The hell with Earth. He wasn't even convinced her decision to return to Karnata wasn't just an after-effect of the eclosion.

She had laid it out in detail, all the things that had gone wrong on Karnata since her father died. They didn't seem that serious to Jake. All she could say to that is:

"Maybe they're not. Maybe they won't ever be, if I go and handle them now. But I've had to review everything that's happened, over and over and— Jake, I can't pretend that abdicating shed me of my responsibilities."

She didn't offer the corollary: he, too, had abdicated in his own way, and he was no more free of his responsibilities than she was. But he got the message when she refused to take him with her.

But it isn't the same, he argued to himself. Dali had already gone.

Earth was a different creature, an intractable, bleeding beast—

And as he had these thoughts and arguments, he remembered what she had said about seeing something in him. That something she saw probably wasn't a coward who ran from his problems.

"The Lost Girls" were disbanded, maybe forever. Mini Kim and Diana had stayed with Derek and The Baron, respectively. Hulda had gone with Dali. Jake noted as a lonely Kurt passed him silently, unseeing.

He didn't know the fate of the other girls. He'd have to ask Min-Hee.

He wandered down to The Lot, surprised to find Mulli cooking away at his old station in the big bazaar.

"Mulli!" he exclaimed. "Who's minding the restaurant?"

"It is closed, Mister Jake. Business got bad when the war started and Chief Weir said he needed the location for a command post." Mulli's accent had lapsed back into its vaguely Balkan muddle from the more refined form it had when he was running the restaurant.

His eyes were not on his favorite customer, however, and following their line of sight across The Lot floor, Jake saw a stand facing Mulli's where a large, brown-skinned man was furiously preparing a mixture that he wrapped up in a tortilla. The line was long, and people seemed to be enjoying the cook's flair.

"Mister Jake, do me a favor. Try this man's food and tell me what you think."

Jake didn't want to tell Mulli he had lost his appetite—possibly for good—and had been hoping some mullis would bring it back, so he crossed the floor and got in at the end of the line and waited. The line moved quickly, however, and the aromas emanating from the tortilla packets were compelling.

People seemed to be ordering The Oscar, so that's what he did when he got to the front of the line. Up close, the man was huge: a bit shorter than Jake but broad and thick. Some would say fat, but Jake had seen a few people in his lifetime who carried around massive weight with incredible command and grace. *Portly*, his grandfather would say.

Unlike Mulli's more cheerful demeanor, this chef was courteous but commanding. One person hemmed and hawed on the order and was sent to the back of the line with an accusatory finger.

Jake didn't get a good look at the ingredients: it looked superficially like traditional Mexican fare, but he got distracted by a glimpse of a black figure out of the corner of his eye and twisted his head around to see it.

A *Myrmidon*?

Not just a Myrmidon, but *Gord*?

When he got a good look, he saw a Coleon, a little black Ip. They didn't look much like the Myrmidons but were about the right size and shape to fool a distracted person.

He felt The Oscar pressed into his hand, and the chef's assistant hustled him out of the line.

He wandered back to Mulli, still thinking about Gord.

"How is it, Mister Jake?" asked Mulli intensely.

"I haven't tried it. Let me..."

Taking a bite, he looked at Mulli apologetically. "It's good. It's quite good. It's not mullis, but—"

"Thank you, Mister Jake. I needed an honest opinion."

The Oscar was convenient to carry around, so he went back to his room to eat it rather than try to mingle in The Lot, which seemed now to have two distinct vibes going on: the humans and a few humanoids preparing for war and the insectoids—mostly Coleons—who were doing—well, who knew what they were doing. High finance and research, probably.

Hogar's lab was dark when he passed. He swung by Doc Blood's clinic and saw the medical assistant who had treated him back on Teila.

"Where's Doc Blood?" Jake asked as the man rushed by.

The man seemed a little overwhelmed and called back, "Just left. Reassigned."

He passed by Doctor Lazar's lab. It looked like the serious hazards had been removed, but the walls had not been repainted, and the glass had not been replaced. The old glass had black streaks and hairline fractures spiderwebbed along it.

He wondered if anyone had taken the time to inventory what had been lost. Lazar had a number of biological samples and alien artifacts that could not be easily replaced—to say nothing of his own samples.

Finally, he wandered "home."

He jumped on the bed and slid back to look at his device.

"What's this?" she asked when he handed her the box.

"When you were stuck on Karnata, I realized that I couldn't think of anything more important than being able to—"

She gasped. "Jake! You got us Q-comms?"

He smiled weakly. "I didn't know we'd need them right away."

"Where did you get that kind of money?"

He never had told her about saving up for a Stretch Ship, so he just shrugged.

She smothered him with kisses and then started crying. "I'll be back as soon as I can," she whispered.

And then she was gone.

No mail.

OK, well, he hadn't expected Dali to contact him so soon. He spent a few moments looking at ways to get to Karnata and join her, but he knew she wouldn't want that.

He might do it anyway, he decided.

He hadn't heard from his grandfather, neither the one he wanted to nor the one he didn't want to, but that wasn't too surprising either.

Mot hadn't written since his visit on Nidus. As he touched the scrambling devices on either wrist, he sent a quick "thank you" note.

And he missed Paul badly. The young missionary with his stiff mannerisms had been like Derek: always there when he needed him. He didn't understand Christianity, but Paul's way of looking at things was often reassuring. He sent him another letter, hoping eventually they'd get through.

He still hadn't heard from Jezz, and that had been gnawing at him since Nidus when he started looking her up in news stories.

Again, he found himself embarrassed by how little he knew of her. Apparently she was a horse breeder of some renown.

POLICE ALLEGE KIDNAPPING IN BOYD CASE

Jezebel Boyd, the proprietress of Boyd Equestrian, who has not been seen publicly in months, may have been kidnapped, according to unnamed police sources.

He read on, but the article was merely alarming and not educational. Jezebel? Was that what "Jezz" was short for? It had to be, right?

He immediately wanted to run back to Earth to save her.

Presuming she were even kidnapped. And what could he do, anyway?

His mind, and indeed his whole life, seemed to be in utter chaos. Nothing made him feel quite so alone as chaos, and nothing made him feel quite so chaotic as being alone.

As he sat, fretting about what to do, if anything, about Dali and, for that matter, Jezz, he heard a knock at the door.

Not quite a knock. More like a "thump."

He carefully threaded his way across the bed and got to the door.

It slid open.

There on the floor lay a woman with short red hair.

A naked woman.

She looked up through cloudy, dark eyes and whispered, "Jake."

He looked up and down the halls, then to the ceiling, as if hoping to see God there, with a little smirk, telling him it was all a prank.

He blinked twice and looked down again.

She was still there.

Swell.

AFTERWORD

Since I started writing the Exopreneurs series, life has become a series of **Baader—Meinhof experiences.** Also known as "the frequency illusion," it refers to one's tendency to notice things that are on one's mind, essentially. You learn about the Roman aqueducts, for example, and soon you're seeing Roman aqueducts everywhere. But sometimes the coincidences are astonishing.

For instance, it's not unusual to see news about bugs, especially if, like me, you're researching them for the books to come. And perhaps that also explains the people around me seeing more bug news than ever. Of course, many of the non-bug concepts I'm writing about are fairly general—memory, culture, community—so it's no surprise they might come up day-to-day.

And I can't *really* be surprised that a haunted maze at Knott's "Scary" Farm this year with a spider theme featured a climactic boogen suspiciously similar to the spider queens of "Silk Unspun".

But I *was* astonished when the final act of the modern slapstick gem "Hundreds of Beavers" mirrored the final act of "Wingless". (I saw *Hundreds of Beavers* in May. *Wingless* was published in April.)

While writing this book, I stumbled across a non-fiction book called "The Heart's Code", which documents instances where people who were given transplants ended up with characteristics and actual knowledge of the donors. It had no impact on the content, which had already been mapped out, but it was the most peculiar coincidence.

They say we live in a simulation and sometimes, the simulation winks. Even if I don't believe it, I can't really argue the point.

Acknowledgements

As always, thanks to my beta readers and advance readers. You're a big part of what makes this possible. Ian Feldman, especially, has always been there with the feedback, and you should check out his fine "The End Is Here" series, which begins with *The Vortex*.

I never know who's going to pop into my life and become indispensable. For this book, I would be remiss in not thanking my pal, Neva, who was a frequent sounding board, reality checker and overall booster, which is an odd thing for someone who proclaimed me her nemesis.

Thanks above all to my readers who, after all, are the point of this series. Your continued support and feedback guide me.

D. S. BLAKE

A long time science-fiction reader, D. S. Blake first put ink to paper after reading "The Martian Chronicles". The author of several technical books and hundreds of articles, he's now devoted to writing fiction and posting piquant observations on x.com. Check out his feed (@idsblake) or drop him a note at his website, dsblake.com.

ALSO BY D. S. BLAKE

The Exopreneurs

Silk Unspun

Foul Brood

Wingless

as Donald Scott Strong

Lair of the White Worm